Hunteress

Book 2

C.K. Franziska

This book is a work of fiction. Names, characters, places, and incidents are the product of the author's imagination or are used fictiously. Any resemblance to actual events, locales, or persons, living or dead, is coincidental.

Cover art and design by Getcovers

Imprint: Independently published

First Edition October 2023

MORE FROM C.K. FRANZISKA

A Speck of Darkness Series

TRIGGERS/CONTENT WARNINGS

Hunteress is a dark high fantasy with gothic vibes and dark world-building. The female lead in this series is cruel, domineering, and manipulative. She goes beyond my typical morally gray antihero and is, in my opinion, an actual villain who has a very disturbing past.

Triggers include:

- graphic violence
- rough and explicit sexual content
- forced proximity
- brutal injures
- betrayal
- graphic language
- trauma

- death
- murder
- intense violence
- graphic depiction of blood
- physical harm inflicted upon the main characters
- & more

Readers who may be sensitive to these elements, please take note, and prepare to enter Hunteress' world...

OCERIS

STARSTRAND

CRYMZON

TERMINUS

ESCELA

ETERNITIE

TENACORO

ONFINES

To the people who are sick of always being the 'bad guy'.
Let them watch, and never give away your next step.

Gods

Zorus

King of the Gods

Lunra

Goddess of the Moon and Love

Otyx

God of the Underworld

Aqion

God of the Ocean and Strength

Emara

Goddess of Vitality

Nelion

God of Destiny

Odione

Goddess of Wonders

Places

Crymzon

Queen Soulin SinClaret/Lunra

Terminus

King Keres/Otyx

Oceris

King Usiel/Aqion

Tenacoro

Queen Synadena/Emara

Starstrand

Queen Caecilia/Nelion

Eternitie

King Citeus/Odione

The Confines

Names

Soulin SinClaret

Queen of Crymzon

Father: King Obsidian (†)

Mother: Queen Ria (†)

Brother: Crown Prince Felix (†)

Moths: Adira, Velda, Storm, Barin

King Keres

King of Terminus

King Citeus Matrus

King of Eternitie

Sons: Prince Cyrus and Prince Cyprian

Daughter: Crown Princess Catalina

Queen Synadena Roja

Queen of Tenacoro

Daughter: Crown Princess Opaline

Son: Prince Crystol

King Usiel Oarus

King of Oceris

Queen: Cleolia

Queen Caecilia

Queen of Starstrand

Myra Eslene

Adviser of Queen Soulin

Wife: Elia (†)

Khaos Zedohr

Grand General of Crymzonian Army

Aemilius Vosdon

Outlaw

Liza

Outlaw

Devana

Outlaw

Father: Wayne (Blacksmith)

Jeremia

Trusted soldier of Crymzonian Army

Remy Cengor

Trusted soldier of Crymzonian Army

Conrad

King Obsidian's trustee

Lady of Fate

Destiny Forgeress. Oracle.

Blake, Kasen, Charli, Rene

Soldiers of Crymzonian Army

PROLOGUE

Devana (14 years ago...)

"Aim right between her eyes," my father whispers as I extend my arm to grab the only arrow I've brought. "Now steady. Steady."

As I notch the arrow onto my bowstring, my fingers delicately grip the sleek wooden handle of my recurve bow. It melts effortlessly with my hand, an extension of my very being. Its taut, honey-colored limbs curve gracefully, bearing testament to countless hours of practice.

I know. Aim right between her eyes, I think, as my gaze wanders over the thousands of spectators watching the new Queen being crowned.

Aiming for her heart would be a much easier target, but that would allow her to use her magic to heal herself. If the arrow pierces through the part of her brain that renders her motor skills and logical thinking useless, we *might* get out of here alive.

The air is crisp and laden with the faint scent of blood from the subject the new Queen hung on the wall after her mother died. The moon slowly creeps over the horizon, casting a warm golden glow upon the Crymzon Palace.

Amid this serene courtyard stands the person I loathe most—the person who is destined to be my Soulmate.

It's rumored that when two souls take their first breath under the same star constellation simultaneously, their bond will be unbreakable.

And I wish it wasn't the truth.

I've been trained to kill the person who shares my constellation all my life. I've watched Monsteress play with her kingdom and her subject like it's a child's game since the moment her family died at her hands just a few days ago.

If my father hadn't been as persistent in erasing the one person holding power over me when he found out about our connection, I would have made that decision alone. I mean, who wants to be bound to a monster?

My time has finally come. If I wait any longer, her magic will be at its highest when Lunra bestows her with her gift. It's time to kill my Soulmate before she realizes I even exist.

"C'mon Devana. Get it done," my father whispers into my ear, and goosebumps flash over my arms.

I've done this thousands of times. My father has trained me in combat and archery for as long as I can remember. But this time, it's different. I'm not aiming for the steady straw sacks placed neatly in the distance.

This time, I'm aiming at a person.

As my deep, focused gaze fixes upon the distant target, I notice her emerald-golden eyes sparkle as her luminous silver freckles shine in the moonlight. Monsteress isn't even Crymzon's Queen yet, and she has brought more violence to Escela than any other ruler in centuries.

Her lush red curls bounce as she moves forward to address her subjects, her smirk beckoning to be wiped away like an irresistible challenge. Dressed in a form-fitting, blood-red dress, she exudes a quiet confidence no thirteen-year-old should have.

My breaths come steady, my heartbeat echoing in my ears as the world around me fades away.

It needs to be done. She will be the ruin of Escela—and me—if I don't stop her.

With measured steps, I position my feet in perfect alignment with the wall, my body adopting a slight sideways stance. Drawing the bowstring back, my arm extends with graceful fluidity, forming a symmetrical line with my arrow. Sinewy muscles tense beneath my skin as I embrace the subtle resistance, channeling it into an unyielding focus.

Time seems to suspend as I find my anchor point, my right index finger resting firmly against the corner of my mouth. The bowstring, taut against my fingertips, whispers a symphony of potential energy waiting to be released. The tension in the air is palpable, a hushed silence intensifying my anticipation as all Crymzonians hold their breaths to hear their new ruler speak for the first time.

My breath slows with her subjects, becoming a steady rhythm, synchronizing with the beat of my heart. In this moment, I become one with my surroundings, every element aligning in harmony. A gentle breeze sweeps through, tousling my flowing black hair as if nature recognizes this moment's gravity.

I visualize my shot, a mental tapestry of flawless execution. The world narrows to a tunnel of concentration, and my peripheral vision fades. All that remains is me and Monsteress, an unspoken conversation between Archer and Aim.

The release comes like a whisper, a barely perceptible motion as I exhale, releasing the tension built within my body. The bowstring snaps forward, propelling the arrow into the air with a quiet swish. Time resumes its normal flow as the slender shaft streaks across the distance, a graceful arc against the backdrop of the rising moon illuminating the Crymzon Palace.

My gaze follows the arrow's flight as my lips form a silent prayer. This has to work.

The target grows more prominent with each passing moment. It's almost done. The tip is mere feet away from Monsteress...

And then, with a resounding thud, the arrow bounces off a protective capsule that forms around my Soulmate out of thin air. Instead of embedding itself between her eyes, piercing the center of her brain, it shatters on impact and drops to the ground.

The triumphant smile on my lips dies as I lower my bow, my entire being suffused with terror.

It should have hit her. My arrows never miss their mark.

"Run," my father growls, ripping the bow out of my hand to toss it on the ground.

Screams cut the air like sharpened blades as my father curls his arm around me and tosses me over the other side of the wall, away from the crowd.

Somehow, I find a hold on the rough rope we used to climb the barrier enclosing Crymzon, but it's too late to create a nozzle around my foot to let me down gently. My fingers heat as the coarse material cuts into my palms, and a groan escapes my throat when I see the fibers covered with skin pieces and blood above me.

Don't cave. You're stronger than those superficial wounds.

But whom am I kidding? Those wounds are now cutting deep enough that I might never be able to use my hands again, not to mention holding a bow or sword.

"Get out of here!" my father yells over the tumult unfolding inside the wall, and my knees buckle when I hit the ground, not even trying to catch my descent.

"Father!" I scream back as he throws his foot over the wall, grabbing the rope.

Tears stream down my face as I press my palms onto the warm, sand-covered ground to stand up. My gaze falls onto my father, who should be almost halfway down the wall...my heart stops when I see him frozen in place, one foot over the wall, as if an invisible force is holding him hostage.

Not a single muscle moves as he looks down on me, his eyes widened and his mouth open.

"No!" I scream, reaching for the rope again to climb it, as I watch him being dragged out of view without anyone ever touching him.

Get out of here; those were his last words.

Despite every fiber of my body telling me to help him, I listen to the logical voice inside me, spin around, and jump on the horse I left behind to get away.

ONE

DEVANA

How did my father make it out of here alive?

Sounds of prisoners wailing and screaming fill the prison, and the musty scent of pee upsets my stomach. My weary eyes glance around the small, barren space, my spirit dampened by the oppressive atmosphere that permeates every corner.

The only light source comes from a narrow, grated window, barely providing enough illumination to pierce the shadows. But it's enough to see a thumb-sized piece of the wall—the Crymzon Wall.

I remember standing on it, taking aim. Now I wish I could replace the thirteen-year-old me trying to assassinate the Crymzon Queen. This time, I would do it. This time, I wouldn't hesitate to release the arrow. No. If I had the chance to go back in time, I would shoot another and another until I'm sure my job is done.

Using my calloused hands, scarred from wielding weapons and saving my life from the coronation incident, I frantically search for an escape route on the rough walls. At this point, I'm convinced I covered every inch of my small stone cell, but I can't stop. I need to get to my father. I need to get to Aemilius and our friends.

Sweat trickles down my forehead as memories flood my mind, memories of a past escape that ended in cruel capture. I remember the day I outsmarted the Crymzonians charging after me. I tasted freedom, only to have it slip through my fingers like sand when they found me almost fifteen years later.

I can almost feel the rush of adrenaline as I jumped onto my horse and galloped through the desert, using every ounce of my expertise to navigate the treacherous terrain during the night. I recall the dark embrace, the stirring of dust masking my presence, and the fear of losing my father.

Then, I refused to succumb to the despair that threatened to consume me.

Now, I have to do it again. I need to be strong.

With a growl of frustration, I renew my assault on the prison walls. The muscles in my arms strain against the resistance, my determination fueling each desperate attempt. There has to be a weakness I can exploit to free myself.

Has Monsteress already figured out who I am?

No, that can't be, for Monsteress wouldn't rest until she crushes my spirit and breaks my will before making a spectacle of my death. When her army attacked our village and took us prisoners, she didn't even look at me when we were led into the Throne Room. Her eyes were focused on the man bringing us in.

What did she call him again? Oh, right. Grand General Khaos.

His name is the second on my kill list once I leave here and bring my father and the villagers to safety.

But what if something happened to them? What if my father is dead already? What if Monsteress got her fingers on Aemilius? As much as I tried to teach him to defend himself, he's no fighter.

Anger settles deep in my stomach when I think about what I will do to Monsteress if she lays a finger on them.

Remembering that time is of the essence, I examined the sturdy iron bars that seal me in, searching for even the slightest vulnerability. I trace the rough edges of the stone, hoping to find a hidden flaw in the design. If I can get one of the iron bars free, I can use it as a tool.

Even though I've tried restlessly to find a weak spot, I still haven't found one.

As I pull on the bars, my thoughts turn to my weapons, which were cruelly confiscated upon my capture. I long for my bow, the familiar weight and balance. In my mind's eye, I see myself drawing an arrow, its tip honed to deadly precision, and releasing it with the speed of a striking serpent.

Nothing will stop me. I will get my hands on a bow, and it will find its mark in Monsteress.

But for now, my weapon is my willpower, and I will use it to chip away at the prison walls until they crumble before me once I get one of those bars out.

With every movement, I feel my energy drain more quickly than the days before. Even though I've fallen into a routine of checking every stone in this cell, somehow, it feels different today. Maybe it's because I haven't received today's meal yet or because I sleep less with each passing day.

Suddenly, a gust of wind blows through the grated slit in the wall, carrying in the smallest temperature drop.

Something isn't right.

I haven't felt a temperature change during my stay until the sun sets. Right now, it's the middle of the day.

Drawing upon my experiences, I analyze the dimensions of my prison cell once more. Nothing has changed. It's still the same bloody shithole they threw me in days ago.

As I lean against the warm wall to peek outside, I sense a slight vibration in the stones beneath my fingertips. Suddenly, a tremor jolts the ground beneath my feet, shaking loose dust particles that hang suspended in the air. My heart races, my body instinctively tensing as the shaking intensifies.

The walls of my cell quiver, and with a resounding crash, a section of the concrete shatters and crumbles away. My eyes widen in disbelief as sunlight floods the once-gloomy atmosphere. Tainted with the scent of freedom, a gust of fresh air beckons me.

I look over my shoulder to check if the opposite wall is still intact, and I'm relieved when I find it unscathed.

Without hesitation, I dart toward the newly formed gap, propelled by sheer hope. I climb over the debris-strewn edge and stand on a narrow ledge high above the ground. Fear grips me momentarily as I survey the vast drop below. The world outside the prison walls sprawls before me, both promising and treacherous.

But the sight brings me back to the day over fourteen years ago when my father grabbed me and threw me over the wall. He didn't care if I survived the fall because, in his opinion, any death that isn't caused by Monsteress is mercy.

"Devana?" a voice asks, and my knees almost buckle when I recognize it.

I whip my head around and almost fall when my father's face appears beside me, just a few feet away. That's when I notice the sizeable gap in the prison wall. It's not just my cell that got hit by the quake. Through the opening, I can see other curious faces peek through.

Frantically, I search the wall for the face that gives me hope in my dreams. But I don't see him.

"She didn't kill you!" I say in relief, my chin wobbling as I gaze at my father to scan his beautiful dark face for any injuries.

"You need to climb," he says, reaching out a hand in my direction to touch me, and my stomach bottoms out as I back away.

I would grab his hand if I weren't standing on such a high ledge. But up here, high over the Crymzon desert, my limbs freeze thinking about the day I almost fell to my death.

He can't do this to me again. He can't just toss me.

Summoning every ounce of courage, I gingerly begin my descent, ignoring his gesture. My hands grasp the crumbling bricks, which are rough and weathered against my skin.

Once I'm out of here, I will never touch another rock again.

"I'm right above you," my father says, and a little piece of rock hits my burning arm as I try to find hold.

My heart pounds in my chest as I carefully maneuver my way downward, inch by inch. The wind whips around me, tugging at my hair and clothes as if urging me forward.

Finally, my feet touched solid ground, and I let out a triumphant gasp. My father only takes a second to drop beside me, his muscles covered in sweat under his ripped clothes.

"I need to get inside!" I say, studying the prison tower and the small bridge connecting it to the Crymzon Wall.

Going back up there isn't an option. We only have a few moments left until guards are going to stream out of the prison gate to inspect the damage. Instead, I sprint toward the wall, my strides fueled by the adrenaline coursing through my veins. Each step carries me farther away from the prison, closer to the life I once lost. My breath comes in ragged gasps, my heart pounding in rhythm with my feet hitting the pavement.

Behind me, I can hear my father.

Every other parent would have warned their child to leave this place at once, but not my father. He knows what I'm about to do. Even though I will probably get killed trying to reach Monsteress, it must be done.

Reaching the wall, I press myself against it, my heaving chest seeking solace in its firm embrace as my father comes up beside me.

Why am I breathing so hard? I'm used to being on foot most of the day, walking the desert to find prey. So why am I in such an awful state?

"What's the plan?" he asks, leaning closer.

"There is no plan," I say, searching the prison gate for any soldiers. Instead, my focus falls on the stable hidden beneath the prison. It would be easy to jump on a horse and ride away before anyone notices our departure.

But that's what a sane person would do, not a warrior.

I close my eyes, feeling the hardness of the bricks against my cheek, and when I open them again, my gaze falls onto a faint line carved into the wall. I search for more scratches but can't find any. Someone must have been out here marking it. But why?

Another shock wave rumbles through the kingdom, and I cover my head with my arms from falling debris. My knees tremble more than they should, and I feel my father's arms holding me steady just before I lose footing.

"The Queen is dying," he says, but instead of joy, I detect fear in his voice.

"She can't. I've done nothing," I answer, trying to stand upright again, but my legs are made of melting clay.

"There's something I need to tell you. But first, we have to find her," he says, urging me forward.

I lean against him to stop him in his tracks. "Wait. Do you see this line? Someone marked this part of the wall, and I need to find out why."

He keeps pushing, but I hold my ground. "We don't have time. We need to get into the palace."

Then his words hit me: *the Queen is dying.*

For the first time since my father started training me to assassinate her, I exhale. Someone did the job for me. Years of preparation, sweat, and training have finally paid off. Sure, It might not be me who is killing her, but who cares?

Without a second thought, I press myself away from my father, steering toward the stables.

"What are you doing?" he asks as I walk on wobbly legs.

"Get a horse and ride far away from this place," I hiss through clenched teeth.

"If she dies now, so will all our friends," my father says, and I halt. "We can't leave them behind."

"Then let's help them escape. But I'm not setting foot into that kingdom again," I say, pointing at the wall.

Another shake rocks the earth beneath us; this time, the barrier before me splits open. An unknown pain radiates through my body, numbing my usual catlike reflexes.

"Watch out!" he yells, bolting forward to grab me by the arm and pull me back.

The pain caught me off guard, and I'm glad my father reacted because otherwise, I would have been crushed by a wall piece.

"Why didn't you move?" he asks, shaking me by the shoulders.

"I couldn't," I say, breathing through the pain. I can't explain where it's coming from. There's a chance that the guards poisoned me slowly with food, and now the effect is finally coming to claim me. But that doesn't make sense.

"We need to find the Queen and save her," he says, studying the prison behind me as if he's trying to figure out how much time we have left until it starts collapsing, too.

"What about our friends?" I ask as another part of the wall drops to the ground behind us. "You forced me into becoming the ultimate weapon since I can think, and now you want to pardon her? Our friends are right there," I say, pointing at the prison. "Let's get them."

"I will explain everything later," he says, pressing my back against the wall. "Trust me on this one."

"Trust you?" I scoff. "The last person who put their trust in you isn't around anymore, and I wonder why. I should've listened to my mother when she told me not to go with you. I should've stayed with her."

My father's eyes fill with tears, and he shakes them away. "That's not fair. Your mother thought keeping you hidden was the right choice. But I couldn't do it. I wanted you to live your life to the fullest."

"Wielding swords and shooting arrows all day? That's not living. It's torture."

"I bet you would say the same thing to your mother if you stayed with her instead."

I know he's telling the truth. I can't blame him for trying to let me experience life outside the sheltered hut in the jungle. He just wanted to help me free myself from the only person who could harm me.

But something doesn't seem right.

"What are you keeping from me?" I ask, searching his face, but he covers his eyes with his hand as if he can't stand to look at me. "Just say it."

"I need to help her," he says, lowering his hand. I want to intervene, but he steps past me as another shake rocks the kingdom, tearing down half of the house now displayed before us.

There's no way I will let him do this on his own.

Slowly, I follow him and watch him climb over the rubble that used to separate us from the Crymzonians, and my heart breaks when I see the extent of Monsteress losing her life.

Whoever is doing this to her enjoys her slow death way more than what I had in mind for her. My arrow would have ended her quickly and mercifully.

“Stay close,” my father says as I follow him into Crymzon.

TWO

KHAOS

"Are you sure you want to return to her?" Opaline asks, her black curls bouncing as she walks to me to hand me a leaf bag filled with dried meat and fruits.

"She needs me," I answer, attaching the bag to my horse.

It has been almost two days since Opaline saved me in Terminus.

My hand goes instantly to the fresh scar hidden beneath my shirt, marking the skin right above my heart. Though it doesn't hurt anymore, its black coloration worries me.

Opaline spent hours trying to find a cure. From herbal pastes and tinctures over creatures she called leeches—nasty, worm-looking things with sharp teeth—to a ritual that is supposed to send evil spirits away.

Nothing worked.

A bit of my magic suffices to cover the darkness of the scar and turn it into a shade close to my skin color. But it's not enough.

I might not see it, but I can feel it.

As I close my eyes, the haunting echoes of distant screams and metallic noises fill my ears, transporting me back to that fateful battlefield. The air was thick with the acrid smell of blood mixed with death and the deafening roar of magic exploding. Each step was a cautious dance around the dead soldiers covering the ground as I approached the frontline.

But it's a single moment that forever seared into my memory—the moment I realized Soulin wasn't there, and the heart-wrenching betrayal that followed.

I was stabbed. I was dying. And then, amidst the chaos, I saw her, a beacon of hope amidst the darkness. Her eyes, once filled with warmth when we were children, glimmered with an unsettling determination.

My mind plays the scene in vivid detail despite my consciousness drifting in and out. I remember the touch of her trembling hands as she pressed against the wound where my heart should have been—a desperate plea for my survival amidst the madness.

I can hear her argue with another soldier and her attempt to heal my wound with magic.

Then she paused. Confusion and disbelief washed over me as I longed for her warm hands to touch me again. I tried to resist, to understand the reasons behind her sudden change, but the next thing I remember was Opaline stopping her from something.

Then shouts filled the air, and just as despair threatened to consume me, a burst of magic rushed through my veins, more potent than an adrenaline rush.

I opened my eyes as Soulin was lifted in the air by her neck, a gasp escaping her lips.

The man before her, King Keres, threatened to crush her windpipe without effort until Soulin kicked his visor up, revealing her father's face.

Her father. The man she despises the most.

That's the last thing I remember from Terminus.

As the memories swirl within my mind, I reach for Opaline's hand and squeeze it tightly. "I can't thank you enough for saving me," I say, returning her warm smile. "But I need to return to Soulin. And don't offer me again to stay here."

A smirk crawls over her lips. "I hope you know what you are doing."

I certainly don't, but I can't tell her that.

Just moments before Soulin found the strength to fight back against her father and cut off his arm to release herself, our connection snapped into place. I'm still unsure why it took so long. It should have happened in the water room. Right then and there, when pleasure rippled through us, threatening to consume us.

In the last few hours, I tried to come up with an explanation. Maybe it was delayed because we never completed the sacred Connection Ceremony under Lunra, or—that's the answer I'm leaning on—that Soulin showed genuine emotions for the first time since becoming the Queen.

While I couldn't see what was happening, I could still hear. The whispers of my soldiers didn't go unnoticed when they pointed out her tears. I've never seen Soulin weep, not in her childhood, and for sure not when her family died.

A mental image of little Soulin flashes before my eyes. Her big red curls rush behind her even bigger personality as she jumps into a stack of hay. Her laughter fills the stables and warms my heart. It was a moment of pure joy and innocence, a memory before her inner war tainted our lives.

The love I once felt for her remains, yet it's tempered by pain and betrayal. The recent scar on my body is a constant reminder of the battlefield, but the wounds in my heart run deeper.

As much as I tell myself to stay away from her, my entire being wants to join her. Every cell yearns to be close to her, to grab her and press her warm skin against mine.

She's mine.

Mine.

With a heavy sigh, I open my eyes, returning to the present, the memories of that fateful day fading. I know the scars of war will never fully heal, but I draw strength from the bond of an old friendship with Opaline and the unyielding spirit of survival that saved me from both the enemy's blade and the betrayal of my love.

"I need her as much as she needs me," I answer, pulling Opaline into a hug.

"You know she will make your life a living hell when you return. She won't be pleased to see you."

"I like my women feisty," I laugh, and Opaline chuckles against my chest. "Seriously though, I will be fine. Now that King Keres is history, there's no more threat."

I wasn't there to watch Soulin hand the self-made King his own ass, but I would have felt if something was wrong with her. No pain means she's alive; if she's alive, Keres must be dead because she wouldn't rest until he's wiped off this planet.

Opaline's big brown eyes fill with sadness. I've seen that look before. She's holding her tongue for my sake. "How are you so sure?"

I release her out of my grip and close in on my horse. "If she hasn't killed me in all those years I've been at her side, she won't do it now."

"But she tried. I stopped her right before her blade could reach your heart," Opaline says, her face covered with sadness. "And the messenger was pretty clear. She will destroy you if you return."

"And I told you it was a misunderstanding," I answer, mounting the steed.

Opaline got me there. I can't come up with an explanation for why Soulin tried to kill me, even though tears ran down her face. Nothing that happened in Terminus makes sense to me, but I'm only a day away from getting all the answers I'm looking for.

Opaline grabs my hand and squeezes it. "I wish there's something I could say to change your mind, my friend," she says, pulling her hand back. "Just know that Tenacoro always has a place for you. May Emara and Lunra watch over you."

I can't thank Emara, the Goddess of Vitality, enough for extending her power to heal my wounds. With the help of a lagoon hidden deep inside Tenacoro's jungle, Opaline was able to speed up my recovery under the watchful eyes of her Goddess. It's unheard of for a God or Goddess to assist a citizen of another kingdom, and I'm unsure what convinced her to help a Crymzonian, but it's a debt I can never repay.

Lunra, the Goddess of the Moon and Love, created my kingdom, Crymzon, which stands hundreds of miles away in the south of Escela.

An everlasting deity oversees each kingdom. The territories of the six kingdoms are safeguarded and guided by three Gods and three Goddesses, each with exceptional talents.

"Don't be so dramatic," I say, a broad, fake grin flashing over my lips.

But Opaline is right.

Soulin won't be happy to see me. She made it clear she never wants to see me again and even went so far as to release me as her Grand General after it became apparent that I wasn't her Soulmate.

But now that we have the confirmation that we're destined for each other, she might try everything she can to rid herself of me again.

If Soulin is known for one thing, it's her incredible determination to be the strongest individual right below the Gods. With the new magic rushing through my veins from being connected to the Queen and Crymzon, I'm as close to the Gods as she is.

We're meant to rule over Crymzon and equally distribute the magic through the land. I'm her anker as much as she is mine, but I bet my life that she isn't as happy to share her power with me as I am to share my life with her.

With a kick of my heels, my horse moves.

"Khaos Zedohr," Opaline calls behind me, and I twist in my saddle to face her. "At least send word about your well-being when you can."

"I will send you an invitation to our kingdom so you can see it for yourself," I answer, burying my heels in the horse's sides, and it gallops through the dense jungle toward the bridge separating Tenacoro from the desert enclosing Crymzon.

The last time I used my magic was to shield Soulin from an incoming attack. Thousands of Crymzonians were gathered before the Crymzon Palace to glimpse at the new Queen.

Back then, I was used to unlimited magic usage. Under Soulin's father, King Obsidian, I experienced no weakness between the throne and the power surging through the kingdom.

Therefore, I used my magic to give Soulin the perfect succession ceremony.

I wiped away any cloud covering the night sky to let the moon through, dimmed the noise from the eager onlookers, and even summoned a low breeze to dampen the heat radiating from the sandstone surrounding us.

I felt my energy draining slowly, but I shrugged it off as nerves for seeing my thirteen-year-old friend descend the Crymzon Throne.

Everything went as planned. The air was filled with tranquility, disrupted only by the distant whispering of the citizens and the faint rustle of Soulin's dress.

But as a gentle breeze caressed our faces, an ominous sound shattered the peaceful ambiance—a sharp whistling noise growing louder by the second. Instinctively, I raised my hand, my palm emanating a soft, ethereal glow, as I conjured a shield of shimmering magic in front of her.

In the blink of an eye, a deadly arrow soared through the air, aimed directly at Soulin's head. The arrowhead's sharp tip glinted maliciously under the moonlight.

With a harsh gesture, I directed my magical shield to intercept the oncoming projectile. The arrow collided with the translucent barrier, causing a burst of energy to ripple through the air. The shield absorbed the impact with a resounding thud, deflecting the arrow's deadly trajectory.

And in that moment, when the Queen stood unharmed, protected by my power, I felt every ounce of magic leave my body.

For the crowd, it must have looked like I sank down to inspect the weapon that almost claimed our new Queen. Instead, my knees caved in, sending me falling to my knees.

With a measured calmness, I did the only thing I could to mask what had happened. I reached out and plucked the defeated arrow splinters from the ground to give me time to find the strength to stand up again. My fingers delicately traced the sleek, broken shaft adorned with carvings. Yet, it was the fletching that caught my attention—only two feathers were attached instead of the customary three.

It was a subtle yet deliberate alteration, hinting at a hidden message or plot lurking in the shadows.

Clutching the peculiar arrow tightly, I stood up on wobbly legs and hid the weapon behind my back while the kingdom erupted into chaos.

How was I supposed to tell her that the arrow belonged to the kingdom she had the strongest connection to? Those feathers didn't belong to Starstrand. Starstrandians use their own pearl white wing feathers to mark their arrows.

That feather I was holding tight against my back was brown. It might have been an unusual color for Tenacoro because their signature is green; I must admit that. But no other kingdom is blessed with winged creatures besides the jungle kingdom.

The next day, Soulin appointed me as her Grand General and gave me the job of recruiting brave souls to join her army. By then, I expected my magic would have returned, but I had to find out I was powerless.

In the following weeks, I tried to make sense of it. Had Lunra punished me for interfering with destiny by saving Soulin? Had I used too much of my power trying to give her the perfect day? Or was it something completely different?

But I had no time to dwell on my predicament. It was my job to turn the new recruits into guards, and while they used their magic in addition to my combat training, I had to train harder to cover my condition.

My lips curl into a smile as I send my magic through the horse's veins to pick up speed. The unbearable heat of the desert has nothing on the cooling sensation crawling over my skin.

I survived almost fifteen years without magic; now that it's back, I never want to miss it again. All those years of sweating my ass off in the sun, healing wounds naturally, and needing twice as much training as anyone else are finally over.

My heartbeat quickens when I see the Crymzon Wall appear in the distance.

Only a few more minutes and I'm home.

THREE

Devana

My lithe figure blends seamlessly with the shadows as I silently make my way through the maze-like structure of the Crymzon Palace.

In the heart of a once-magnificent palace lies a desolate scene of destruction. Crumbling walls, fallen pillars, and shattered remnants of what was once grandeur are scattered across the expansive halls.

Whatever caused the prison wall to burst open also affected the buildings outside and Monsteress' palace.

I tread lightly through the labyrinth of ruins, but I can't say the same of my father. Even though he taught me everything I know about tracking down prey, hunting, and dismantling it, it doesn't mean he embodies the same values as I do.

While my steps barely make a sound against the stone floor, he stomps behind me as if we're taking a stroll through the desert.

"Can you be any louder?" I whisper, pressing myself against a wall.

"There's no one here."

"Yet," I hiss, watching him march through the corridor with no sign of concern on his face. "They have magic, and we don't even have a weapon to defend ourselves. If they catch us, we're dead."

My words roll off his massive body like water on a boulder.

"How are you feeling?" he asks, coming to a halt beside me.

"I would feel better if you at least attempted to stay alive."

He grabs me by the hand and pulls me into the sunlight falling through a shattered wall behind him to study me. "I'm taking this seriously, Devana. That's why I need to know how you're doing."

"I'm fine," I hiss, ripping myself free. "Stop acting so strange."

"We haven't encountered a single soul since we entered."

Frowning, I nod my head. Besides the destruction lurking in every corner of the kingdom, we haven't seen a single soul. But that doesn't mean we can let our guard down.

Dust swirls through the corridor as a gust of wind blows in, and I suppress a cough that has been itching my throat since we entered.

Where is everyone?

I should be happy to find this place empty. Instead, a strange feeling washes over me every time I dodge a brand-new piece of palace stone falling out of its place.

"Explain to me again why we have to help the Queen," I say, pressing myself against the wall as we continue our search.

Our mission is to find the elusive Queen whose treachery plunged the kingdom into chaos and destroy her.

Damn, no. I meant we have to *help* her. Or is it to help her so we can destroy her *then*?

"With her magic, she might be the only one who can help with your...impairment." His last word comes out in a hushed tone, and I almost didn't hear it.

"It's about my disability? That's what this is all about?" My nostrils flare. "You can say it: this is my *disabled* daughter. She's struggling with weakness of her limbs, lack of coordination, and electric shocks."

My father goes silent, his eyes resting on me.

It's hard for him to say it.

He's trained me to be an ultimate weapon for almost thirty years. Despite that, he struggles to admit that I'm not flawless.

Not that he wants me to be.

No.

He can't voice my condition because he can't find a way to help me. He wants to take this burden off my shoulders and carry it himself.

But he can't.

This is my little package to carry through life, and even on the worst days—plagued by tingling sensations and electric impulses rushing through my body—I'm just glad to experience another day.

My condition forces me to slow down at times and inhale. But what's so wrong about that?

He must stop treating me like I'm broken and finally say it.

I know he blames himself for the way I was born. I also know he would have given me perfect health if it was in his hands.

I know I'm his most valued possession. I mean, that's why he left Tenacoro behind to shield my imperfections. He protected me from being sorted out of being a warrior and took the role of being my mentor in his own hands to see me thrive. Even though his motives for my harsh training were more profound than just being able to provide food for myself and fit in, I owe him my life.

My mother, on the other hand, couldn't handle my flaws. My constant pain was a sign of weakness she couldn't live with. If it were up to her, she would have handed me over to the silent sisterhood for them to take over my care.

I was her burden. Nothing more than a broken toy with no hope of repair.

Thinking about my mother stings, but this mental pain has served as motivation countless times.

Somehow, I will show her I can do great things, even with how I was born. I'm more than a fearless warrior—more than a broken individual that needs saving. I'm stronger than most people I know because I have to work three times as hard to get even.

Just as we make our way up the broken stairs into the second story, unseen mechanisms rumble into motion. As if driven by some unseen force, sections of the palace begin to shift and rebuild themselves. Walls, once mere piles of debris, morph into solid structures. Corridors realign, creating alternative paths while closing off others.

Caught amid the ever-changing labyrinth, I'm suddenly separated as an imposing wall rises between my father and me, sealing off our paths.

"Father," I call out, my voice echoing through the lonely halls. But my pleas are met with a haunting silence. "Stay there. I will find you."

Fear and determination intertwine within my heart as I realize I must continue my mission alone. With a deep breath, I press forward, my steps becoming more resolute.

As I venture deeper into the reconstructed palace, the atmosphere becomes a haunting echo of its former splendor. But it's not done yet. More stone sections scramble past me, mending the broken walls enclosing me.

I need a door—just one.

Frantically, my steps turn into a run as I search the wall for an opening. I must get to my father. Without me, he's a sitting duck.

Through the twists and turns of the rejuvenating palace, my senses heightened, alert for any sign of the Queen's presence. The sound of my footsteps reverberates, an unwelcome reminder of my solitude amidst the fractured kingdom.

I long for my father's reassuring presence and know that time is running out.

Eventually, I arrive at a towering doorway, its solid frame standing as a testament to the palace's past glory. I approach it cautiously, my hand gently grazing the warm surface.

As I listen, the faintest sounds from the other side reach my ears—an indistinct murmur of voices intermingled with occasional footsteps.

Hopeful, I press my ear against the ancient wood, desperate to glean any information that can aid me in finding out if it's my father or strangers.

It can't be him. My father isn't the talkative type, and what are the odds that he knows someone inside the palace walls to talk to?

Should I open the door and confront the unknown voices just a wooden board away, or should I wait until the air clears and sneak out?

As I weigh my choices, the broken sandstone palace seems to hold its breath for a moment. Its silent corridors and shattered halls echo with the weight of my decision before it continues to repair itself.

I prepare myself to take control. I have to do it if I want my father back.

My heart pounds in my chest as I extend my hand, my fingertips brushing against the warm metal of the doorknob. It burns on my skin as I fasten the grip on it.

Just as I'm about to twist it and jump at the danger on the other side, my neck flings to the side. A sharp and unexpected pain rushes through my body when something heavy connects with my head.

The impact echoes through the hallway, and time seems to freeze momentarily as my body goes limp.

My hand slips from the doorknob, the door remaining steadfastly closed as if mocking my failed attempt.

The pain is so intense that I close my eyes as I crumple to the ground, my body folding like a marionette with severed strings. A cascade of dark hair conceals my vision when I try to see what has struck me.

The last thing I hear is the distant sound of footsteps fading away before everything goes dark.

FOUR

DEVANA

Slowly, consciousness seeps back into my world. My eyelids flutter, fighting against the weight that holds them shut. A dull ache throbs at the base of my skull, a painful reminder of the blow that stole my awareness.

As my vision clears, I find myself lying on a warm stone floor. The bright light that filters through high, narrow windows paints elongated shadows across the hall.

At least the sun is still out.

The longer I look at it, the more I realize it isn't the afternoon brightness anymore. It's morning. How is that possible? Have I slept all day?

With a groan, I gingerly press a hand against my temple, feeling the tender skin beneath my fingertips.

Memories flood back, jumbled and fragmented. I remember the door, the anticipation that filled me moments before, and the sudden darkness that enveloped me. And then, my purpose crystallizes in my mind: I need to find my father.

With a grunt, I push myself up, wincing at the sharp pain from my protesting muscles. As I rise, my surroundings come into focus. It's still the same corridor I lost my father in, but the floor is clear of stone fragments, dust, and debris.

Squinting against the residual pain in my head, I steady myself and take a tentative step forward. Whatever caused me to black out must have been a piece of rock returning to its original spot.

I press my ear against the door again, but there's no one on the other side this time. I crack it and squeeze through, checking my surroundings for any guards.

Someone must have seen me lying on the ground. There's no way an entire day can go by, with no one noticing a stranger's still body on the floor.

Unless...

Unless we're the only two people remaining in the palace.

But why did they evacuate the kingdom?

As I navigate through winding corridors and shadowed hallways, my head throbs with every heartbeat, a constant reminder of my miserable attempt to get to my father. But I push through it.

It has nothing on me. I'm used to feeling stabbing discomfort and shooting pain daily. Somehow, my regular, ever-existing discomfort is gone. But I know better than to waste my time on it. It's just a matter of minutes until the first ache settles inside my muscles and a few hours until every movement is a fight. My body may be bruised and weary, but my determination remains unyielding. It's a fire that refuses to be extinguished.

I will not falter until I find my father.

As I traverse the maze of corridors and halls, my sharp senses catch the sound of primal grunts from a nearby room. My curiosity peaks as I creep toward the source of the commotion, my hand resting on my hip where my blade should be.

Shit. I still don't have a sword or a bow.

But that can't hold me back.

When I reach the massive door, partially damaged by the relentless sands of time, I pause to listen. I know I should turn around and keep searching for my father, but it's the first noise I've heard since I woke up.

The muffled sounds of a fierce struggle reach my ears, mingling with grunts of exertion and the clash of magic. Without hesitation, I push the door open, careful to avoid drawing attention to my presence.

Quickly, I scan the room, absorbing every detail as a scene of an intense stand-off unfolds before my eyes. Two figures engage in a life-or-death struggle in the center of a spacious yet cluttered chamber.

The Queen, her signature red dress flawlessly hugging her body, stands in the middle of the room. Her opponent is a mysterious massive creature, formed out of twisted vines.

What in the Gods' name is that thing?

It possesses the same lethal grace that matches Monsteress, and my throat constricts the longer I look at it.

An otherworldly screech rips through the air. The beast jolts towards the Queen, and I have to blink twice as I watch the vines form into sharp talons before embedding into Soulin's chest.

Seeing her getting injured is enough to feel her pain in my body. I bring my hand up to my chest to ensure I wasn't struck. But there's nothing. It's just my imagination.

Behind the creature, another emerges, and I don't have enough willpower to wait for its transformation to end.

I pull the door shut and run. I run as fast as my legs carry me. My breath comes in quick gasps as I push myself to my limits, my body driven by sheer fear.

Did Monsteress notice me? Even worse: Did the creatures see me?

As I round a sharp corner, my eyes widen with alarm as I collide with an unexpected obstacle. The impact sends me sprawling to the ground, the force jolting through my body as a scream escapes my lips.

The beast found me. It cut me off.

Shaking off the shock, I quickly regain my senses and scramble to my feet.

That's when my eyes lock with another human.

It isn't a beast I ran into. It's a frail man dressed in the blood-red Crymzonian uniform. But I don't have time to figure out who this man is or why the only guard inside the palace looks older than Crymzon.

"Monsteress..." I pant out between sharp breaths. "I mean, the Queen. She needs help."

I point back to the corridor, but another wave of fear grips me when I realize how much time I already wasted.

Without missing a beat, I resume my frantic pace, knowing every second counts. The fleeting thought of stopping to check on the man I collided with flickers in my mind, but the urgency of my panic compels me to continue.

My legs hurl forward, the rhythmic thud of my footfalls blending with the sound of my labored breath. The corridors blur as I push myself harder to suppress the pain and exhaustion.

The scene shifts again as I navigate through the winding passageways, weaving and dodging with practiced precision. My eyes are fixed on an unknown destination. I'm unsure where I'm going, but I refuse to let the collision slow me down. Instead, I use it as fuel to speed up.

With every step, I grow stronger, my body adapting to the strenuous demands I place upon it. The air rushes past me as I fly towards a giant door that seems to be the entrance.

The image of my father flashes back into my mind, and I draw up short, just feet away from leaving this god-awful place.

I need to turn around and search for him. There's no way I can leave him behind.

But I'm also no good if I'm dead.

Against my better judgment, I step over the threshold and run.

FIVE

KHAOS

I'm not sure what I expected.

Maybe that Soulin is waiting at the gate for me because she can sense my nearness as much as I do. Or a crowd of Crymzonians filling the streets, greeting me as I pass. But when I canter into Crymzon, the roads are empty. Not a single soul stands between me and the Crymzon Palace, and the closer I draw to it, the stronger the feeling of unease gets.

My dream of being received by my kingdom's citizens is too bizarre to be accurate, but not crossing a single person until I reach the courtyard is banal.

What in Lunra's name is going on? Where is everyone?

I'm aware it's not nighttime, but Crymzonians are nosy, and whenever they hear someone entering the gate, they at least open a blind to peek outside. They must be exhausted and sleeping. I mean, we just went to battle.

Shrugging the superstition off, I keep riding until I reach the courtyard.

My heart yearned to return to Soulin since I woke up in the lagoon, and now that the moment is here, I freeze.

I've fought against the odds to regain my strength and return to the palace, but how will Soulin react when she sees me?

My steps reverberate through the silent hallways. Usually bustling with life and activity, the palace is strangely muted, as if awaiting my arrival. With each stride, my brain tells me to turn around while my heart tugs so strongly in my chest that I want to rip it out.

As I approach the throne room, the anticipation of reuniting with my Queen fills my heart with joy and trepidation. It has been three days since I last laid eyes on her. The thought of her kept me going, igniting a fierce longing to return to her side. Still, I pause for a moment to gather my thoughts.

What is the worst she can do to me?

Well, that's a stupid question. I've seen Soulin kill people in the most cruel ways. No, that blood isn't on her hands.

I executed people in *her* name in the cruelest ways.

I take a deep breath, adjusting the weight of my sword, now more ceremonial than functional, and push open the towering doors to the Crymzon Throne.

I'm back. I can't believe it. I'm finally here after our forced separation because of my injury, and I'm eager to reunite with her and fulfill my duties as both, a soldier and her Soulmate.

A curious sound catches my attention as the doors swing open—a series of muffled grunts and clinking armor.

The circular, red-tinted window casts a warm glow over the room, while tapestries depicting the lunar cycle and moths adorn the walls. At the far end of the room, atop an elevated dais, sits the Crymzon Throne, a symbol of power and authority.

My breath hitches as I take everything in, and my heart skips a beat at the sight of my Queen.

In the center of the opulent throne room, Soulin stands surrounded by a group of guards, their helmets and weapons scattered about. The air carries a smell of sweat, mingling with tension.

The Queen, draped in a red dress, possesses an intensity in her gaze as she meticulously inspects the guards one by one. Three nasty creatures follow her as she strolls through the rows of soldiers.

Confusion clouds my mind, unsure of the situation that unfolds before me. I hesitate, my footsteps faltering as I try to make sense of the scene.

The guards, stripped down to their undergarments, stand with a mix of discomfort and respect as Soulin examines them, her discerning eyes scanning their bodies for unknown reasons.

My gaze locks on the Queen, my heart torn between the relief of finally seeing her and the bewilderment of the unexpected sight.

What the fuck is she doing? Why is everyone undressed? And what are those nasty-looking creatures doing behind Soulin? Is she aware she's being followed by beasts formed out of nightmares?

Rows upon rows of half-naked soldiers fill the room. Some stand proud and tall, while others cower before her, trying to hide as much skin with their hands as possible.

Sensing my presence, Soulin turns, her expression briefly revealing surprise before settling into a composed demeanor.

Her eyes meet mine. "What are you doing here?" she asks, her voice tinged with disgust.

I shake my head. My voice catches in my throat as I struggle to find words. When I fail, I approach slowly, the weight of my armor almost invisible compared to the importance of uncertainty in my heart.

"What is this?" I ask, my voice laced with concern as I point at my soldiers.

The Queen's gaze softens, and her posture straightens as she walks in my direction, the beasts following her as if they're on a tight leash. "The kingdom has faced challenges in your absence," she begins, her words formal and emotionless. "I have taken it upon myself to ensure the well-being and readiness of my guards. It is my duty to protect and defend my people."

Her guards and *her* people?

And in *my absence*?

I was gone for three days, not a year or a decade. Three fucking days.

With every step she draws closer, my body reacts to her. My palms sweat, and my heart rate spikes when the silver freckles surrounding her wild green-golden eyes dance across her face. Her red curls are divine, and my eyes widen when I see the white hair strand marking her flawless appearance.

She still has it. Even though her magic is back, a piece of her hair is still drained of color, and she doesn't mind showing it.

"You're not welcome here," she hisses between clenched teeth, coming to a halt.

In a blink of an eye, she reaches into the slit of her dress, and I'm not fast enough when her arm shoots in my direction.

Of all people, I should know how fast she can pull out her whip. For years, Soulin has worn all kinds of jewelry, covering the entire surface between wrist and elbow. Only under close inspection, those bracelets turn out to be whips neatly curled around her arm.

She's also tested a prototype of an even bigger metal whip on me that was fastened around her thigh.

I braced myself for a magical attack when I decided to return to Crymzon. But when the sharp metal of her whip she hid under her dress around her thigh closes around my neck, I'm surprised.

You're not welcome here. The sentence echoes through my head over and over again.

The warm metal cuts into my skin, but I use my magic to absorb the pain and press against it to ease her grip. My eyes fall on her hand and then on her arm. My stomach tightens when I see the scar her dead brother inflicted on her.

Yes, her dead brother.

With the help of a necromancer, the self-appointed King Keres, he was resurrected from the dead just to torture Soulin.

But that scar isn't the one that worries me at the moment. My eyes land on a bunch of newly healed scratches across her arms and chest.

What happened to her in the days I was gone?

"This is my last warning, for old times' sake." She pulls on the whip's handle to apply more pressure. "Turn around and never come back," she said, her voice cool and distant. Her words pierce my heart like a dagger, shattering the fantasies I wove during my time away.

As I absorb her words and the scars marking her olive skin, I realize the depth of her commitment and the burdens she shouldered in my absence. A wave of admiration washes over me, mingling with the desire to be by her side, to support her in any way I can.

Slowly, I kneel before her, the sharp claws of the whip cutting into my throat. "I may have been away, my Queen, but I have returned to stand by your side. Let me share the weight of your burdens. Let us face the challenges together."

The room is quiet enough for me to hear the shivering soldiers around us. For a moment, I forgot we were not alone until their whispers filled the silence.

"Clean yourself up!" I yell at the soldiers before looking up at Soulin again.

Her eyes practically shoot fire at me as the room turns into motion. "I'm your Queen, and I command you to stay!" she barks, but most soldiers are already halfway out of the door with or without their armor in tow.

Soulin pulls on the whip, and I sprawl forward, closer to her. "How dare you address my army?"

"*Our* army," I answer, squaring my shoulders.

"One pull, and your head will come clean off," she snarls, and I watch the slight tremble in her hand.

The door swings shut behind us as if the last soldier is trying to save their souls from what's coming next.

I know Soulin killed her father and brother in this room. Even though the charcoaled stone beneath us is covered with new flooring, I remember the stench of burned hair and flesh hanging in the air for weeks.

"Do it," I say as my heart slows in my chest. "You're all I have."

SIX

Queen Soulin

Khaos' eyes wander over my arm again.

I now have enough magic to cover the scar inflicted by my brother and the ones I received from the creatures submerging the device in Khaos' room.

But I want him to see them.

I want to see them.

They remind me I can't trust anyone on this planet, including the person destined to be my Soulmate.

I pull on the handle again, and Khaos slides even closer to me. I can feel his warm breath caressing my thigh as he straightens up again.

"Were the beasts inside your room meant for me?" I ask, my voice deeper than a growl.

Khaos raises his gaze to meet mine. His expression shifts from confusion to surprise as his eyes wander from me to the creatures behind me and back. "Soulin... I have no idea what you are referring to," he stammers, his voice laced with genuine bewilderment.

It almost brings me to my knees when he says my name. My brows furrow as I take a deep breath to suppress the feelings inside me, my voice stern but tinged with frustration. "Do not play coy with me. The creatures you harbored in your chamber—monstrous beings that nearly killed me. Tell me, how could you bring such danger within the very walls of my palace?"

His confusion deepens. "I assure you, I know nothing about those creatures. I would never purposefully put you in harm's way," he pleads, his eyes widening.

The room seems to hold its breath as we lock eyes, the weight of my accusations and the intensity of the moment hanging in the air. Anger and doubt cloud my mind, and conflicting emotions are warring within me.

I've known Khaos almost my entire life. He's a lot, but not a liar.

"Stop playing stupid and just admit it," I say, my eyes searching for any indicator of a lie.

"Look at me, Soulin," he says, grabbing my whip to pull me closer and relieving some pressure around his neck. "I would *never* hurt you."

Amidst the tension between us, an unexpected shift occurs inside my heart. The fire of our heated conversation transforms into something else entirely—an unfamiliar spark of desire. I feel a palpable electricity, a connection that tries to break through.

My heart flutters as I see the sincerity in Khaos' eyes, his confusion giving way to a genuine plea for understanding.

"If what you say is true, why did I find a gadget from Eternitie inside your chamber?" I ask, leaning back to put more space between us.

Something flickers in Khaos' eyes, and I know he knows what I'm talking about.

"The gadget," he whispers, more to himself than me. "I found it in the prisoner's hut."

Immediately, all the puzzle pieces click into place.

Of course. I sent Khaos to check Cyrus' hut for any companions. He was the one returning with Cyrus' whore, who turned out to be a Starstrandian traitor.

Cyrus Matrus, the prince of Eternitie, fled his kingdom to escape his father's plan of being betrothed to me, and through sheer luck, he ended up in my kingdom as a prisoner.

Eternitie is known for its baffling gadgeteers and genius inventors. I should have known the gadget belongs to my once-again missing prisoner, who happens to be running loose since my return from Terminus.

But not for long.

Khaos, still on his knees, nods earnestly. "I didn't know what the gadget was. I tried to hand it over to you, but..." he stalls momentarily. "You were preparing for war against the North."

I know what he wanted to say. His mind wandered to our steamy encounter in the water room, followed by his demotion as my Grand General.

As the weight of the accusation lifts, my mind fills with the images of his naked body. His hot breath against my neck. Our shared heated kisses. His dick thrusting into me. The warm waves washing over me as I let loose.

I watch his eyes darken as if he's seeing the same images.

My body trembles and my breath quickens as I look into his brown eyes.

It was so much easier holding onto the belief that he tried to kill me. After all, that's what most people want to do when they see me. And I don't blame them.

But seeing him kneeling before me, his eyes pleading for more...for me...I can't hold back any longer.

Before I can react, Khaos grabs my dress with the other hand and pulls me in. His face collides with the thin fabric separating him from my pussy, and I gasp as he rips again on my dress, and the delicate silk shifts to the side to give him a glimpse.

I want to retaliate. I need to. We can't do this again.

But he's faster and presses his arm against my ass to pull me closer, and another gasp escapes my throat when his tongue finds my clit.

Oh, fucking Gods.

This can't be happening.

What is he doing?

As much as I want to push him down and make him pay for how he's handling me, my core and heart work against it.

I need him. Right here and right now.

Whatever he is doing, it feels so good.

Warmth spreads through my lower abdomen with each lick of his tongue, and I'm surprised when I hear my whip falling to the ground beside me. Now that my hand is free, I fist his dark curls as wetness spreads between my legs when I hear his groan.

Fuck.

His tongue swirls around my clit, and my legs shake as I stand my ground.

I will not falter. He can't just march in here, command *my* army to leave, and then take from me what he wants.

"Lie down," he whispers between sliding his tongue through my seam and sucking on my clit.

"Never," I say between ragged breaths, but somehow, my body follows his command against my inner war of keeping the upper hand.

My ass touches the warm stone beneath us as I let myself down slowly, his tongue still attached to my clit as if he's scared, he will lose his hold over me if he lets go. When my back presses against the floor, he pushes my thighs apart as far as they can go, grabs my ass with both hands to angle my pelvis up, and keeps sucking on me harder.

My nerves go wild as he spreads my legs apart.

Pressing my hands against my mouth, I try to stifle the moans escaping my lips, and that must be the sign he has been waiting for to up his game.

A familiar burn begins to build in my lower belly when he slips two fingers into me, turning them sideways to rub my inner wall while his tongue moves over my clit, again and again.

My senses overstimulate as I buck against his face, grabbing his hair to push him deeper into me.

"I need you," I whimper, spreading my legs even wider to give him more access.

Instead of untying his pants to thrust into me and give me the relief I crave, he adds another finger and sucks even harder.

"I can't take it any longer. I want you," I moan, my back arching from the pressure building up.

He never stood a chance. Before he can move his other hand to release his dick, waves of pleasure rush through me. The release is so intense that my screams echo off the walls back at me.

When my muscles finally stop twitching from my release, he pulls his fingers out and lifts his head to look at me, a smile tugging on his lips.

"Stop smirking," I breathe out, my skin coated with a thin film of sweat.

"You don't know how beautiful you sound when you let go," he says, wiping his mouth with his sleeve.

Scrambling to my feet, I pull my dress down and straighten my posture. "What are you really doing here?" I ask, trying to push aside the touch of his tongue I can still feel on me.

It's wrong of me to act like he wasn't just face deep in my pussy, but I have to. I've already given him more power over me than I ever wanted.

Khaos uncurls the whip still attached to his throat, and my heart aches when I see the deep puncture wounds before he heals them with his magic.

I warned him. This is his own damn fault.

As Khaos steps before me, his eyes are brimming with emotions he struggles to contain. His voice wavers as he speaks, the words heavy with remorse. "Soulin, I fought with all my strength and courage for you and our kingdom. Let me come home."

"You should have considered the consequences when you left me alone, burdened with the weight of fighting a war while you went behind my back to speak to Queen Synadena. I needed you here by my side."

"You sent me away."

"I know," I say, my heart twisting in anguish as I realize the pain I caused Khaos. "I didn't know what else to do. The only way to protect you was to send you away. You were always a friend before a soldier. I feared my feelings were a fleeting dream, destined to be shattered by the reality of my position."

A tear wells up in Khaos' eye, his voice choked with emotion. "I would give up everything to be by your side again. My life is nothing without you."

Those words stir something deep down in my heart. As much as I want to push him away to shield him from the fate I mark the people surrounding me with, my heart won't let me do it again.

I've tried and failed now twice to keep him away from me. I'm not sure if I can do it a third time.

For once, I need to act against my better judgment. For once, I need to let my guard down and accept that I'm not alone because, no matter what I do, Khaos *will* return again.

"Then help me figure out who the mole is. Somehow, King Citeus already knew about my defeat in Terminus and declined my invitation to hold a Council meeting."

Khaos' eyes widen. "Defeat?"

I don't want to relive the moment again when King Keres, better known as my father, vanished before I could unleash my new powers on him. But Khaos deserves the truth after all I put him through. So, I tell him how I tried to end his life to give him an honorable death; how Opaline showed up upon his request for aid; how I sent them away because I couldn't function feeling him close; and how I destroyed Keres' entire army before losing sight of him.

"He's still alive?" Khaos asks, his mouth hanging open.

"He's not my father anymore. He's just one of Otyx's puppets he uses to play with me."

Otyx, the God of the Underworld, is the only deity who hasn't made a mark on Escela yet. Well, until he resurrected my dead father to build a fortress in Terminus.

Khaos shakes his head. "Why you?"

"I asked myself that question multiple times, and I concluded. When I spoke to Lunra, she mentioned that her history with Otyx goes way beyond our time."

"You spoke to her?"

I forgot how much Khaos has missed since I forced him to leave Crymzon. "How do you think I got my powers back? She granted me seven nights to lure a reaction out of Otyx."

He claps his hands together. "Then let's start with her. And maybe the mole shows itself during the process."

That's not a bad idea.

Feeding the Painite to the Heiligbaum is the next point on my agenda, anyway. If we play it wisely, we may catch Eternitie's spy along with it.

SEVEN

Queen Soulin

"Can we talk about them?" Khaos points at the creatures lurking in the shadows, their eyes resting on me.

"What about them?" I ask, brushing my tangled hair into a manageable mane.

Khaos stares at the beasts hiding in plain sight. "Why do they follow you?"

I cackle and lower my brush to look over my shoulder at him. "Because I'm their alpha. It took little to overthrow them with magic."

Khaos walks to the closet without breaking eye contact with my new pets. "Can't they stay in another room?"

I spin on the chair to admire the creatures. "Are they frightening you?"

"No." He coughs. "But they're ugly."

A creature bolts into the low sunlight, and I can feel Khaos' heart skip a beat inside my chest. Or maybe it was mine.

No, I'm pretty sure it was his.

I laugh. "Maybe they think the same about us. By the way, you need to control your emotions better. Whatever you feel, it feels like it's rubbing off on me."

But who am I to judge? My plan to rid myself of Khaos went up in flames when I looked into his dark eyes. It only took one second to lose my grip on my emotions; now, it's all I want.

I want him. *Only* him.

Khaos ignores my words as he fishes something out of the closet. "Queen Ria took my breath away every time she wore this gown for a ceremony," Khaos says, and my stomach bottoms.

Why, in Lunra's name, isn't my magic strong enough to suppress my feelings? It has worked for over a decade, so why does it suddenly hurt so much to think about my mother? And why does it keep slipping, forcing me to make irrational decisions?

My eyes fall on the stunning creation, designed to captivate, and mesmerize with its unique combination of elegance and charisma. Crafted meticulously, the gown he's holding is made of the finest burgundy silk, chosen for its luxurious texture and rich color. The silk drapes gracefully, and I can see the fabric hugging my mother's body form-fittingly, accentuating her figure and exuding confidence and beauty.

The allure of her dress lies in its intricate embellishments. Adorning the entire garment surface are delicate red moths, carefully crafted from various materials such as silk, organza, and even feathers. These moths are arranged to create an ethereal pattern that dances across the silk they have spun before dying. Each moth is intricately detailed, with their wings displaying myriad shades of red, from deep crimson to vibrant scarlet.

It features a plunging neckline that accentuates the collarbones and draws attention to the decolletage. At the same time, the back reveals an elegant, low-cut design highlighting the graceful contours of the spine.

The dress extends to just above the floor with a deep slit cut into the left side, showcasing the legs, and allowing graceful movement.

Khaos notices my silence and pushes it back into the closet. "Maybe you should wear a new dress."

"No," I say harshly.

He looks at me, his hands holding onto the dress like it's poisonous.

"I want to wear it," I say, my eyes stinging with tears.

He studies me for a moment before pulling it back out. "It's going to look even better on you."

My heart throbs when I try to compare my mother and me. I'm nothing like her. She embodied everything I'm not.

"Let's get this over with," I say, swallowing my emotions. "The sun will set soon."

I didn't have to ask Khaos to stay after our intimacy. He followed me to my chambers without saying a word.

I thought our connection was strong when I felt it for the first time, right before the evil meat bag of my father's corpse tried to crush my windpipe. But since I accepted Khaos to touch me, I can feel his emotions, his longing for me, and something else I couldn't put my finger on until now. I can hear his thoughts. It's hushed like a whisper, but it's there.

Can he hear my thoughts also? Does he feel what I feel?

This is precisely why I wanted to distance myself from him.

And it shows me that whatever façade my father put on when he sat on the Crymzon Throne was just a lie. He must have felt my mother's agony when she held on to life while trying to push the winged child out. He had to hear her scream inside his mind.

Their connection was stronger than what Khaos and I have. We're at the beginning of our Soulmate Connection and haven't even completed the ceremony yet, while their Connection Ceremony was over three hundred years before they died.

My insides boil when I think of him sitting before me on the throne, not a single emotion clouding his face when he told me about my mother's fate.

"You're nothing like him," Khaos says, holding the gown inches from my face.

I blink up at him, my body trembling with hate. "How can you say that? How can you be so blind?"

He drops the gown to cup my face. "Because I know you. Because this version of you was created by what your father put you through."

"I almost killed you," I whisper, channeling all my magic to banish all those pesky feelings stirring inside me.

His warm, brown eyes search mine. "Only because you thought I was suffering. You tried to relieve me of my pain."

"You find an excuse for everything I do. You're not thinking clearly. I've hurt you so many times."

"But you were never cruel to me. The easiest way to be free of me would have been to kill me, yet you sent me away. Why? And why didn't you use your whip to rip my head off? Why did you let me leave Crymzon instead of hanging me on the kingdom's wall?" He pauses for a moment and continues when I don't answer. "Because you can't. You thought my life would be easier without you in it, and you could keep your composure as the Queen. But is it so bad to have someone by your side?"

I take a few moments to think about his words.

I tried. I really tried to imagine a life without Khaos. But every road I take leads back to him. I'm his flame he returns to every time we stray apart.

With one last push, I force more magic through my veins to stop my trembling and seal my emotions away. “I’m not going back. I’ll never turn back into the frail girl you used to know.”

He pushes a strand of my hair behind my ear. “I know. But I’m not here for the girl I used to play with in the courtyard. I’m here for the woman you’ve become.”

He wants to say so much more. I can hear it inside my head, calm and blurred, but he closes his mouth and leans in to kiss me.

After a while, he pulls back. “Now let me admire you one more time before you put the gown on,” he whispers into my ear, and goosebumps shoot over my skin.

As the golden rays of the evening sun filter through the temple’s stained-glass windows, casting vibrant hues upon the ancient sandstone floors, hushed murmurs fill the air. The chamber is adorned with intricate tapestries depicting the tales of our Goddess, their vibrant colors shimmering in the soft light.

I stand at the entrance, dressed in the flowing burgundy gown my mother used to wear when I was a child.

I never thought the day would come when I step into her footsteps. I’m wearing the gown, I admired as a child.

My eyes fall on the heart of the temple, where a magnificent tree stands. Its branches and lingering fire coming from inside the bark, reach towards the heavens like outstretched arms. But the Heiligbaum isn’t any tree. Over the centuries, it stood as a symbol of Crymzon’s divine connection to our Goddess, Lunra, a source of strength and magic for my kingdom.

However, the tree's flame has withered, its once lush fire now tinged with the desolation of a dying spirit as the stone fueling the Heiligbaum slowly runs out. And with that, the connection to Lunra and the magic she gives Crymzon is compromised.

Amidst the gathered crowd, clad in shining armor of regal red, I stand tall. I scan the room as I step forward, carrying a smooth stone cradled in my hands. The stone, a relic from ancient times, is said to possess the power to enhance the Goddess's influence and restore the vitality of the Heiligbaum.

I've witnessed what the Painite can do. Not only did it almost cost me my life to find it in the coldest part of the land, Terminus, but it's also so rare that I thought I might never get my hands on it.

Well, that's a lie. I didn't find it. Thinking about Conrad's smile when he delivered it to me makes me roll my eyes. For a brief moment, I wonder how he's doing since he's reunited with his family.

Shaking my head, I turn the stone in my palm. If I'm lucky, I never have to see that old man's smile again.

The air is heavy with a pressing aura as moonlight streams through the stained-glass windows, casting warm hues across the assembled soldiers standing in solemn formation. I search the ranks for Khaos until I remember I left him behind in my chamber to look after my new pets. Although he may not currently like them, he must adapt to them eventually, regardless of his preference.

There's also still the problem, that he doesn't know yet that most of the Crymzonians are currently spending their days in my prison. I need to keep it that way.

As I approach the water surrounding the Heiligbaum, my gaze pierces through the crowd. My subjects, dressed in their finest attires, await my words.

I can't fuck this up. Not again.

Silence envelopes the temple as I speak; my voice, resonant and commanding, echoes through the temple's vaulted ceilings, cutting through the peaceful atmosphere like a sword through the air. My words have no warmth, only the icy edge of disappointment.

"People of Crymzon. We stand here today on the brink of a pivotal moment in our history. The time has come to restore the connection between our land and Goddess."

I motion to the Heiligbaum, its ancient roots gripping the earth as if yearning for something long lost. Slowly, I look at the large rock in my hand, heavy and unyielding, poised to be sacrificed in the name of redemption.

"The Heiligbaum, our lifeline to Lunra, has withered, its connection severed by our failure," I continue, my tone laced with disdain. "We fought a war, a war we did not win. Our enemies thought they could defy us, but they underestimated our resilience. They will learn the consequences of their folly."

The soldiers stir, a mixture of shame and defiance on their faces, but none dare to interrupt as I resume my speech.

"Our losses are an affront to our kingdom's pride," I sneer, "but today, we take a step towards redemption. We offer this Painite, symbolizing our hardships, to appease our Goddess and restore her favor upon our lands."

A faint flicker of pride glimmers in my chest as I raise the Painite high above my head, ready to cast it into the gaping maw of the sacred tree. The soldiers watch, their breaths held, as I continue.

"Let this sacrifice remind us of our past failures and ignite a fire within us," I declare, my voice resonating with a chilling intensity. "We will rise from the ashes of defeat, fueled by the vengeance that burns in our hearts. The energy of our Goddess now courses through its roots, bolstering our magic and granting us a power that shall bring victory in our darkest hour. Our enemies will tremble before us, for we embody ruthless magic. We possess a power born from our undying devotion, which shall lay waste to those who dare to oppose us!"

As I approach the ailing tree, a hush falls over the temple, broken only by the soft rustling of my ceremonial gown. I carefully kneel before the Heiligbaum, my fingers gently caressing the rough, gleaming bark as though seeking solace in the embrace of the ancient guardian.

I place the Painite at the tree's base, the smooth surface of the artifact glimmering in the dappled light coming from within. A collective gasp ripples through the onlookers as subtle energy emanates from the stone, permeating the air with a tangible sense of power.

The temple vibrates with sizzling energy as I, infused with unwavering conviction, call upon Lunra. My words carry a melodic resonance, blending with the harmonious chants of my ancestors. The sacred language fills the chamber, entwining with the ethereal whispers of the wind, as though nature responds to my plea.

With each invocation, the Heiligbaum responds, its withered branches quivering with newfound vitality. Leaves, once dry and brittle, unfurl in a breathtaking display.

A chorus of gasps and murmurs erupt from the crowd as they witness the rebirth of our Heiligbaum, its renewed vigor a testament to Lunra's benevolence.

With a swift and forceful motion, I pick up the rock and hurl it into the tree's hollow trunk. It disappears within, swallowed by the very essence of the land, as I brace myself for the consequences of my action.

As the echoes of my chants subside, the Heiligbaum shudders before bursting into wild flames, licking my face.

I did it. I fucking did it!

I turn to face my army again, my skin burning as the Heiligbaum ignites into a blazing fire, its flames reaching toward the ceiling as if longing for the divine touch.

Gradually, a gentle breeze swirls through the temple, carrying the essence of the Goddess herself over my subjects.

Narrowing my eyes, a twisted smile on my lips, I speak my last words: "War is not for the weak-hearted. It's time to reclaim what is rightfully ours. We shall march forward, leaving only a trail of destruction in our wake. No mercy, no quarter. Victory will be ours, and our enemies will forever regret crossing paths with the wrath of our kingdom."

With that, the temple erupts with the thunderous cheers and cries of the soldiers, their allegiance sealed by fear and my unwavering longing to bring the North to its knees.

Otyx thought he was clever in luring out the strongest kingdom in Escela, but soon he will learn he made a horrible mistake.

EIGHT

CYRUS

Has it been two days already or three since we escaped Crymzon? I've lost track of time as we trudge through the unforgiving expanse of the desert under the scorching sun, our footsteps leaving imprints on the arid sand. Liza's face is etched with weariness, but each night, the gaping wounds Monsteress inflicted on her back heal as if the starlight took it upon itself to revive her.

This must be a Starstrandian ability I wasn't aware of until now. But it doesn't explain why it didn't help her when she needed it the most: when her wings were clipped.

I lead the way, and my strides are purposeful, even though I'm unsure where to go. It's my first time being so far away from my kingdom, Eternitie. When I fled my role as the Prince, leaving my sister Catalina, Crown Princess of Eternitie, and my brother, Prince Cyprian, behind, I only made it to the outskirts of Crymzon, not even a day's ride away from the Brass Palace and the Crymzon Wall.

Where we're heading now is unfamiliar territory for me, but not for Liza.

As we press forward, she matches my steps. The barren landscape is endless, with dunes rolling on the horizon. The oppressive heat threatens to sap the last of my strength, but the yearning for freedom pushes me onward. Each step brings us closer to the edge of the land, where the vast ocean awaits us.

I need to get her as far away from Monsteress as I can.

After what feels like an eternity, our weary feet carry us to the end of the desert. As we reach the pinnacle of a sandy hill, my eyes widen in disbelief. Before us lies a breathtaking panorama—a kingdom floating high above on a massive cloud and another shimmering beneath the crystal-clear waters.

The floating kingdom, with its white structures and reflecting windows suspended in the sky, looks like a realm pulled from a dream. Its towers and spires pierce the sky, casting a shadow on the water below.

In contrast, the underwater kingdom shimmers with a mystical beauty. Its architecture mimics the graceful forms of marine life, with buildings adorned in pearls and corals. Sunlight filters through the azure waters, illuminating the kingdom's depths in a mesmerizing display of colors.

I look at Liza, and we exchange glances, her eyes reflecting uncertainty.

Our escape from Crymzon granted us a chance at a new life, but we must decide. Should we ascend to Starstrand, where the skies hold limitless possibilities, and the touch of starlight is tangible? Or should we descend into the depths of Oceris, where a hidden world awaits, teeming with secrets and untold wonders?

If neither of us had any relation to those kingdoms, it would have made our decision easier. But Liza fled Starstrand and never told me why, even though I tended to the wounds inflicted on her back for weeks.

"So..." I begin, and I feel my lips crack.

"We only have one option," Liza says, her eyes resting on the kingdom in the sky.

"We have a choice," I say, pointing at Oceris. "King Usiel won't dismiss us."

"And how are we going to breathe underwater?"

I shake my head and instantly make the headache I've been carrying around for days worse. "I haven't gotten that far yet."

"Exactly. Starstrand is our only option."

I know exactly what I would do if someone would give me the option between Eternitie and Oceris. I would rather drown trying to reach King Usiel to ask for refuge than setting a foot into my kingdom again.

But what is Liza hiding?

Whatever it is, she must think that her Queen forgives her. Or maybe she knows what consequences are coming her way and accepts them to save me.

No, I wouldn't let that happen.

Still, the question burns on my tongue, but I swallow it. Liza never asked me why I fled Eternitie, so I won't press my curiosity on her now.

"She's my grandma," Liza says slowly, her eyes cast to the ground. "I was supposed to guard her until it's my turn to take over her position in the palace, and I failed her."

My head hurts even more trying to figure out who she's referring to without asking her. Apparently, she thinks I know her family's history, but I know little about Starstrand.

Queen Caecilia is the ruler. I know that. She used to have a companion and a daughter, but both died in mysterious ways just days apart. No one, and I mean *no one*, ever talks about it. If I hadn't read about it in the Brass Palace's library, I wouldn't know it.

But I do, and I tucked that info away for later use.

"You don't have a clue what I'm talking about, do you?" Liza asks, her eyes directed at me.

I shrug my shoulders. "Am I supposed to?"

"I suspected everyone in the village knew," she says in a hushed voice, her cheeks blushing.

"If they did, they didn't trust me with it," I answer, trying to force a smile on my lips, but the dry skin makes it impossible.

"My grandma forms starlight into candles," Liza says as she studies me.

Oh, shit.

The wrinkles on her forehead grow deeper when she catches my reaction.

Her grandmother is the Lady of Fate. *The* Lady of Fate.

"What are you saying?" I ask, my voice trembling.

"I guess the other kingdoms give her many names. The Lady of Fate. Destiny Forgeress. Oracle. Starspinner. Those are the most common ones I've heard during my exile."

"Exile?" I cut in, not believing what I'm hearing.

"My grandma turns fate into candles. She plucks it from the stars, each star representing one individual on this planet."

"So she shows people their destinies?"

Liza bites her lip. "Could you please stop cutting me off? I'm trying to explain everything," she says, exhaling sharply to calm herself down. "No, destiny has nothing to do with it. That's where people get it wrong. Your destiny is every decision you have made that led you to this present moment." She points to the ground to get her statement across. "Your fate is something you can't change. It's not determined by your decisions. It's a flicker of your future."

"So your grandmother sees the future?"

"I guess you can say that. But it's not just her. I see it, too," Liza says, straightening her shoulders.

The silence hanging between us is unbearable.

Liza can see the future.

She can see the fucking future and never told me about it?

Okay, I guess that's cool...

But is she serious?

"Did you know..." I can't finish that sentence.

"That our village would be attacked?"

I cringe. "You knew all this time?"

Liza nods with closed eyes, as if her agreement hurts.

"Why didn't you say anything? Why didn't you warn us? You could have spared us so much trouble."

"Because even if I see a person's fate, I can't change the course of it. It wouldn't have mattered if we tried to run from the village. One way or the other, fate *always* comes true."

My head throbs as I try to absorb what she's saying.

"What about your wings?" I say, rubbing my temples.

"As I said, I'm the next Lady of Fate. Once my grandma dies, I will take her place. But for the gift to fully expand, she must die a natural death."

"That doesn't explain why you're clipped. And what about your mother? Why isn't she the next in line?"

"Because the firstborn female of every other generation can only receive the gift. If every Fate would have the sight, it would be catastrophic."

Liza Fate.

Oh gods.

Liza *Fate.*

I never ask her for her last name. It wasn't needed. And while I never knew her given name, she doesn't even know my real first name. She thinks I'm Aemilius Vosdon, the name I chose to protect my identity.

"Wait, you said it was your duty to protect your grandma. What happened to her?"

"Monsteress," Liza says, and a shudder runs through me. "Queen Caecilia clipped my wings to ensure I would find my grandma after she didn't return from Crymzon's market to get more wax for her candles. In return for her safe recovery, I will regain my wings."

Starstrandians are proud people. Their most valuable possession is the wings protruding from their shoulder blades, hence the kingdom in the sky. Besides their feathered body parts, their kingdom thrives when bathed in starlight, just like Crymzon runs under the moon.

Only those two kingdoms live in the dark, while Oceris, Tenacoro, and Eternitie accomplish their daily routines when the sun is up. I guess Terminus belongs to the daytime kingdoms, but it was uninhabited for thousands of years until King Keres, God Otyx's creation, claimed the freezing part of Escela.

"What will happen if you return without her?" I ask, looking up into the sky.

"I really don't want to find out," she says, grabbing my hand. "But I can't run any longer."

"Can't you see your own fate?" I mumble. "I mean, isn't there a way to tell what's going to happen next?"

She squeezes my hand. "Just because I can see other people's fates doesn't mean I can abuse my gift. So no, I'm not able to see my future."

There's still time to opt for Oceris and ask their King if he knows a way for us to live underwater with him. But Liza is set on her kingdom, and there is nothing I can do to change her mind.

"It's so humiliating," Liza whispers, inhaling sharply. "Queen Caecilia. Please lend us your wings," she screams into the sky as she closes her eyes.

"No. We didn't come this far for you to be punished again. Let's leave."

"I'll be okay. I promise," she whispers, but the strength in her grip says differently.

I lift my head and expect Starstrandian soldiers to drop out of the sky to evacuate us, but nothing happens.

Our escape from Crymzon was fueled by the desire to escape Queen Soulin, to breathe freely, and to reclaim a life without being prisoners. Yet now, faced with choosing between the two extraordinary realms, I regret marching west. Whatever awaits Liza once we reach Starstrand might not compare to what the Crymzon Queen has done to her, but it can't be uplifting either.

Hand in hand, we stand there, awaiting Queen Caecilia's approval.

"No matter what happens next, you know nothing about my mission," Liza whispers, just before the sky darkens above us.

NINE

DEVANA

My father would never return to Tenacoro, I tell myself as I stumble over the bridge, crossing into Eternitie's territory.

Oceris and Starstrand are also out of the question because he has no wings or fins to survive in those kingdoms.

That leaves me with the only remaining kingdom: Eternitie.

As I make my way toward my destination, a heaviness weighs upon me physically and emotionally. The effects of wandering through the land for days have taken their toll, leaving my body fatigued and my movements labored. Each step feels like an uphill battle, like invisible chains burden my legs.

The journey seemed longer than usual, as my symptoms sapped my energy, causing my muscles to weaken and my coordination to falter. My body, once full of adrenaline when fleeing Crymzon, now feels confined by the limitations I'm used to.

After a few hours, I approach the towering metal gates that mark the entrance to Eternitie, and unease courses through my veins, making me forget my strained muscles momentarily.

The gates, designed with gears, cogs, and coils, creak open as I'm about to reach out to push them aside.

Is it that easy to gain excess to another kingdom? If I had known that Eternitie opens its gate to anyone, I would have convinced my father to flee here instead of living off the grid in the Confines.

My eyes widen with wonder as I find myself immersed in a bustling metropolis of steam and gears.

Hissing condensation and rhythmic ticking resonate through the air, hinting at the mechanical wonders that lay beyond.

Odione, Goddess of Wonder, really knows how to impress newcomers.

With each step, my eyes dart from one fascinating invention to another. To my left, a group of engineers in leather aprons tinker with a colossal steam-powered machine, its metal limbs moving in precise motions. Its glowing brass exterior contrasts with the smoke from the nearby iron furnace, casting a vaporous glow.

On my right, another weird-looking device takes flight, its propellers spinning vigorously and emitting a soft whirring sound. The vessel sails above me, suspended by a confusing network of metal cables and pulleys. Its sleek metallic exterior gleams in the fading sunlight as it slowly approaches the sky, trailing steam plumes.

Continuing my journey, I follow a winding path paved with brass gears and copper rivets, leading me deeper into the kingdom's heart. Steam-powered lamp posts illuminate the way, casting a warm, amber glow upon the streets while carriages glide past, their mechanisms whirring and sputtering with every movement. The lamps are nothing like the candlelight I'm used to.

The air gets thicker with the scent of oil and the hiss of escaping steam with every corner I take. I pass a bustling marketplace where vendors display their wares: shiny brass goggles, leather-bound journals with copper engravings, and delicate pocket watches.

My pace is slow and deliberate, but my determination burns brightly within me. Though exhaustion threatens to overpower me, I press on, my father's training serving as a guiding force.

Finally, I reach my destination, the grand centerpiece of Eternitie—the Brass Palace. Rising majestically against the sky, the palace is nothing like I imagined it and yet everything I expected it to be. Its domed roof is covered with intricate filigree that glimmers in shades of bronze and gold, reflecting the last rays of sunlight, while colossal clockwork mechanisms adorn the exterior, functioning both as decoration and functional pieces of art.

Crossing the threshold into the palace, I marvel at the luxury within. Heavy chandeliers, crafted from a mosaic of gears and glass bulbs, bathe the grand hall in a warm, flickering light. Everywhere I look, metal servants are performing various tasks with mechanical precision. The clicking of gears creates an atmosphere of perpetual motion; somehow, I miss the silence of the Confines.

The colossal fountain in the center of the hall takes me by surprise. Water cascades from its brass spouts, propelled by a complex network of interconnected pipes and pressure valves. The flowing water and the rhythmic clanking of gears create a symphony of an unknown melody.

Why is no one stopping me? Those outside the palace might not pay attention to a stranger entering their kingdom, but at least the guards marching in front of the palace must have noticed me.

Fatigue washes over me in relentless waves, slowing my progress and forcing me to pause for breath. I lean against a nearby wall, seeking support, and close my eyes momentarily, drawing strength from the depths within.

I made it this far. I need to keep going.

The world around me blurs, the vibrant colors muted by my weariness. As I push myself off the wall, my body sinks to the ground, the weight of my exhaustion finally overwhelming me. My breath comes in ragged gasps, and my body trembles with the effort it took to reach this point.

"What is she doing here?" a voice asks, and I try to lift my chin to look at the person running in my direction. "How did you get in?"

I feel my eyelids growing heavier with every heartbeat, and as much as I want to stand up and state my case, I don't have much time. "Queen Soulin might be dead," I say before I lump to the side, and the world darkens.

Slowly, I fade back to reality.

"This seems important. I think we should let the King know," a female voice says in the distance, and I keep my eyes shut while feeling which body part experienced the most damage during my days of hiking through the desert.

My legs, for sure.

"And if it's useless information, he will replace us with his new robots," a male voice answers in front of me.

I'm unsure what a robot is, but I know enough that it can't be good being exchanged for something else.

"It's my first week at this job. If I get thrown out, I have to go back to my parents to help them with the aircraft shop, and I can't do that," the woman says, and the longer I listen, the less their conversation makes sense.

With an exaggerated grunting noise, I open my eyes to draw their attention to me. As my groggy eyes flutter open, I find myself in an unfamiliar room. I'm not in the entrance hall anymore. The air is filled with the scent of old wood and metal, and the soft glow of morning sunlight seeps through the dusty windows, casting long shadows across the worn furniture.

"She's waking up. What do we do?" the man asks, panic lacing his voice.

As far as I know, one of them must have seen me collapse, which puts me at an advantage. All that person saw was an individual stumbling into their palace, too weak to stand. For them, it must have looked like I'm delicate and helpless.

But beneath my fragile surface, my mind is clear as day.

I can take them down with two simple steps. But first, I have to locate where their swords are.

Slowly, I open my eyes, and two soldiers clad in armor materialize before me. The metallic gears and intricate brass adornments of their attire glint in the sunlight as they take me in.

So this is what Eternians look like.

I cautiously rise from the bed I have been placed on and inspect them, my gaze shifting between their armor and faces. I scan their bodies for swords, hidden blades, or anything that can help me get out of here.

But as I study their demeanor, I sense something unexpected—there is no hostility in their eyes, no threatening intent in their stance. Plus, they are unarmed.

Realizing that these soldiers pose no immediate danger, I decide to engage them in conversation. I approach them, my voice filled with caution. "Who are you? And why have you brought me here?"

The man steps forward, his helmeted face giving away nothing. "The bigger question is: who are you, and why did you break into the palace?"

Break into the palace? That's a strong way of putting me strolling through half their kingdom and entering the palace without force.

"Do I look capable of forcing my way through Eternitie?" I ask, twitching my hand a little.

I need them to believe I'm weak. If push comes to shove, I need the upper hand to get out of here.

"We are the Vanguards of the Steam Corps, tasked with protecting this kingdom," the woman says, her eyes resting on my hand. "We apologize for any inconvenience but must ensure you're not a threat."

No, I'm not *a* threat. I'm *the* threat.

They would be terrified if they knew whom they dragged even deeper into their palace.

"You're from Tenacoro," the man says, studying my golden-brown skin and dark coils.

"Why does that matter?" the woman hisses at him, shaking her head.

He covers his mouth to whisper to her, but his attempt fails. "They are excellent hunters and warriors."

So he knows my roots. That's good.

What he doesn't know is that my education goes well beyond the average Tenacorian. If he already thinks my kingdom is known for its animal hunting techniques that have a ninety percent success rate, he hasn't seen what a Tenacorian trained to kill humans can do.

Instead of letting his suspicion spiral down, I force a mild smile on my lips, as innocent as I can muster. "Not everyone in Tenacoro is a hunter," I say, knowing that my explanation will hit a sore spot because why be a soldier if you can be a gadgeteer? "And while I was born in Tenacoro, I grew up in the Confines."

Both look at me, their mouths wide open. The woman takes a step back, guarded yet intrigued. "Then why did you come here if you're a godless soul?"

Just because I left Tenacoro doesn't mean I stopped praying to Emara, the Goddess of Vitality.

"Because I was a prisoner of the Crymzon Queen. I came all this way with vital information about her well-being," I answer, intensifying my shaking limbs. "But I don't have much time. It might be too late if I don't get an audience with the King soon."

The man pauses, considering my words. "What can you offer to back up your claim?"

"My word. It's all I have," I answer, spreading my arms out to showcase I'm no danger.

They whisper to each other audibly. How did those two make it into the Steam Corps? If I'm up against this, I don't need a weapon to break out.

Finally, the woman looks at me and sighs. "Alright, we'll bring you to him. But on one condition: If you betray us, you will die a slow and painful death."

I chuckle on the inside but manage to put a sweet smile on and nod solemnly. "You have my word. I'll ensure the King knows what you have done to save his kingdom."

Escorted by the pair of guards, I'm being guided down a corridor lined with tall, arched windows that offer glimpses of lush gardens and clockwork sculptures. The faint aroma of lavender rises into my nose, adding a soft touch to the otherwise metallic ambiance.

Elaborate cogwork covers the walls, interlocking with polished copper pipes that snake through the ceiling. Crystal chandeliers hang overhead, while gears embedded in the floor emit soft mechanical whirrs with every step.

Finally, we stand before a colossal double door at the end of the corridor. The doors swing open with a hiss of escaping steam, revealing a grand hall bathed in golden light. A long, polished oak table stands in the center, surrounded by high-backed chairs.

At the head of the table, resplendent on a magnificent throne made of polished bronze, sits King Citeus. He's dressed in a regal, steam-punk-inspired attire that exudes authority. Goggles rest atop his head, and a monocle gleams in his eye, reflecting the flickering light of a nearby chandelier.

Even though he looks like a King, I know he's all bark and no bite. Compared to Monsteress' aura, he seems like a side figure in the big game.

But what catches my attention are the figures seated around him—the other Kings and Queens, each representing a different kingdom.

As the guards lead me closer to the table, I notice the astonished glances and raised eyebrows from the monarchs. They exchange curious whispers and sideways looks, their eyes fixed on me before returning to a piece of paper in the middle of the table.

Queen Synadena, my former ruler, studies me curiously.

There's no way she recognizes me. It has been twenty-six years since she laid eyes on me for the last time.

Yet, she looks at me like she knows exactly who I am and what I'm doing here. But I could ask her the same.

Slowly, I count the royals before me to avoid her eye contact.

One. Two. Three. Four.

Four?

I count again.

No, I didn't make a mistake counting the first time. Only four of the six rulers are present at the table. I didn't expect King Keres to sit here since he's the one invading our land from the North. But I expected five rulers.

Still, it's only four.

Citeus Matrus, King of the Gadgeteers, Ruler of Eternitie.

Caecilia Estella, Queen of the Winged Warriors, Ruler of Starstrand.

Usiel Oarus, King of the Saltwater, Ruler of Oceris.

And Synadena Roja, Queen of the Jungle, Ruler of Tenacoro.

So, where is Monsteress?

My mouth opens and closes repeatedly as I search for the right words.

Am I too late? Are the kingdoms already aware that Crymzon has fallen?

I take a deep breath. My heartbeat pounds in my chest as I press past the guards. When I draw closer to King Citeus, the room hushes, and all eyes land on me again.

"Your Majesties," I address the rulers collectively, my voice resonating with a quiet strength, "I stand before you as a humble fugitive from the fallen kingdom of Crymzon. I traveled far to bring you the news of Queen Soulin's downfall."

My words hang heavy in the air, drawing gasps and whispered conversations among them, but I continue unwavering, "The Queen who rules over the desert was on the brink of death when I fled her kingdom."

Silence falls upon the grand hall as the weight of my words sinks in. The royals exchange glances, their expressions betraying a mix of empathy and concern. King Citeus, his face etched with lines of disbelief, leans forward on his throne, his eyes fixed on me.

With a measured breath, I keep going, "I implore you, Kings and Queens of Escela, to lend your aid and wisdom in this time of dire need. The people of Crymzon, scattered and broken, yearn for hope and the chance to rebuild their lives."

This is the part I have been dreading. Of course, I don't want all Crymzonians to suffer when Crymzon turns into dust once Monsteress dies.

But that's not the reason I came all this way.

I hoped to run into my father on my way to Eternitie. He always finds me. *Always.* But since I'm still alone, the chance that my father is still inside her palace is high. Plus, I left all my friends behind; their survival is also my priority.

If Crymzon gets evacuated, I will see all of them again. My father. Aemilius. And everyone else I hold dear.

King Usiel taps his dark brown fingers on the table. "What's your name?" he asks, his eyes as cold as stone.

"Devana," I answer, straightening my shoulders to match his tone.

"If your statement is true, it's too late to aid Crymzon. If Queen Soulin has passed, her kingdom is lost."

"No," I whisper. "It can't be."

"Why did you come all this way to help a kingdom you don't belong to?" Queen Synadena asks, sending a wave of goosebumps over my body.

There's no fooling my former Queen. She might not remember or have watched me grow up, but she knows my father and mother. If my father is right, I'm a spitting image of the woman who tried to hide me for the rest of my life.

"The Queen has my father," I say calmly.

Chaos breaks loose.

"I told you we should invade Crymzon. This is getting out of hand," King Citeus barks, hammering a hand on the table.

"It's not our responsibility. All Crymzonians have the right to leave the kingdom," King Usiel says calmly, tapping his fingers against his chair.

"She didn't give them that option. Crymzon is a ghost town. I've watched it crumple to the ground twice in less than a moon's cycle. And the last time I checked, the streets were empty every night. We must do something," Queen Caecilia says, her wings rustling behind her.

King Usiel leans back. "None of us is strong enough to survive an attack from Queen Soulin. Her magic is strong enough to take half of us out in a blink of an eye."

King Citeus reaches out to twist his mustache. "So, what's your plan? Watch her destroy her kingdom and then us because she's running out of entertainment?" he growls. "I'm sick of pretending everything is fine when it's not."

Queen Synadena stands up, and the room falls silent. "If we start a war with the Crymzon Queen, we won't walk away from it. But I agree with King Citeus. I can't watch any longer."

"If you want to dig your own grave, go for it, but I'm not sending my subjects into a battle they can *not* win," King Usiel says, rising from his chair.

He brushes past me as if I'm invisible, and in the next moment, he's out of the door.

Three.

Only three rulers remain.

"What's in it for you?" Queen Caecilia asks, searching King Citeus' face.

Her question hangs in the air like a stormy cloud.

King Citeus perks his lips before turning his attention to the other side of his mustache. "I'm in their crossfire. King Keres presses against my border in the north, and Queen Soulin massacres her way to him from the south. It's just a matter of time until they meet in the middle. I won't let that happen."

His point is valid. Yet, something seems off. Eternitie isn't known for strength and battle tactics.

"How do you want to approach this?" Queen Caecilia asks, pointing at the piece of paper before her.

"We must move now when her body and land are the weakest. One army marches against her, while the others raid her kingdom and free every poor bastard incarcerated inside and outside her wall."

"We won't stand a chance," Queen Caecilia says, shaking her head.

"I'm not asking you to fight against her. My army will divert her long enough for you to extract most citizens. If Queen Soulin dies during the process, I can't promise your soldiers will get out in time, but I will do my best to keep her alive for as long as possible."

His move is pretty bold, but it's completely justified. My life's mission is to kill Monsteress. Still, something seems fishy.

"You don't mean that," Queen Synadena says, her eyes narrowing on King Citeus. "What makes you think you can harm her?"

King Citeus laughs. "A Gadgeteer never reveals his secrets. Besides, she's just as mortal as we are."

The smile forming on King Citeus' face forces a shiver down my spine. Whatever he's planning on doing to Monsteress, he must have been planning it for a while now, because there's no way he's making a plan up as he goes.

The atmosphere is electric, and an underlying tension tinges the air. It's clear that this gathering I walked into is no ordinary meeting of royalty. They came together behind Monsteress' back to discuss what was to become of the youngest ruler in Escela, and to my satisfaction, I can't wait to offer my help.

A memory forces itself into my head. My father's voice is loud and clear: *I need to help her.*

Maybe *he* does, but I say: screw her. She has my father, and for that, I will make her pay.

TEN

Queen Soulin

"What do I have to do for you to trust me?" Khaos asks, and my mouth goes dry.

Trust.

What a simple word with such a monstrous meaning.

"It's not that I don't trust you," I answer, but it's precisely that. "There are some things I'm not ready to share yet."

Because if he knew that I'm hiding a Starstrandian...no, not any Starstrandian... that I'm hiding the Lady of Fate inside my palace, he would lose his mind. Once he knows my secret, what will stop him from freeing her?

Even though the Oracle has served her purpose, I can't give her up. She's the only leverage I have against the kingdom I loathe the most, and after losing Cyrus, I can't risk having her being taken away, too.

"Whatever you're about to do, I know you do it for a reason," Khaos says, and his innocence breaks my heart.

"Stop doing that," I say, shaking my head.

"What?"

"Pretending I'm something I'm not."

He cocks his head, and his face turns into stone. "It's not Myra, is it?"

His question startles me.

The image of the woman who helped birth me, my mother's maid and companion, flashes before my eyes. She was the one who raised me after my parents' deaths, and who stood beside me even after I earned my cruel nickname.

Not a day goes by that I haven't thought of her. Commanding my guards to seize her still haunts me. But it needed to be done. I needed her to play her role outside the palace.

"She's not in my possession," I say, watching his brown eyes scan my face.

I wondered if he noticed her absence. After all, she was my advisor and always at my side. She was also close to Khaos. She watched us grow up together and helped to shape us into who we are now.

"Do you know where she is?" he asks, sadness clouding his voice.

"Do you?"

The silence between us is insufferable. After a long moment, he shakes his head. "I'm waiting for her to walk through this door and act like nothing happened, but she's not there every time I open my eyes."

I have nothing to say because if I do, he might discover what I did to her.

"I need to go," I say after a few minutes, pulling the dress over my head and securing the small buckle around my waist to keep it in place. "It won't take long, I promise. To keep yourself busy, you can claim your title back."

Grand General Khaos Zedohr.

That's the name everyone in my kingdom knows him by. Most servants and soldiers might not realize I stripped him of his title right before the battle.

But I do.

"I don't want it back," Khaos whispers, closing in on me. "Serving you is the most time-consuming job, and I don't want to miss a second of it."

I study him for a moment. His brown eyes drive over my body, and my core heats when our eyes meet.

"Is that really all you want in life? Following me like a pet?"

He smirks and brushes my hair back. "Don't be ridiculous. I would follow you to the Underworld because a long life with you is still too short for me."

Oh, Khaos.

"I hope you're true to your word because I might end up there sooner than later," I whisper into his ear, and a quiet growl escapes his throat when my lips touch his skin.

My opulent red gown trails behind me as I walk past the dais to the tapestry on the wall. The fabric shows scenes of the lunar cycle and, of course, moths.

Behind it is the Silk Room, a chamber renowned for its ethereal beauty only known to a handful of people. Its walls are lined with rows upon rows of delicate cocoons spun by many of my moths.

As I approach, I hear the faint fluttering of their wings, a soft symphony of delicate whispers. The room glows with the gentle luminescence of a human-sized lantern, casting a magical ambiance that dances in my peripheral vision.

A gust of air escapes as I push the door closed, stirring the silken threads, and causing the moths to take flight in a whirlwind of delicate grace. Like fragile petals, their wings flutter against my face, evoking a brief sensation of happiness.

Those are the only babies I will ever have; I spend every free minute looking after them.

"Adira," I whisper, searching for my most valuable moth.

As I take another step into the room, a sudden chill races down my spine, causing me to shiver involuntarily. I pause, my eyes widening as a whisper of fear tugs at my heart. Sensing a presence, I turn slowly, my gaze fixing upon a figure that materializes before me in the shadows.

An unexpected apparition stands before me, bathed in the soft glow of candlelight.

My fingers curl into fists as my eyes fall on the Goddess, the embodiment of the moon's radiant beauty and the allure of love itself.

What is she doing here?

Her skin has a mesmerizing red hue, like the blush of a thousand blood moons. Her long, dark flowing hair shimmers with silver strands that seem to capture the very essence of the moon's gentle light—the same sparkle she blessed my freckles with.

Lunra wears a gown that flows like liquid ruby, a vibrant cascade of red silk that clings to her graceful form. Its embroidery and delicate patterns mirror the moon that adorns the night sky. Her eyes, pools of endless warmth and compassion, are fixed upon me.

The room grows still as if she's forcing my moths to hold their wings shut.

I straighten my posture to regain control of the situation, but my voice falters, reduced to a mere whisper, as the weight of the Goddess's gaze bears down upon me.

"Goddess Lunra," I say, knowing I should lower my gaze, but I can't ignore her. "What brings you here?"

Lunra steps out of the darkness into the light, and my breath hitches.

"I came to check on you. I saw the pain etched on your face, and it grieves me deeply. But fear not. Your defeat is merely a stepping stone."

"My defeat?"

"Against Otyx."

Oh, right.

So much has happened since I returned home that my loss seems like a distant memory. It's not like I've forgotten how the God of the Underworld sent my father to fight against me, but I pushed it to the back of my brain until I could figure out what to do with Khaos. It's not like there's much to decide because he still returned to me even after multiple warnings about staying away from Crymzon.

"I'm not grieving," I say, regaining the strength in my voice. "That wasn't my father on the battlefield. Otyx has to do much worse if he wants to upset me."

The more time I have to think about his choice of resurrecting my father, the calmer I get. I already killed him once, and I know with the help of the other kingdoms, I can do it again because my magic won't be sufficient this time.

Therefore, my grudge is with the immortal being himself. I want a fair fight against him for exploiting my brother's corpse. That I will never forgive.

"I also saw that you finally accepted your Soulmate."

"Accepting is a strong word," I snarl, but the memory of Khaos' face between my legs makes blood rush to my face. "Why didn't you tell me it was him?"

"Would that have changed anything?"

"Maybe," I answer, stretching my hand out to pick up a moth from the nearby wall.

I would have probably just laughed and brushed her comment off as a fantasy; nevertheless, it would have been nice to know.

Lunra takes a step forward. "How does it feel having your full power back?"

"You're not here to learn about me and my feelings, are you? You're here because Otyx is still left unpunished." My words come out harsher than expected, but that doesn't make them less valid.

Lunra was the one steering me to teach Otyx a lesson. Because of him, she granted me magic for seven nights. Then, I thought nothing of it because it also benefited me.

But now?

What happened between those two immortals? What grudge can be deep enough to let their subjects battle it out?

"I'm sure you have reason to be cross with him, but I don't want to get involved. This is something personal between me and the God of the Underworld, and I can't taint it with your hatred."

I shouldn't be speaking to Crymzon's Goddess this way, but I'm sick of being everyone's toy. I'm not responsible for the beef between them. Even though I'm destined to live a couple of centuries, I'm mortal and weak compared to the Gods.

"You can't challenge Otyx," Lunra says, her voice turning cold. "But you can hit him where it hurts most: his creations."

"You're starting to sound like you don't know me," I laugh, curling my hand around the soft little creature in my palm. "I don't care what you think I can and cannot do. He overstepped, and I'll ensure it won't happen again."

Somehow, I expected Lunra to help me. Therefore, her reaction catches me off guard. If she doesn't support me, I will find a way to lure Otyx into my realm. Sooner or later, everyone ends up in Crymzon, whether or not they want it.

"The loss you suffered has ignited a fire within you that will guide you to victory," Lunra says, turning away from me. "I need you to prepare your army once more. Remember that I shall be by your side, guiding your steps and lending you my strength when needed. But be warned: My hands are tied if the God of the Underworld enters the war."

"You can't help, or you won't?"

"No mortal or immortal walks away from Death himself," Lunra whispers, and before I can say a word, I'm alone in the room.

ELEVEN

Cyrus

It's ridiculous how many times I've been held prisoner over the last few weeks. I escaped Crymzon—twice, just to be clear—to find myself in a cell with Liza in Starstrand.

The air feels lighter, and the surroundings are cloaked in a thick mist that dances with every step I take. Under closer inspection, I realize that the floor is made entirely of fluffy white clouds, and we're trapped inside a cell made of these billowing cotton-like formations. They're soft, shifting, and swirling like an indestructible breeze. The ceiling above seems endless, stretching into a vast sky sprinkled with shimmering stars.

While the conditions are way nicer than what Queen Soulin offered, I'm fuming inside.

When the clouds above us turned dark in the desert, I expected winged warriors to rain from the sky to seize us. I didn't expect a part of the cloud to fly down to pick us up and give us a ride like it's a damn carriage.

Trying to contain my rage, I reach out to touch the cloud wall again, my hand sinking into the cushiony substance. I turn to Liza. "I've heard the saying *being on cloud nine*, but I never thought we'd end up inside one."

Liza chuckles nervously, her eyes scanning the cell. "Only you can try to rip a joke in our situation."

What else am I supposed to be doing instead? Crying and screaming won't help us get out of here any faster.

"Let me recheck your wounds," I say, stepping in her way.

"I'm healed," she chuckles, waving me away. "How often do you need to check on me before you believe it?"

"No one heals this fast."

"Now you understand how important starlight is for Starstrandians. Without it, we can't thrive."

Monsteress must have known that when she had Liza thrown into my dark chamber. I'm sure of it.

The question of what would happen if a Starstrandian doesn't see starlight for a long time lingers inside me. But before I can ponder further, a soft, melodious voice echoes through the cloud cell, captivating my attention. "Welcome, travelers," a female voice says, carrying a regal tone. "I've been informed of your unexpected arrival. Don't be frightened."

As the voice dissipates, Liza and I exchange glances, and I see in her expression that she's as clueless as I am. What should we be afraid of? It's just her and I in this cell.

The walls vibrate with a palpable energy as if awaiting the arrival of our enigmatic captor. Finally, a radiant figure descends from above, bathed in an aura of warmth and light.

Queen Caecilia.

She's clad in a flowing gown of white fabric that imitates diaphanous clouds. Her blue eyes pierce through me while her wings whirl her blonde hair around her face like a halo.

I cover my face, fearing getting caught in her feathers as she lands before us.

With a gentle smile, the Queen approaches us, her voice soothing yet commanding. "I'm Caecilia, Queen of the Winged Warriors, Ruler of Starstrand. Tell me, what purpose brings you here?" Her facial expression changes when her gaze falls on Liza. Her youthful, bright smile turns into a frown. "Have you completed your mission?"

Apparently, the informant didn't know who he led into his kingdom, and the Queen is as shocked to stand before Liza as she is.

Collecting my thoughts, I step forward, my voice filled with sincerity as I lower my head and bow. "Your Highness. We mean no harm or intrusion. We seek refuge from Queen Soulin."

Queen Caecilia inspects me and then Liza again, who has her eyes cast on the ground. "You come here empty-handed, escorted by another Outlaw, and expect me to shield you from the Crymzon Queen?"

My stomach turns. We should have tried our luck in Oceris, far away from our haunting pasts.

The Queen chuckles and waves her hand. "I'm glad you returned." Her eyes soften. "It might be an accidental arrival, but it's just in time."

"For what?" Liza asks, her eyes finally wandering up to meet Queen Caecilia's.

I've gotten used to Monsteress' reactions so quickly that I have to rub my ears to ensure I heard correctly.

She's *glad* of her return?

"I'll bring you up to speed in private," the Queen says, looking at me.

"I'm sorry," Liza cuts in, grabbing me by the arm. "This is—"

"Cyrus Matrus," the Queen finishes, and my legs wobble.

How does she know my real name? That's impossible. Cyrus Matrus is dead to Escela, and only Monsteress knows who I really am. So, how did Queen Caecilia figure it out? Has Monsteress reached out to her to warn her about me? Is my father somehow involved with her?

Liza tightens her grip around me to keep me upright.

"There's no need to worry," Queen Caecilia says, noticing my distress. "I find no pleasure in interfering with other kingdoms' business. Whatever forced you to fake your own death, it's your matter."

I can feel Liza's eyes burn into my skin. This isn't how she was supposed to find out who I am. I had so many opportunities to tell her I'm the *dead* Prince of Eternitie—at least dead to everyone besides Monsteress and my father.

My father spread the word about my death and held a funeral with a beaten-up body he found on the streets to cover up my escape.

"Aemilius, is that true?" Liza's voice breaks as she lets go of me.

My heart throbs when she steps back as if I'm a stranger. "I wanted to tell you. I did. But I feared what would happen to you if my father found out you've been hiding me all this time."

That's the truth.

I would never forgive myself if Liza came in harm's way because of me. She's been through too much to put my burden on her.

The silence in the room threatens to eat me alive.

I can't lose Liza. She's everything I got.

"It looks like you two have some catching up to do," Queen Caecilia says, her words cutting the air like lightning bolts.

Liza steadies herself. "No. Whatever you have to say, Cyrus stays with me."

The wrenching feeling of my intestines being torn out vanishes.

She used my name. My *real* name.

"Are you certain?" the Queen asks, her eyes studying Liza closely.

"Yes."

Queen Caecilia raises her eyebrows and waits another moment for Liza to interject before continuing. "Your father," the Queen looks at me, "is planning to attack Crymzon come sunrise."

I swallow hard. "Pardon me?"

The Queen clears her throat. "King Citeus is marching against Queen Soulin. He's preparing his army as we speak."

The room spins around me.

"He can't," Liza says in disbelief. "She will turn him into dust before he can even set foot in her kingdom."

Queen Caecilia nods. "I expressed my thoughts about his attack, yet he's convinced he will walk away."

No.

No. No. No.

"No one walks away from the Crymzon Queen," Liza whispers, voicing what I'm not saying aloud.

My mind races, trying to come up with all the ways this battle can end, each ending with my father's death. His inventions are nothing—*nothing*—compared to her magic.

But isn't that what I want?

If my father is gone, I'm a free man. My sister Catalina, the Crown Princess of Eternitie, will welcome me with open arms.

Everything would work out perfectly if it weren't for my brother, Cyprian.

"Are you aiding him?" I ask, slowly regaining my composure.

"While Queen Soulin needs to be stopped, I don't want to see her dead. I don't want to be responsible for an entire kingdom to fall."

I didn't even think about that. We're not talking about one person here. We're talking about the *entire kingdom.*

"Our friends are in Crymzon," I say, thinking about all the villagers I left behind to take Liza away.

I care for all of them, I do, but my chest constricts when I think about leaving Devana behind. Did she find a way to escape? Did Monsteress harm her?

Queen Caecilia bites her lip. "So I heard. My job is to evacuate as many people inside and outside the wall as possible before King Citeus takes Queen Soulin down."

I can't let that happen. I need to warn Monsteress. Whatever my father has planned, it will be deadly if he's convinced to have even the slightest chance of going head-to-head with the most powerful ruler in Escela.

If Monsteress dies before Queen Caecilia can rescue the villagers, they will die. Devana will die.

I've seen how fast Crymzon reacts to its ruler. I was there when the palace crumbled like a sandcastle.

And what if my father uses Catalina for the attack? What if he sends her like the coward he is? I can't let her go up against Monsteress. She won't stand a chance.

If it were just my father and brother I have to worry about, I would let them go, but only because I know they have the shorter end of the stick.

But my sister and friends? They don't deserve that horrible fate, and I must do everything I can to protect them.

"I need to go back," I say steadily.

Liza's mouth pops open. "Are you mad?"

"The way my father insists on fighting Crymzon, I promise you, whatever he's planning on doing will have devastating consequences for us. Something must have happened that he thinks he has the slightest chance of winning, and I need to figure out what it is."

I'm almost sure that it's my invention my brother stole from me right before I fled. And if that's true, I can't just stand here.

He might have stolen and duplicated my concept, but it's my fault that it's in his hands. I should have destroyed it the minute I found out how much damage it could do.

"I'm not letting you go," Liza says, her brows almost touching each other. "No one walks away from Crymzon, and you've done it twice. Isn't that enough? You're lucky to be alive, and you want to go back a third time?"

"That's not your decision to make," I say, facing Queen Caecilia. "Please send me back to warn her."

"Why?"

It's a simple question I don't have an answer to.

Because the blood of my friends will stick to my hands if my father kills her. Because if I'm wrong and he doesn't use my invention, there's a chance I will lose my sister if my father takes her with him. Or because we need Monsteress alive in case Otyx reappears with another army of resurrected soldiers.

Only Crymzon's magic is powerful enough to slice through those abominations. I was there when Monsteress took down a dozen of them with her bare hands like it was nothing.

As much as I want to see the Crymzon Queen dead, her well-being outweighs the horrible things she has done.

"I will bargain to get the Lady of Fate in return for my intel," I say, and Liza's eyes throw daggers at me.

I promised I wouldn't say anything, but here I am, blasting her secret mission out like it's common knowledge.

But Liza can see the future. Can she see mine? Does she already know what's going to happen to me?

If she does, I don't want to know.

"Irrational acting seems to be your family trait," Queen Caecilia says, and my cheeks burn. "What makes you think she's going to listen to you?"

"Because she knows who I am."

It's out. Now, everyone in this cell knows how I survived Monsteress twice. I'm more precious to the Queen than any other prisoner.

The Prince of Eternitie. Her secret weapon to the Brass Palace; to my father.

"If your attempt to reason with Queen Soulin fails, I have no other choice than to stick to King Citeus' plan and free her people," the Queen says slowly, folding her hands together. "If you free my subject unscathed, I promise you will have a home here in Starstrand, and I *will* ensure that her prisoners are being released."

That's all I need to hear.

Even if I die, Devana will be safe. Even if I die, Queen Caecilia will help the villagers to escape. It's a foolish plan, but the only way to right my wrongs.

TWELVE

QUEEN SOULIN

First of all, how dare Lunra drop into my Silk Keep unannounced, scaring the living hell out of me? And second, what the actual fuck?

On top of finding Eternitie's mole, Khaos' return before he literally swept me off my feet, and figuring out a plan to hit Keres again, I don't have time to waste on a Goddess' empty warnings.

I don't care if Otyx will be the end of me. I would go to war with Zorus, the King of the Gods, if he had the nerve to mock my family.

I swat the moths fluttering around me out of my way and search for the tiniest hole in the wall.

There it is.

In one quick motion, the whip curled around my arm drops to the ground, and I hold on to the handle to inspect the only key for the desolate stone cell tucked away in the Silk Keep. As I turn the key, a clicking sound rings in my ears, and I push against the stone slab separating me from my destination.

The room before me is dark and cold, and the air inside the dimly lit dungeon is heavy with dampness and the faint scent of decay.

A frail figure sits hunched over the table, her gnarled fingers tracing invisible patterns on its surface.

The old lady, with her clouded eyes and wrinkled face etched with a lifetime of secrets, seems to sense my presence. Slowly, she lifts her head, annoyance and suspicion clear in her expression. Her voice is tinged with bitterness as she speaks. "So, the Queen seeks counsel from the wretched old crone yet again. What brings you here, Your Highness?"

Undeterred by the old woman's tone, I step forward and reply with a calm yet determined voice, "I come seeking answers. My kingdom has a mole. I need your help to uncover their identity."

A faint smirk creeps across the old woman's lips as she leans back in her chair. "Why should I help you? You've ignored the plight of the oppressed and turned a blind eye to the suffering of those who truly need you. Now, you seek my help only when your power is at stake."

My nostrils flare as I try to keep calm. "My people deserve justice, and I will do whatever it takes to secure their safety. Tell me what you know."

"The only justice to end their suffering is your death."

I jolt forward, and before she can figure out what's coming, my hand buries in her hair, and I pull her head back to force her to look at me.

I know it's useless. She's blind, for goodness' sake, but I need her to listen carefully.

The Lady of Fate's features soften slightly, her skepticism giving way to a hint of curiosity. "Very well, Your Highness. But remember, the path to the truth is treacherous, and the knowledge you seek comes at a price. The future you seek may not be the one you desire."

As I nod, the old woman reaches out her weathered hand, beckoning me to come closer. The flickering light from the lamp inside the Silk Keep casts eerie shadows on her face as I lean in, our eyes meeting for the first time. At that moment, I sense the weight of the woman's wisdom, as if the secrets of the kingdom and my destiny hang in the balance.

I might be the strongest individual in Escela, but I have nothing on the Lady of Fate.

The woman lets out a dry, humorless laugh that fills the cell with a sense of bitter irony. "Ah, the great Queen, in need of guidance from an old, blind woman. What a farce this has become." Her voice holds a touch of resentment and skepticism.

As I intensify the grip on her hair, her eyes widen. "I do not seek to undermine your wisdom nor underestimate the value of your perception," I hiss through clenched teeth. "I believe that even in darkness, you can still see what eludes the rest of us. You've done it before. So tell me, Lady of Fate, what do you see for the future of my kingdom?"

"The future? Do you truly believe there's a happy ending for you? You come to me seeking answers, but fail to recognize the suffering you have inflicted upon me and your kin."

I'm one move away from ripping her head clean off.

"Very well," she says. "I will help you."

Slowly, I release her hair and step back, but her grin brings my blood to boil.

Why is she still smiling?

"There are depths of darkness that even you cannot fathom. And in seeking the truth, you may lose more than you are willing to sacrifice."

"Stop talking in riddles."

"He's coming for you."

My heart skips a beat. "Who? Otyx?"

The Lady of Fate laughs again, rippling through me like icy waves. "Whatever you tried to cover up, he will resurface it. He will break you. He will punish you for what you've done."

Fuck.

Otyx is coming for me.

"And I will be waiting for him," I say, turning on my heels. As I storm out of the cell, I can hear her laugh.

"You can't hide from him."

I halt. "I'm more powerful than ever. The Heiligbaum is restored, giving me more magic than I can hold."

"The stone, oh yes, the stone," she muses, her voice carrying a melodic cadence that seemed to blend with her breathing. "Each stone holds a secret, as hidden as the stars in daylight. But you think there's only one important one."

I turn to face her.

"The sparkling sapphire cradles the wisdom of ancient skies," she continues, her eyes glinting like the gem she spoke of. "Its touch gives clarity upon the wandering mind, and within its depths, visions of futures yet untold may arise." She holds her breath to build tension. "Then there's the fiery ruby," the old woman whispers, a hint of excitement in her voice. "It pulses with passion, igniting hearts with ardor and courage. But beware, for the intensity of its flame can consume the unprepared."

As she speaks, the old woman gestures toward the ground, where small stones shimmer like fragments of starlight. Each stone seems to hold a tale of its own, waiting to be unlocked by her cryptic words.

But it has to be a trick of the light because those gems can't be in her windowless cell. Beside a bed, table, and chair, she has nothing.

"Ah, but the emerald, a verdant soul among stones," she cuts in, her eyes alight with reverence. "Its touch is a balm for weary hearts, nurturing love and healing even the deepest wounds. Within its green embrace, life blooms anew."

"Stop it," I say, curling my fingers into fists.

"And do not forget the Painite," she says, her voice softer and almost mystical. "A kaleidoscope of emotions reflects the ever-changing tides of the soul. Its play of colors mirrors the complexities of our being, teaching us to embrace the myriad hues within. But beware, dearest Queen," she warns, her tone solemn. "For these stones are both a gift and a burden. There are so many more powerful gems you don't even know of. They hold the power to heal and to harm, to empower and to ensnare. It is the path of the wise to wield them with care and respect."

Her words linger in the air like venomous snakes.

I shake my head. "We're done here."

"But you're about to find out how much damage they can do," she concludes, her voice a whisper.

I spin around, and with a twist of my hand, the stone slab slams into place. As I walk away, I can still hear the Lady of Fate's hysterical laughter.

He's coming for me, and he's prepared.

But so am I.

THIRTEEN

Khaos

Making love differs entirely from how Soulin and I approach our new Soulmate Connection. During every intimate encounter, we let our primal instincts take over and fuck like it's our last time. It's like we try to get it done as fast as possible.

She deserves more than that. Soulin deserves someone who shows her how beautiful it can be to love someone instead of submitting to the urge of the Soulmate Connection.

As I contemplate creating a romantic evening for Soulin, my mind buzzes with excitement to make this night memorable. I know that spoiling her means going above and beyond, leaving no detail unattended. With every decision, I have to show my love, and maybe, just maybe, I can crack through the hardest-as-fuck-of-a-shell a person can build around themselves.

Selecting the perfect location is first on my list. I ponder various locations that resonate with my Queen's heart. I need a place that exudes intimacy and elegance, where we can be free to express ourselves without the outside world's distractions. Perhaps a secluded garden covered with twinkling fairy lights or a lavish private dining room in the palace, where we could have a breathtaking view of the moonlit landscape.

No.

I can't take her to places she already knows and so close to any servants. It needs to be somewhere where no one can see us.

The East Tower is out of the question because the last time I found her there, her resurrected brother almost killed her. But what about the other tower? I've never seen her spend time in the West Wing, where her father's chamber used to be.

I guess I will find out how she reacts to the West Tower soon.

Next, I need flowers. Nothing suits Soulin better than the Crymzon Veil.

It's a rare and captivating bloom that encapsulates beauty and death in its intricate petals. This extraordinary flower emerges from the depths of the desert's mysterious tapestry, a testament to the delicate balance between life's vibrancy and its inevitable demise. Like the rich fabric of Soulin's gowns, its velvety petals blend the deepest shade of burgundy, reminiscent of a moonlit sky at twilight. Each petal is veined with dark, almost black streaks resembling intricate smoke tendrils, intertwining, and curling upon themselves like whispers of death.

The velveteen texture of the Crymzon Veil's petals, so soft to the touch, beckons admirers to caress its surface, only to be met with an enchanting, delicate chill. It seems to keep the coolness of a midnight breeze, evoking a sense of nightmares.

Its fragrance is an intriguing blend of opulence and decay, a delicate dance between the intoxicating sweetness of life and the subtle hint of mortality.

The Crymzon Veil's beauty lies not only in its striking appearance but also in its symbolism. It is a poignant representation of life's transience and the ephemeral nature of existence. Its profound burgundy hues speak of passion, love, and vitality, reminding me of the vibrancy of life's fleeting moments. Yet, the somber undertones of its dark streaks allude to the inevitability of mortality, a reminder that beauty and life are inextricably intertwined with the eventual embrace of death.

Pairing the Crymzon Veil with Soulin's favorite dishes is a must. I must seek the expertise of the kingdom's finest chefs to curate a delectable, multi-course meal.

Knowing that Soulin's responsibilities often demand much energy, I also must arrange a spa-like setting with a fragrant bath in her water chamber and soothing oils to provide the perfect relaxation to soothe her body and mind.

I'm unsure if I can control myself seeing her stand inside the pool again. My mind goes straight to her bare skin, my warm touch on her breasts, her nipple perked just for me.

Damnit, Khaos. Keep it together.

No, I won't take her to the water chamber. I will hold off until I take her to the secluded West Tower, where we can stargaze under the clear night sky.

I know that spoiling my Queen isn't merely a display of grand gestures but an earnest desire to make her feel adored in every way.

However, Soulin possesses a fiery spirit and a tendency to challenge even the most well-intentioned gestures. This makes my task even more challenging.

One misstep and she will eat me alive.

As Soulin finally enters the room, her regal presence fills the space. Her eyes, filled with anger and skepticism, survey the scene before her.

Standing in the room's corner, I study her. She's as beautiful as ever!

Slowly, I approach her with a gentle smile and extend my hand, inviting her to come closer. With a playful glimmer in her eyes, she hesitates. I hold my fingers out steadily until she finally places her hand in mine.

I guide her to a table covered with a feast fit just for her, saying nothing. There's no room for words.

The scent of delectable delicacies fills the air, tempting my palate. Wine glasses stand tall, waiting to be filled, while a bouquet of Crymzon Veils takes over the table's centerpiece.

"What is this?" Soulin asks, trying to pull her hand out of mine, but I strengthen my grip.

"It's just a little distraction from—"

Soulin moves so fast that I can't finish my sentence. One minute, I'm holding her hand by the table, and the next, she pins me with my arm against my back against the wall.

"A distraction from what?" she growls into my ear, pressing her weight into me.

"From everything that happened to you," I say, pushing her back, but I can feel the sharp edges of the whip curled around her wrist against the back of my neck.

I should have known better. I should have known that the word *distraction* would set her off faster than her father's name.

What was I thinking?

"Soulin," I beg, softening my voice. "I was trying to show you how someone is supposed to treat you. This wasn't an evil plan to deceive you."

The pressure against my neck and back slowly lifts as she steps back to give me space. She looks at the food as if it's poisonous, then at the Crymzon Veils, and back at me. "Whatever this is, I don't like it."

My heart pounds in my chest. I spent all day creating this romantic gesture just for her to turn it down.

I have no clue why I thought it would work on the first try. She hasn't experienced affection since her mother died, and it will take quite some time to normalize it again. The defense she has built up over the years won't crack with one meal.

"You're mistaken. This *thing* between us is nothing more than a mutual agreement. I take what my Soulmate Connection wants from you, and you do the same. We're not some power couple destined to ride into the sunset together. I'm me, and, well, you're you. This will be nothing other than just getting our needs met."

Each word cuts through my heart like broken glass. "What happened today?" I ask, taking a seat and loading my plate full of delicacies.

"Nothing," she snaps back, looking at my plate. "How can you eat right now?"

"If nothing happened, I have all the time in the world to enjoy my dinner," I answer, filling my glass with wine.

Soulin watches me as I bring the first fork to my mouth. The marinated pork is so tender and delicious that my eyes roll back.

"I can't believe you," Soulin hisses, strolling over to the other side of the table. "It's not the time to relax right now."

"Then tell me why? Why should I stop eating the perfect meal when everything in Crymzon is fine?"

Her nostrils flare, and she grabs her fork and jams it into a piece of the same pork I had taken from as if she's still not convinced that the other courses are deadly.

I watch her bite into the tender meat and how the corners of her mouth lift briefly before she stabs her fork into another piece.

"Do you want to sit and enjoy the meal in silence?" I offer, but she shakes her head and goes in for a third serving.

Chuckling to myself, I try the vegetables, a weird-looking red sauce—which I think is some fruit—the chicken, some kind of other meat I can't put my finger on, and finally, a chocolate dessert. Meanwhile, Soulin watches me closely, and while she stands during her meal, she tries everything on the table right after she watches me consume it.

This is not how I expected our meal to go, but hey, she stayed and hasn't tried to kill me—again.

I'm torn between showing her the West Tower or calling it good after this meal. But the longer I think about her reaction, the clearer my decision becomes.

Something must have happened. Otherwise, Soulin wouldn't be so on edge. Showing her the tower will probably be my death sentence, so I change my plans.

The chair scratches over the ground as I push myself off the table. "If you need me, you can find me in my chamber," I say, marching to the door.

I reach my hand out to grab for the doorknob and stop mid-motion when I notice Soulin's red magic sparking around it. If I touch that knob, I will either be electrocuted, or she uses her power to hold it shut. Both options are not favorable.

"Who said you can go?" she whispers, and when I turn around, my eyes fall on her burgundy gown on the floor between us. "My connection is not done with you yet."

Slowly, my eyes wander over her curvy body, up her legs, belly, and breasts, and then to her face.

There are only ten steps between us, and I want to launch forward and feel every inch of her body. She's offering herself to me. To *me.* I need to take the bait and run with it.

Instead, I turn back around and touch the knob. To my surprise, she hasn't used her magic to cause me any harm. Despite that, the door won't open. Her chuckle behind me makes me aware that she has the upper hand until...

I force my magic into the knob, undoing her spell.

Her chuckle dies off behind me when I open the door and shut it behind me.

She might be stronger than any other Crymzonian, but she forgets I'm her equal now. And just because her connection tells her she wants me, I want *her* to want me. I don't want to be one more addition to her pets.

As I walk away, I expect the door to fly off its hinges and Soulin's hands to curl around my throat to hold me back.

But it stays closed.

The anger that pushes through our connection forces a little smile onto my lips.

Good, she's pissed. But so am I.

FOURTEEN

Devana

The training grounds are filled with soldiers clad in armor. More soldiers gather around a designated area, eagerly waiting for me to showcase my skills with a sword.

Just because I'm from Tenacoro, everyone believes I'm a warrior. And they're right.

I stand at the center of the training arena outside the Brass Palace, dressed in loose-fitting armor, my hands clutching a poorly crafted sword.

If my father could see this weapon, he would laugh and break it in half. Eternians might be genius inventors, but they lack the art of sword forging.

Despite holding on to the excuse of a blade and my outward composure, a persistent pain courses through my body, reminding me of the battle I fight daily that no one knows about besides me. Each step comes with a wave of agony, yet I push through, determined to prove myself.

They wouldn't believe me if I acted like I'd never used a sword. But I also can't show them my skills surpass everything they know. After all, Eternians weren't created to fight.

The captain of the soldiers, a burly man with grizzled features, barks out orders. "Prepare yourselves, men! We'll see what this recruit is made of!" His voice echoes across the training grounds as the soldiers tighten their grips on their weapons.

The first soldier lunges forward, his blade flashing in the sunlight. I dodge his attack, my movement graceful yet controlled. I dance around the battlefield, skillfully dodging and deflecting the soldier's strikes. Every action is deliberate yet designed to give the appearance of weakness.

The soldier, confident in his numerical advantage, grows bolder. "Jump in," he yells at his comrades.

They come at me one by one, their strikes growing more fierce and relentless. I absorb each blow with careful precision, never revealing my true strength. Sweat mixes with the dirt on my face as the muscle pain gnaws at my body. It whispers a cruel symphony of agony in my joints, but I refuse to relent.

The soldiers, caught in my whirlwind of feints and counterattacks, exchange glances. Their skepticism morphs into arrogance, encouraging them to press harder, to strike faster.

With every swing of my sword, I fight against my opponents but also against my body's limitations. My muscles quiver, and my limbs grow heavy.

This is the reason my father focused on archery. I can't do this for long. Not if my body grows weary so fast.

Their swords slash through the air. My movements become more sluggish and weak, as if I'm merely going through the motions to stop them from hurting me and nothing more.

I purposefully hold back, my strikes lacking the power I'm truly capable of. The soldiers sneer and scoff as I deflect their blows.

My muscles rebel against my will, growing weaker and more unresponsive with every passing moment.

I need to do something. I need to make them stop.

Despite the torment coursing through my body, I grit my teeth, refusing to let it show.

I'm not a quitter.

I'm not a quitter.

My vision blurs, my grip on the sword weakens, and my fingers tingle with numbness.

I could take these fuckers out. Right here and right now. My energy would be enough to make them regret the day they were born before my body caves. But I know that revealing my true abilities would only expose my vulnerability to those who sought to undermine me.

A sword swings in my direction, and I command my arms to move up to block it, but they don't react. The dull blade crashes into my metal chest piece, forcing the air out of my lungs.

The soldiers, now convinced of my incompetence, exchanged mocking glances.

"She's useless for battle," a soldier laughs, throwing his weapon to the ground. "You want us to fight alongside a broken Tenacorian?"

My grip on the hilt of my sword grows firmer, though hidden tremors threaten to betray me as I look at his exposed neck.

I could end him. I could show him how fast a *broken* Tenacorian can move.

But I don't.

I can't.

I need to play by King Citeus' rules if I want to take the slightest chance of rescuing my father.

"She's going with us," the captain barks, ripping the sword out of my hand.

"But—"

The captain turns around to silence his soldier. "End of discussion. She's coming with us, and if I hear one more word, you will stand beside her at the end of the formation."

The soldier glares at me before he picks up his sword and storms off. I look after him, memorizing every detail. His hair is short and almost white, his eyes blue as the sea, and he must weigh twice as much as me. But that won't stop me from teaching him a lesson once I find my father, Aemilius, and my villagers.

No one calls me *broken.*

I clutch onto a pendant in my trembling hand, an object small enough to hide between my breasts from curious eyes. The charm, carefully crafted by my father, holds a secret known only to me. It's not an ordinary pendant but an extraordinary treasure—a feather from Erinna.

Why? Why am I doing this to myself right now? Why am I thinking of her?

Erinna wasn't just my pet; she was my Glimmarum—a faithful companion who understood me like no other.

Every time a Tenacorian is born, an animal steps forward to claim the new babe as a companion and exclusively bonds to it. It's a creature supposed to bring solace and friendship in times of darkness.

A Glimmarum may display remarkable physical or other traits that reflect the unique nature of its relationship with its human confidant.

As my fingers curl around the brown feather, its color of rich, earthy tones, I feel its power resonating within my grasp. The feather's surface is velvety, with each barb and vane crafted to perfection.

Delicately, I trace my fingertips along the spine, feeling the ridges and contours that embellish its length. Glimmers of golden highlights dance across its texture at certain angles as if it holds a hidden luminosity. These flecks of gold mimic sunlight filtering through a dense forest, casting dappled warmth upon the feather's surface.

Though small, the pendant holds an undeniable presence for me—a symbol of a connection to a kingdom long forgotten, a world I had to leave behind to save my life.

Maybe my Glimmarum can forgive me for leaving her behind someday, but until then, I'm well equipped to fight my way through this world alone.

As the sun stands at its highest point, casting harsh shadows upon the cobblestone streets, I find myself wandering through the heart of Eternitie again. Somehow, I managed to slip away from the guards leading me back to the Brass Palace.

Alone, I explore the bustling streets alive with the sounds of hissing steam, rhythmic clanking, and the distant hum of machinery. Each step I take sends a gentle echo reverberating through the narrow alleys.

Along my path, I come across a small workshop tucked away between towering buildings. Its windows glow with warm, inviting light, drawing my attention. I push open the heavy brass door and enter.

Inside, shelves lined with gadgets, mysterious contraptions, and inventions fill every corner.

A tall, bespectacled Eternitian greets me, his eyes shining with disbelief as he takes me in. He's wearing a disheveled lab coat, and his hands are full of gears and cogs. He holds out an invention, a small brass device resembling a pocket watch.

“Behold, madam,” he says, stepping closer. “I present to you the Chrono-Locator, a device that allows you to navigate this wondrous city easily.”

My eyes widen as I reach out to accept the invention. Its polished surface gleams under my touch. Tiny gears move in perfect synchrony, creating a dance within the device.

I press a small button, and the Chrono-Locator springs to life, emitting a soft hum. A mesmerizing holographic display materializes above the device, projecting a three-dimensional city map. The streets, buildings, and even airship routes are rendered in astonishing detail.

My eyes soak up the hologram as I trace the winding cobblestone streets and hidden pathways.

“I can’t accept it,” I say, handing it back, but my eyes can’t stop scanning the map to memorize every single detail.

“Sure you can. What good is a Chrono-Locator to me if I know every corner of this kingdom blindfolded?”

“But I can’t pay you,” I whisper, pressing the button again, and the hologram disappears.

“Some things are priceless,” he smiles, closing my hands around the device. “You will need it more than I do.”

With the Chrono-Locator in hand, I step back onto the streets, and my gaze is drawn to a street performer standing at the corner, manipulating a contraption. It looks like a monkey, but it’s crafted in polished brass, its gears visible through a transparent casing. The animal juggles small, glowing orbs with smooth motions, captivating an audience that gathered around.

As I draw nearer, it begins to sway to an unheard rhythm, its limbs moving without losing a beat. Whirring mechanisms beneath its metallic exterior propelled the creature, allowing it to mimic lifelike gestures and expressions. It claps its mechanical hands together, emitting a soft clanking sound. It's adorned in a miniature vest with buttons and tiny cog-shaped patterns. A top hat embellished with a feather sits jauntily upon its head, adding a whimsy touch to its appearance.

The monkey performs a dazzling display of acrobatics, effortlessly leaping from one platform to another. As the performance climaxes, the monkey descends to the ground, landing on its feet with a gentle thud. Its metallic eyes meet my gaze, and for a brief moment, I feel fear—if the Eternitians can turn metal into lifelike creations, what holds them back to create a weapon strong enough to destroy entire kingdoms?

The onlookers erupt in applause, showering the monkey and its performer with praise. I join in, clapping my hands slowly.

Eternity might not have strength on their side like the other kingdoms do, but I have underestimated their skills. If King Ceitus truly wants to go head-to-head with Monsteress, he has to be damn sure that whatever he has created is strong enough to injure the Crymzon Queen.

"Don't trust it. It's the King's spy," a woman whispers into my ear as the monkey makes its rounds to collect coins from the crowd. I whirl around to face her, but my eyes lock with a guard behind me.

He grabs me by the arm and pulls me away from the crowd. "It's time to report to the King. He will be pleased to hear that a Tenacorian will join his army in the last row."

His loud chuckle vibrates through my arm into my body. I stare at his Adam's apple, knowing that one punch would be enough to force him to his knees. Instead, I chuckle back and let him guide me back into the Brass Palace.

FIFTEEN

Cyrus

Two winged men lead us down a corridor to a room.

As I stand at the threshold of the cloud room, my breath catches in my throat as I behold the wondrous sight that lies before me. The room is a vast, open space, its walls and ceiling formed entirely of swirling clouds. It feels as if I've stepped into a dream, a realm where the ordinary rules of reality no longer apply.

My eyes adjust to the celestial hues, and I tilt my gaze upwards. Above me stretches a seemingly infinite expanse of the night sky, a mesmerizing tapestry of stars.

I've never been so close to the sky before.

The stars twinkle with a brilliance that defies description, casting a soft glow upon the cloud walls. The constellations sparkle across the night sky, their patterns intertwine in a cosmic dance. I trace the lines connecting the stars, my finger brushing against the fabric of the cosmos.

Time seems to lose all meaning. The worries and cares of my everyday life fade into insignificance as I immerse myself in starlight.

I feel the cool touch of the clouds beneath my feet, their soft texture adding to the surreal experience as I step inside. Soft wisps of mist swirl around me, carrying on gentle currents of air. It's as if the very atmosphere of the room is alive, responding to my presence and the grandeur of the night sky above.

With a deep breath, I reluctantly tear my gaze away from the mesmerizing lights.

"It's beautiful, isn't it?" Liza asks beside me, startling me.

"It's...marvelous," I answer, my mind returning from wandering through stars and darkness.

I understand why Liza is drawn to the skies and stars. She closes her eyes for a moment, allowing the starlight to bathe her face. Watching the warmth of celestial energy seep into her being is another thing I've never seen before. It's invisible yet there.

As I watch Liza charge herself, my sense of responsibility grows, and impatience eats away at me.

I fidget, glancing back towards the entrance where the two guards block the exit.

I let out an exasperated sigh, glancing at Liza, who stands there with a serene smile. "Our friends need us. We can't afford to linger here any longer," I urge, my voice tinged with frustration.

Liza opens her eyes, her smile still evident, though she must sense my vexation. "I know, but can't you feel it? This place, it's so close to starlight and God Nelion," she replies in a dreamy tone. "It's been too long since I've been home. Let's just stay for a little while longer, please?"

My heart softens, knowing that Liza has always seen beauty in places where others might miss it and she yearns for the celestial—her home. But my concern for our friends overshadows my ability to enjoy the present moment any longer.

I brought Liza to safety. Now I need to return and do the same for the villagers. For Devana.

I step closer to Liza and gently take her hand. "I can't deny that you want to stay, but our friends need us just as much as you need to be here," I implore.

Liza looks into my eyes, her starlit gaze meeting mine, and nods. "You're right. I can't let my love for the stars blind me. But I can't go even if I wanted to," she says, her voice filled with regret. "Queen Caecilia won't return my wings until I retrieve my grandma."

"That can't be the reason you're staying. I don't have wings, and somehow, I will make it back to land," I say, my eyebrows pressed together.

"I'm scared," Liza says, walking over to the wall to touch the clouds.

"Of what?"

What a stupid question. I know exactly what she's afraid of. But I'm scared, too. That can't be the reason to stop moving forward.

"I still feel her whip cutting into my back every time I think of her. I'm worthless to her. She only kept me alive to torture you."

I want to tell her she's wrong, but she's not. If Monsteress hadn't seen me begging to spare her life, she would have killed her.

"I understand," I whisper, stepping beside her.

We just stand there, watching the clouds swirl before us, when I hear a rustling noise.

"I meant to ask you earlier: do you know someone named Devana?" Queen Caecilia asks, flowing into the room.

My throat closes when I hear her name.

Devana.

I could never forget her. *Never*. But I tried to suppress the intuition that something terrible happened to her. Besides Liza, Devana and her father are the only other people I grew close to while living in the Confines. She taught me how to use a sword while her father made me a few blades to protect myself. And while I lived with Liza, it might have looked like we were a couple, but another woman stole my heart.

"Yes," Liza says, bringing me back to reality.

"She made it all the way to Eternitie to ask for your father's aid to free the villagers you're so concerned about," the Queen says, directed at me.

I exhale sharply.

She's alive. Of course, she is. Of all the villagers, she's the one with the highest chance to survive imprisonment: Devana *and* her father.

So why does my heart hurt so badly thinking about her? I should be happy that she's well. I should be smiling.

Yet, I can't.

Monsteress might be our biggest enemy, but my father is just as lethal without magic. Devana traded her freedom for an equally disturbing fate. I never thought about warning her. It was my responsibility to tell her who I was, and I didn't out of fear they would reject me, or my father would use that knowledge someday against them.

What a fool I was.

"How was she?" I ask, regaining my voice.

Queen Caecilia and Liza look at me. I don't care if they can hear my broken heart. I should have saved her. Instead, I've been running from Crymzon ever since we got captured.

"She looked fine to me. Her face was covered in dirt, her clothes filthy, but she was fine," the Queen answers, and my heartbeat slows.

Devana's face is always covered in a thin layer of sweat and dirt. She says she uses it to block the sun from frying her skin. I imagine the mud she carefully mixes to match her golden-brown skin. I've watched her do it several times from a distance when she thought no one was watching.

"Please tell me she won't fight against the Crymzon Queen," I say, fully aware that's exactly what she's preparing to do.

"At sunrise," Queen Caecilia says, walking over to the wall opposite me. "I'm sorry."

"I will never make it to Crymzon in time. If Eternitie starts marching at sunrise, they will arrive before me."

"Not if you use these." With a graceful wave of her hand, the Queen's touch awakens the slumbering power within the cloud wall—the misty barrier ripples and shifts like a liquid mass responding to her command. Soft tendrils of clouds separate, revealing a small section that floats gently in front of her.

With a tender smile, the Queen extends her hand toward me, presenting the precious fragment of cloud wall. It appears weightless, shimmering with a radiant light that dances across its surface. As I reach out, my fingertips brush against the delicate material.

In an instant, the cloud particles respond to my touch. They begin to swirl and dance, weaving around my outstretched hand.

I try to pull back, but it's too strong.

Like a thousand tiny feathers, they caress my skin, eliciting a tingling sensation that spreads through my body. The cloud particles continue to twist and turn as they transform into magnificent wings extending from my back.

The wings, an iridescent curtain of gossamer clouds, unfurl gracefully and elegantly. They gently embrace me, their touch firm yet gentle, and a rush of exhilaration courses through my veins. As the wings stretch wide, I can feel the weightlessness of flight lifting me off the ground.

"Think of it as a present to return my subject safely," the Queen says, her eyes shimmering as I struggle to keep my balance.

"If Queen Soulin sees those wings, she will know that you send me," I say, moving my arms and legs to work against the flapping wings that keep me off the ground.

How am I supposed to steer these?

"They are an extension of your being now. Just imagine what you want them to do, and they will follow your command."

Easier said than done.

My eyes meet Liza's, and I can see the deep hurt as she watches my wings move behind me. "I'm sorry. I can't do this," I say, concentrating on returning to the floor.

Surprisingly, the wings listen, and I carefully descend back to the ground.

Queen Caecilia looks at me and then at Liza. "I will ensure Liza gets her wings back while you're gone."

I stare at Liza momentarily, searching her facial expression to see if I can trust her Queen's word. I've been burned too many times to trust a ruler—by Monsteress and my father.

Liza nods slowly before turning to her Queen, and it's enough to make me understand.

"Be careful," Liza says, coming closer to me.

I want to answer and assure her I'll be fine, but it's impossible. Outrunning Monsteress twice is unheard of, but returning freely to her kingdom three times is preposterous.

As I close my eyes, I spread my arms and wings wide, allowing the delicate clouds to embrace me. The radiant starlight filters through the open ceiling, and a content smile curves across my lips as I lift off the ground again.

Devana is fine—as of now. She might be in my father's grip, but hopefully, he hasn't realized that she knows me. If he does, he will use her to get to me.

But I can prevent that.

Hopefully, I can get Monsteress to free the villagers and the Lady of Fate so Liza can keep her wings. After that, it's time to face my father and end this game of hide-and-seek.

SIXTEEN

Queen Soulin

I'm on fire—literally.

Anger washes over me in hot waves.

How dare he turn his back on me?

Flames shoot over my skin, licking every inch of me without causing me any harm.

I fucking knew it. Not only is the Soulmate Connection binding me to Khaos, but he also gained a significant amount of magic that reaches almost my potential. This makes him superior to anyone inside the Crymzon Wall beside me.

Fuck!

The only thing that keeps me sane is the knowledge that he would never use it against me.

Oh, wait. I'm wrong.

He just did not even a few hours ago. He used his power to break the magic I put on the door and did it without even moving a muscle.

Not only was his magic strong enough to counterattack mine, but I also felt his gloating through our connection.

What if he turns out to be just like my father? All charming and loving on the outside, but waiting for me to die on the inside? What if I don't know the real Khaos? What if—?

I storm through the palace after I'm sure he's gone to get my mind off it. I'm not giving him the satisfaction of running after him. After all, it's he who keeps following me. He will come back, I know it.

In the depths of the palace in the moonlit Silk Keep, I stand amidst a flurry of my delicate, luminescent moths. Each moth, no larger than a palm, flutters about without acknowledging me.

I pull my hair together and braid it into a loose tail before stepping close to the wall to handpick a few moths.

Before I can think about the next step, Adira lands before me and throws her oversized, fuzzy body into me, almost tipping me over.

"Oh, now you come to see me, you coward," I hiss, pushing her back playfully. "Where were you when I needed you?"

My deep red gown billows gently in the breeze when Adira flaps her wings to get away from me.

The giant moth, my first Fighter Moth, with red shimmering iridescent wings that glistened like precious gemstones, perches gracefully on an ornate stone pedestal. Her antennae gently sway as she watches me with big, expressive eyes.

"Come down here, Adira. I have something to discuss with you."

Adira descends back to the ground and presses her head against my shoulder.

I gently place my hand on her enormous head, its silky touch akin to the finest fabric. "You have been by my side for so long, through trials and triumphs. And because of that, I need to create more of you," I say, petting her scales.

Adira's antennae twitch with curiosity. She lets out a soft, melodic hum, and I hear more wings fluttering in my direction.

My other three Fighter Moths appear between the hundreds of tiny, ordinary silk moths.

After my success in turning Adira from a regular moth into a horse-sized one, plus equipping her with a working mouthpiece and organs, I created Velda, Storm, and Barin as her companions. Each of my winged creations has a unique personality. While Adira seems to have the mentality of a firstborn child, a perfectionist, and a rule follower, Storm turns out to be the stubborn one. Barin is the most playful, and Velda is my teenage moth.

"I will need all of you this time," I continue, my eyes scanning their perfect bodies and wings. "Four is just not enough."

As I speak, I raise my other hand, and tiny, delicate drops appear in my palm, resembling miniature, luminescent orbs. Each orb glows with a radiant light, a reflection of my magic.

"I will need you to teach the other moths how to transport my soldiers," I explain, my gaze never leaving them.

With a gentle gesture, I release the glowing drops, and they disperse into the air like glowing insects. I watch as my magic scouts the little moths surrounding us, carefully picking their targets.

"Your legacy won't be forgotten," I assure them. "Through your kin, the skies shall forever be ours."

Adira lets out another soft hum, almost like a contented sigh, as if she understands my intentions, while Barin jumps around us excitedly. Velda looks unimpressed while Storm shakes her wings in protest.

From the shadows, tiny, glowing moths emerge. They shimmer and pulse with energy, their wings picking up speed like a race to get to me.

What took me days before happens now within moments.

As the magic courses through their tiny bodies, they grow, expanding to become giant insects with wings that span several feet. The once diminutive creatures transform into majestic Fighter Moths, their bodies now visible with distinct patterns and vibrant red and black hues. Their delicate wings, once almost translucent, now display myriad colors, resembling stained glass windows reflecting moonlight.

I smile, my heart gleaming with excitement as I witness the birth of my enchanting creations. These magnificent moths are no ordinary insects anymore; they possess the agility and grace of their smaller counterparts but now wield a strength that matches their newfound size.

As my new moths hover in the air, their colossal wings fanning the night breeze, I whisper an ancient incantation, binding my magic to their essence, ensuring their loyalty and obedience. The moths respond to my words, their antennae quivering as if attuned to my every command.

With my army of Fighter Moths at my side, I gaze towards the throne room, where darkness looms.

It's too early to release them into my kingdom to watch over the wall or to mount them. But in a few days, I can start testing them to determine which moths suit riders and which are staying behind as guards.

SEVENTEEN

Khaos

There's only one place I can go from here.

The heavy wooden doors of the training hall swing open with a resounding creak as I step inside, my heart pounding in my chest. Dressed in my polished armor, my eyes run over the rows of soldiers gathered before me.

As I approach the hall's center, whispers flood the air. I have once been known for my exceptional power in combat—hence, that's why Soulin picked me as her Grand General—but that seems like ages ago. What the other soldiers don't know yet is that I made a name for myself without using any magic.

Once thought to be extinguished forever, my long-lost magic grants me a newfound advantage in battle.

The chamber buzzes with energy as my fellow soldiers eye me. I take a deep breath, centering myself as I draw upon the wellspring of my magical essence. I close my eyes, channeling the energy that surges within me, and when I open them again, a soft glow emanates from my palms.

The first soldier steps forward, unsheathing his sword with a determined expression. "It's really you," Remy says, holding his sword in my direction.

It has been five days. *Five fucking days* and Remy already acts like he's the leader since he took his first breath.

"I'm just here to train," I say, lowering my hands to extinguish my magic.

"Bullshit. I know why you're here."

I cock my head. "And why am I here?"

"You came back to crawl onto the Queen's lap like the good boy you are." He shakes his head. "No. She won't let you touch her. That's why you're always so angry because she doesn't put out."

"What has gotten into you, man?" another soldier behind him asks, stepping away. "You're talking about our Queen."

He shrugs his shoulders. "So what? What is she going to do? Lock us away like our families?"

I'm not sure what I walked into, but this wasn't the welcome I expected from Remy. After all, it was *me* who promoted him to Grand General, and *me* who trained him and taught him everything he knows.

"I know a scared boy when I see one," I say, stepping back to ease the tension between us.

Remy takes another step forward. "Let me guess. She's not holding your family hostage, is she?"

What in Lunra's name is he talking about? Why would Soulin hold my father hostage?

"She probably spared them because you're her *favorite.* The man who can do nothing wrong."

Yeah, right? When was the last time Soulin pressed him against a wall to demonstrate her power?

"Leave my family out of this," I hiss, backing away again.

This is not the time and place to educate Remy, not while everyone is watching. Apparently, he doesn't know that my father is the only family member I have left.

"You don't want to do this," Jeremia cuts in, pulling on Remy's shoulder.

I'm relieved to see Jeremia. Not only did he try to warn me about the sword that pierced my heart on the battlefield, but he's also the soldier I trust the most.

"He can't just walk in here and reclaim what I worked so hard for."

"So, this is what all this is about?" I ask, watching him struggle against Jeremia's grip. "I'm not here to reclaim anything. I just want to train."

Remy huffs before elbowing Jeremia into his unguarded ribcage. Jeremia hunches over, and his painful expression sends me over the edge.

Before Remy can take another step in my direction, I raise my hand, and a brilliant bolt of lightning crackles through the air. It strikes the ground beside Remy's feet, scattering stone pieces and causing a gasp to echo throughout the chamber.

With a flick of my wrist, I create a protective shield around myself, shimmering with a golden glow. Remy's sword clashes against the magical barrier just seconds later, his strikes rendered futile against my enhanced defenses. I retaliate with a wave of my hand, and the air erupts into a whirlwind, lifting my opponent off his feet and sending him sprawling across the chamber.

This feels so good! I forgot how it feels to wield magic.

But my display of power isn't limited to defense alone. With precise control, I conjure orbs of fire that dance through the air, scorching the other soldiers with intense heat. The flames lick at Remy's armor, forcing him to retreat as he struggles to extinguish the magical inferno that threatens to engulf him.

"I'm going to say it just once," I growl, watching Remy squirming on the ground to rid himself of the flames. "If you ever talk ill about our Queen again, I will make sure those flames will feast slowly on your flesh and bones."

I pull my hands back, and the heat and flames evaporate before I turn on my heels.

"Like mother, like son," Remy whispers.

Everyone knows what he means: Soulin burning her father, brother, and the entire throne room to the ground, and now I'm threatening to do the same.

But I won't stand for it.

I whirl around, reaching for every ounce of power fueling my body to flail him. But when I'm about to release it, I see Jeremia standing between us, holding out his hands.

"Not like this, Khaos," he says, holding his ground.

"Step away," I bark, building myself up to my entire height.

He extends his arms further to cover more space. "No."

I take him in more closely. I've known Jeremia for a long time, and whoever stands before me isn't the same person I know. His eyes are harder than usual, his eyebrows drawn together as if he's in pain, and he looks like he hasn't slept in days.

"I need to talk to you," Jeremia says, slowly lowering his arms. "In private."

I nod and drop my hands.

As the training session picks up again around us, a seamless blend of swordsmanship and magical abilities, I turn around to walk out of this place finally. Jeremia follows me quietly, and I don't look over my shoulder to know that men are storming Remy to help him.

"I'm so glad to see you," Jeremia says as the door falls into place behind us.

I'm trying to remember if I saw him during the awkward encounter with half-naked soldiers when I arrived. I didn't pay close attention to the underdressed men and women because I only had eyes for Soulin. But now that I think about it, I'm sure Jeremia wasn't one of the poor souls who had to strip bare before her.

"What happened while I was gone?" I ask, leading him away from the corridor to my room to let him know it's not an option to go there.

"Didn't she fill you in?"

"Would I ask if she had?"

Jeremia sighs. "I still can't believe you're alive. I saw that sword piercing your heart. You should be dead."

I should be, and the black, itching scar covering the stabbing wound is a gruesome indicator that I barely made the cut. It's better to keep that detail to myself.

"You're the only one who will tell me the truth," I continue, ignoring his comments. "What did she do?"

"When we returned, the entire kingdom was...empty. Not a single soul greeted us when we arrived."

Jeremia seemed to have the same experience I had when I got here. I'd never seen the streets empty before, but I thought everyone was sleeping. I should have trusted my guts.

"Where is everyone?"

"Supposedly, Soulin keeps our families in the prison."

I scoff. "That's insane. Why would she do that?"

"To use them as leverage against us? I don't know. All I know is that everyone who didn't make the cut as a soldier is gone."

I never thought about checking in with my father after my return. It should have been the first thing to do. Jeremia, on the other hand, doesn't have any family members left. They either left Crymzon to live in the Confines or died peacefully within the Crymzon Wall.

"What else?"

Jeremia shifts from one foot to the other. "She made everyone strip almost naked for no apparent reason. After that, she restored the Heiligbaum, and since then, I haven't seen her."

I wasn't there to watch the ceremony in the temple because I had to babysit her nightmare creatures, but I did witness the humiliation in the throne room.

"What happened to you after the Crown Princess took you away?"

If I didn't know better, I would say Jeremia sounds jealous. He was with me in Tenacoro when I tried to convince Queen Synadena to aid Soulin's fight against King Keres. He also spent quite some time with Opaline alone while I rested, and when he returned, he was full of energy. Maybe I read the situation wrong. Or perhaps something happened I don't know about.

The thought of someone I know falling for Opaline makes me feel uneasy. She's like a little sister to me.

"She let me use one of their lagoons to heal my wound," I say, keeping it short. "Is there anything else I need to know?"

Jeremia shakes his head. He looks just a breath away from wrapping his arms around me to squeeze me tight to ensure I'm real.

"I need to check on my dad," I say, coming to a halt right before his chambers.

"Do you want me to come with you?"

"No, I'll be fine," I answer, patting his shoulder. "You've done enough."

There's so much more I want to ask him. For example, since when is Remy so defiant? Or what happened to him in Tenacoro? But my father is now my priority, and if Soulin really incarcerated him, I need to find out why.

EIGHTEEN

DEVANA

As the sun casts long shadows on the polished brass and copper walls, a gentle breeze carries the scent of oil and smoke.

I brush my hands over the dirty ground and am surprised when the color matches my skin perfectly. With a few swipes, I cover my face and arms, inspecting myself in the bizarre reflection of the polished metal, my face illuminated by the warm glow of an oil lamp.

Even though I'm a prisoner again, I find solace in the small room the soldiers put me in, surrounded by books and sketches that depict the wonders of the world I yearn to explore. I pick up a leather-bound book and inspect the drawings of a machine so foreign to me. Whoever used this room before must have been an Eternian.

Suddenly, a soft knock resonates through the room, causing my heart to skip a beat. With wide eyes, I carefully set the book aside and approach the door, my hand trembling slightly as I reach for the brass handle.

As the door swings open, a breathtaking sight greets me. Before me stands a figure resplendent in a green beaded gown. Her regal bearing exudes grace and wisdom, and a crown of leaves and roots rests gently on her head.

"Queen Synadena," I say, lowering my head. "I didn't expect to see you here."

What *is* she doing here?

"Good evening, young Devana," the Queen's voice reverberates like the chiming of a grand clock tower as she smiles warmly at me. "May I come in?"

I want to say no and slam the door in her face. Instead, I nod, stepping aside to allow her entry. Once inside, the Queen's eyes sweep across the room, taking in the scattered sketches and books.

"I've been watching you from afar, Devana," the Queen says, her voice tinged with sympathy and urgency. "War is looming on the horizon, and the world outside this palace needs brave souls like you. I come to offer you a chance to return home with me, where your dreams can flourish, and your spirit can soar."

My heart races at Queen Synadena's words, and my mind fills with images of a daring escape and a future beyond the constraints of Crymzon or Eternitie.

I glance back at the sketches, realizing they are glimpses of what Eternitie can do to Monsteress and my father, and take a deep breath. "Your Majesty, I'm honored about your offer. But I yearn to see my father again and explore the wonders beyond all the kingdoms."

Queen Synadena notices my internal struggle and extends a hand. "I know this is no simple decision, my dear," she says, her eyes filled with empathy. "Take your time to consider, but remember, you possess a unique gift. You're not weak or broken. You're one of the strongest Tenacorian I've ever seen."

My heart stumbles over her words. I wasn't enough for my mother, and in all those years, Queen Synadena didn't come looking for me. I always suspected she knew about the aches and pains I went through and didn't see me as worth her time.

But maybe she has been watching from the shadows. Perhaps she has been waiting for this exact moment.

"I can't go with you," I say, grabbing her hand to squeeze it. "I owe it to my father to find him. He needs me."

In return, Queen Synadena squeezes my hand and pulls me in for a hug. I haven't hugged another person in so long. It feels stiff and intrusive, yet warm and comforting.

As I pull back, I study her brown eyes. "How's my mother?"

The Queen releases me and takes a moment to find the right words. "She hasn't been the same since you left."

Now, that can mean so many things. Is she happy or miserable? Does she regret letting me go?

"She's proud of the woman you've become."

Those are not the words I want to hear. I don't doubt that she enjoys seeing her daughter become the warrior she always wanted me to be.

But that's all I am to her—strength.

"When you see her, tell her she can go to hell," I say, squaring my shoulders.

My mother doesn't deserve to call me *hers.* She doesn't deserve to reap what my father sowed.

Queen Synadena smiles at me. "She knows."

And those are the words that mend my broken heart. It feels cruel to hope my mother knows what she has lost. I shouldn't feel this way about the woman who birthed me. But she was an adult when she made the decision, and I was just a child.

For years, I imagined how it would be to stand before her again, to see her again. I imagined how she would wrap her arms around me and sob.

Now, I don't need her affirmation anymore. I don't need her at all. I never have. She's dead to me as I was to her the last twenty-something years.

"You know how to call home," she says, pressing her lips together. "Just because one person turned their back on you doesn't mean the rest did."

I grab my pendant tightly and watch Queen Synadena leave without another word.

NINETEEN

Queen Soulin

As I open the door to escape, I run into Conrad.

"Your Majesty. I'm so incredibly sorry," he says, stumbling a few feet back.

I haven't seen Conrad since the beasts in Khaos' chamber attacked me. He came to my rescue, but I already had everything under control when he arrived.

The smile he gives me adds fuel to the fury blazing inside me. On top of feeling that Khaos is distancing himself from me—mentally, but more importantly, physically—I'm not in the mood to entertain the oldest Crymzonian I can't get rid of.

But I should feel content, maybe even happy. I have an entire army of Fighter Moths at my disposal. Our Connection gives me everything I need to build the army I always wanted.

"My Queen, you have a visitor," he says, breathless.

My eyebrows shoot up. No one visits my kingdom unannounced. If someone wants an audience with me, it's scheduled way in advance and typically not in Crymzon.

"Who is it?"

Conrad leans against the wall to take a few deep breaths. "He says his name is Aemilius."

For fuck's sake.

Aemilius Vosdon, or should I say Cyrus Matrus, the Prince of Eternitie?

What is it with that man that he keeps returning after breaking free? Last time, I lured him back with the girl he was hiding beneath his hut in the Confines. But this time, I have nothing that might interest him.

"What does he want?" I ask, strolling past Conrad, who lets out a whimper before following me.

"He didn't say. He's in the throne room."

I clap my hand against my forehead. "Did you not notice the moths when you let him in?"

Conrad gives me a puzzled look.

I guess I'm about to discover how hostile my new creations can be.

When I push the doors open, I expect Cyrus to be cowering in a corner surrounded by my new Fighter Moths. My annoyance goes to a new high when I see Barin happily jumping around Cyrus and his laughing face. But the moment he sees me, the corners of his mouth drop, and he pushes Barin to the side, who's not getting the message and keeps tackling him.

"Why are you here?" I ask, marching past him to descend the Crymzon Throne.

"No need to get all formal," Cyrus says, pointing at the dais. "I thought we were starting to become friends."

Friends? Really?

"How did your girl enjoy her whipping? Any permanent marks I should know about for next time?"

Cyrus' mouth tightens, and he steps closer, his hands balling into fists. "Funny that you speak of a Starstrandian. That's why I'm here."

That grabs my attention. "I don't have her," I say, inspecting my nails. "If she didn't escape with you, I don't know where she is."

"I'm not talking about her. I'm here for the Lady of Fate."

He could have said any name, but I wasn't prepared for this one. How does he know about her? Besides Queen Caecilia, no one should have that information.

"I don't know what you're talking about."

"I know she's here, and I've come to strike a bargain."

A laugh escapes my throat. "Oh, that's entertaining. And what do you have to offer in return?"

I hold his gaze, studying all his micro-expressions to figure out if he's lying.

Cyrus holds out a hand to scratch Barin's body to stop him from nudging into him. "I have some vital information about my father that concerns you."

Ugh. I should not be entertaining this. I should throw him back into the dungeon and be done with him once and for all. Instead, I step closer. "What information?"

"Do we have a deal? In return for the details, will you let her go?"

Never.

But I nod, grinning on the inside.

"Add Wayne to it," Cyrus says quickly, holding his breath.

"Who?"

"I was told you're still holding the villagers."

"You have to be more specific. My prison is bursting out of its seams with Ordinaries."

The way he's reacting seems off. Why is he only requesting one prisoner and not all? If his information is as vital as he says, why not bargain for his entire village?

"He's a blacksmith. About this tall." He holds his arm about three inches over his head. "Tenacorian."

"Doesn't ring a bell," I answer, scratching my forehead. "But you can check the prison afterward."

And this time, I make sure you will never leave again; I want to add but keep it to myself.

"So, tell me: What is your father up to now?"

Cyrus holds my stare as if he's trying to figure out whether I'm serious. Then he caves. "He's marching against you as we speak."

That's it? That's all he came here for?

"I'm not afraid of Eternitie's puny inventions."

"But you should be."

"Why?"

"Because if my father decided to go to war against you, he must have found a way to kill you. He won't choose a battle he knows he will lose."

"And *how* is he going to do it?"

"I'm not sure. But I know he's dangerous. Trust me."

I chuckle. "Trust you?"

Gosh, can everyone stop using that word?

"I hate you after all you've done. But I fear my father more. If you die, nothing will stand in his way."

I spread my arms. "To do what?"

"I'm not sure."

"What do you want me to do? Open the gate to let him in without fighting back? Fleeing Crymzon so he can't *hurt* me? His toys are nothing compared to my magic."

"You're insufferable," Cyrus says, clearing his throat. "Just listen to me for once, from a concerned royal to another. My father will attack, and even though I don't know what he has up his sleeve, it will be destructive. You're underestimating him."

Another laugh ripples through me. "And you underestimate my power. Nothing will stand in my way with the Heiligbaum intact and my Soulmate Connection."

Still, deep down, an unknown feeling of unease grips me. What if he's right?

Cyrus' face turns with disgust. "I made good on my part of the deal. Now, I need you to release the prisoners."

Our eyes meet, and I can see in his face that he knows. I won't give in easily. "Until I know King Citeus is coming, I won't release anyone."

Cyrus contemplates for a good minute before he nods his head. "I'm not going back into that dark room," he says, pointing to the ceiling. "At least let me check on my friends in the prison while we wait, and the second my father's army is visible on the horizon, promise me you let us go."

He knows I won't, yet he holds out his hand to shake it.

"Why should I believe you *again*?" I ask, looking at his palm.

"I only lied before because otherwise I would be a dead man. You left me no choice but to make you believe I know where to find a Painite."

It hasn't slipped my mind that he betrayed me. But he also saved me. He could have left me in Terminus to die at the hands of the Undead when I depleted all my magic.

Slowly, I reach out to grab his hand and squeeze it. "If this is a trick, I will know where to find you," I say, and Cyrus' scream rips through the air.

He pulls his hand away and stares at the fleshy mark on the back of his hand—a red crescent moon.

"Think of it as a leash. If you step too far outside the wall, I will know."

"Is that really necessary?" Cyrus yelps, rubbing his hand.

"You have a track record of fleeing my kingdom," I snarl back, turning to inspect my moths.

Without even knowing, I created my new fighters just in time. If King Citeus is as close as Cyrus says, I must break them in now.

TWENTY

Khaos

The same silence as when I entered the gate greets me when I walk through the courtyard into the streets of Crymzon. By now, the moon is casting its silvery glow upon the houses.

As I approach my childhood red sandstone house in the middle of the kingdom, memories flood my mind, blending the past with the present. The house stands sturdy, bearing the marks of time, its walls weathered but resilient, just like me. With each step, my heart grows heavier.

Pushing open the creaking stone door, I enter the dark foyer. Dust particles dance in the rays of moonlight that filter through the worn-out silk curtains, casting a cold glow on the worn wooden floors covered with a threadbare rug that my mother wove long ago.

The familiar scent of polished furniture and aged books envelops me, triggering vivid memories. The faded wallpaper showcases remnants of a mural I painted as a child; my imagination encapsulated in vibrant strokes of color.

My eyes trace the family portrait on the wall. The stone image captures a time of innocence and joy before my life took an unexpected turn.

A young boy with bright eyes and a mischievous grin stands beside his parents. His father, a figure of strength and wisdom, holds him firmly, while his mother's warm smile radiates love and comfort.

My gaze shifts to the worn-out armchair in the room's corner. It was my father's favorite spot, where he would sit, pipe in hand, telling tales of ancient gods and far-off lands. Those stories fueled my dreams when I was young and ignited a desire to serve my kingdom.

As I traverse the house's corridors, I venture into the kitchen. My mother's worn apron still hangs on a hook, and the scent of her cooking lingers in the air, transporting me back to when he would sneak samples of her delectable treats. The aroma of freshly baked bread and simmering soup fills the air, conjuring memories of family meals shared around the worn wooden table. Laughter and animated conversations echo through the room, mingling with the clinking of cutlery.

Ascending the staircase, I reach the bedrooms, each holding a different story. My mother's room, with its frilly curtains and delicate dried flowers, reminds me of her infectious laughter and the way she used to braid wildflowers into her hair.

Moving down the corridor, I find myself standing in my bedroom. Once adorned with maps and drawings, the walls now seem bare, stripped of their youthful vibrancy. My eyes fall upon a tattered book on the shelf—a reminder of countless nights spent exploring distant kingdoms between its pages. It was within these walls that my dreams took flight.

As I continue my search, I enter my father's study. The shelves are lined with books on Escela's history and Gods—my father's prized possessions. Running my fingers along the spines, I deeply long for the wisdom and guidance my father gave me.

He knows way more about Escela than anyone. After leaving Soulin's services, he ventured outside the Crymzon Wall to find a cure for my mother's sickness. He turned every stone to find a way to heal her.

Finally, I reach the attic, a treasure trove of forgotten relics. Among the trunks and forgotten belongings, I stumble upon a weathered soldier's uniform. It's a suit I built to present to Soulin when I was just a boy, pledging my life to hers at such a young age. Seeing it brings forth a mix of pride and sorrow, realizing that my feelings for Soulin go way beyond the Soulmate Connection.

A gust of wind blows through the open window, causing the curtains to dance gracefully. My eyes fall on my reflection in the dusty mirror, and I see a tired, scared face staring back at me. The SinClaret family has transformed me from a carefree stable boy into a hardened soldier. But at this moment, surrounded by the remnants of my past, I yearn for the simplicity and warmth of my childhood.

With a heavy sigh, I close my eyes, allowing the memories to wash over me once more. The echoes of laughter and the scent of home mingle with reality—my father is not here, so I need to speak to Soulin.

As I turn to leave, I call out once to make sure I'm not wrong. Silence greets me again, and I leave my home without looking back.

The closer I get to the palace, the more I can feel the Connection to Soulin getting stronger. It's like an internal compass leading me through the entrance hall to the throne room. I don't knock and just lift my hand; the doors jump open without touching them.

Amid a few dozen horse-sized moths stands Soulin with her back to me, her red hair falling down her curves. Slowly, she spins around to face me, and I'm just a foot away from her when our eyes meet.

"Where is he?" I ask, calmer than I feel.

"He just left," she answers, looking past me at the doors.

My eyebrows draw together. "My father?"

If my father had been in the entrance hall, I would have seen him. I didn't notice anyone else besides servants and a handful of soldiers.

"Oh," Soulin says, turning back to the moth she was attending to before I arrived. "He should be at home like—"

"He's not," I cut in, grabbing her arm to whirl her back around. "The entire kingdom is a fucking ghost town."

Her eyes darken when she faces me. "Maybe he went for a stroll."

"Stop bullshitting me, Soulin. Where is he?"

My blood boils the longer I look at her. She presses her lips together and closes the distance between us. "I've never seen this side of you," she says, caressing my chest.

A wave of arousal pushes back the anger surging through my veins—but it's not mine.

Through our Connection, I can feel Soulin's desire for me. It rushes through me in waves.

This is wrong. So wrong.

"This is not the time for your twisted games," I growl, pushing her away from me.

"Then stop fighting me," she whispers, forcing goosebumps over my skin.

How can she do this to me? Why now?

A couple of hours ago, I tried to be romantic and show her what it's like to be desired. But right now, all I want is an answer.

"Where are all the Crymzonians?" I ask, widening my scope.

It's not just my father who's missing. While I expect empty streets during the day, the kingdom should now bustle with people.

"He's fine," she says, coming closer again. "I would never hurt him."

"That means nothing anymore. I need to see him."

Her hand touches my cock, which is already hard. She presses against me, her fingers gliding over the fabric, and I can feel my dick twitching under her touch.

Her need for me almost drowns me. She might not be saying it, but I can feel the heat radiating from her and the tug inside my heart.

With every stroke, my anger ebbs away.

"Stop it," I say, pulling back, but she holds on to the seam of my pants to hold me in place. "Not now. This is not the way."

I'm not fast enough to stop her from using her magic to unbuckle my pants and slip it over my ass to my ankles.

One moment I'm looking at her, and the next, I can feel her fingernails bite into my cheek while her other hand closes around my cock. Her nails cut into my skin as I try to move away, and just when I'm about to use my magic to force her to release me, I feel her tongue licking over the tip of my cock.

My pleasure mixes with the one she forces down our Connection, and every thought I had moments before evaporates.

This is madness. I can't do this...I need to...

A moan escapes my throat, urging her to take my entire length into her mouth. The wicked pleasure running through my body as Soulin sucks on my cock makes me shudder. I watch as my erection slides in and out of her, leaving her saliva all over my length.

I moan in disbelief as she takes me in again, her eyes looking up.

There she is—my Queen—kneeling before me to suck every ounce of lust for her out of me.

Soulin's grip tightens around my cock to continue what her mouth isn't doing, and my lips part with my ragged breaths as she licks over my length before sucking me back in.

I pick up the pace, thrusting deeper into her mouth. Into her throat. I don't stop when silent tears slide down from the corners of her eyes.

She wants this. She started it.

But it's not enough. I need more.

I dig my hands into her hair and rock against her mouth, and my body shudders.

"I'm so close," I moan, almost slamming into her. "I need to be inside you."

Ignoring my wish to let me take her, she rocks faster, and I feel the warmth spreading through my lower belly.

"No," I whisper as I cum inside her mouth, and my eyes widen when I see her swallow my pleasure.

"Now we're even," she says, wiping away the tears from her cheeks.

TWENTY-ONE

Devana

I feel sick to my stomach when I wake up. I'm unsure if it's the greasy food bothering my stomach, my condition, or the knowledge that it's finally time to march against Monsteress.

Somehow, I'm still torn between what to do when I face the Queen. Even though my entire life I've been training to aim for the Crymzon Queen's head, I can't stop thinking about what my father said: *we need to help her.*

Maybe I don't have to decide, and those monsters in the room with her took care of my problem after I ran. Maybe we get there, and Soulin is already dead. The odds weren't in her favor when I saw her.

I'm so close to the palace's garden that it only takes the guards assigned to me a few minutes to get there. As I'm led into the brass garden, I can't stop myself from grinning.

Personally, I wouldn't call it a garden. This place, where fantastical contraptions and eccentric designs thrive, shimmering under the golden rays of the rising sun, has no real flowers. Its pathways are lined with gears, clockwork flowers, and steam-powered fountains that spray mist into the air. The air is filled with a soft hissing sound and the unmistakable scent of oil, blending with the earthy fragrance of dirt patches beneath my feet.

The garden looks like an organized junkyard, and I halt when a resounding echo of synchronized footsteps reaches my ears. Curiosity mingles with excitement as I follow the source of the sound. Suddenly, I'm led into a clearing, and my eyes widen at the sight that greets me.

Before me stands an army of metallic soldiers, their appearances reminiscent of Eternitie's signature metal fused with weaponry. Each soldier wears intricate brass armor adorned with elaborate engravings and gears, their helmets equipped with goggles that reflect the fiery determination in their eyes. A soft glow emanates from the mechanisms embedded within their exoskeletons, emphasizing the depth of their craftsmanship.

I laugh.

"What's so funny?" the guard beside me asks, his eyes directed at the hundreds of soldiers.

"You guys will never make it to Crymzon," I say, shaking my head. "Your armor must weigh hundreds of pounds. If you don't die of exhaustion, the sun will melt you inside those metal cans alive."

The guards look at me and then at their comrades. It takes them a moment to realize what I mean.

Eternitie might be colder because of its higher altitude and being in the middle of Escela, but it's hot and miserable where we're going. There is no way more than half of those soldiers will make it.

These soldiers, numbering in the hundreds, maybe thousands, stand in perfect formation, their polished boots clanging against the brass-covered ground. As if moved by an invisible force, they part, creating a path leading to the front line where I stand. My attention turns to a man, and a peaceful silence falls over the ranks as they do the same.

A resounding horn blares, signaling the King's approach. Stepping out of the formation, the King emerges, his presence commanding and regal. He wears an intricately designed coat decorated with gears, chains, and steam-powered insignias. His crown is a masterpiece, a fusion of brass and clockwork that symbolizes his dominion.

A gust of wind sweeps through the garden, carrying with it the whispers of the frozen army until King Citeus stops right before me.

"Have you gotten all the rest you need?" he asks, studying the armor they handed me this morning. It has to be the prototype of the uniforms enclosing me. Luckily, mine is made of mostly fabric and leather with the least amount of metal.

"Yes," I lie, trying to control the trembling of my muscles.

"She says we will never make it to Crymzon," the soldier behind me cuts in, and my stomach bottoms.

"Is that so?" King Citeus asks, looking over his shoulder to study his troops. "How come?"

My eyes throw daggers at the man behind me. "The soldiers' armor might be protective enough to shield them from magic, but the weight and material will slow them down in the desert."

King Citeus takes me in for a heartbeat, from toe to head, and the soldiers who stand behind me. His piercing eyes, framed by goggles, glimmer. "You think the armor needs to be redesigned?"

I'm not sure what forces him to listen to me. It could be my heritage as a Tenacorian or because I had just fled Crymzon myself. Whatever it is, something makes him consider my statement.

"The armor they gave me would do just fine. It won't be as protective as those," I point at the men facing me, "but it also won't kill me trying to get to my destination."

King Citeus' eyes narrow. He spins around and walks through the first row of soldiers, inspecting them from front and back.

"Take the first layer off," he yells, and the line before me moves within seconds.

The noise of metal falling to the ground is deafening, but I keep my head high as I watch the soldiers peel out of the metal exterior.

I stand there for a few minutes, waiting for King Citeus to return to me to tell me I'm wrong. Instead, he strolls through the formation, one row at a time, until the tumult subsides.

With a flourish of his hand, the King silences the last murmurs that fill the courtyard. The soldiers snap to attention, their eyes fixed on their ruler on the opposite side of the formation. The King's voice, strong and resolute, echoes through the courtyard. "Soldiers of Eternitie!" he begins, his voice reverberating with a mix of authority and passion. "Today, we embark on a journey through the unforgiving desert to face the Tyrant Queen and liberate our kingdom from her clutches!"

A surge of anticipation ripples through the ranks as the soldiers exchange glances.

"Our new inventions, born from the brilliance of our engineers and craft workers, will be the key to victory!" the King continues, raising his arms dramatically. "With their revolutionary contraptions, the Queen's magic will pale in comparison! Our mechanical wonders will level the playing field and tip the scales in our favor!"

Behind the King, an array of moving, steam-powered machinery, towering war machines, and gleaming steamships stand proudly, ready to be unleashed upon Crymzon.

I marvel at their mighty engines' unusual designs, gears whirring, and steam venting. But with every passing second, my heart sinks. There's no telling what his creations are capable of. At least, I can't. But seeing the excitement wash over the rows gives me a clue about how destructive they are.

As he speaks, the King's voice swells with conviction, igniting a hunger within his army. "Through the scorching desert, we will march as one! We shall overcome every obstacle in our path and prove that the power of innovation triumphs over sorcery!"

A thunderous cheer erupts from the soldiers, their voices echoing through the courtyard, merging with the clanging of gears and the hiss of steam. The ground beneath me trembles as they march to embark on bringing war to Escela.

King Citeus raises his fist, a symbol of unity and defiance. "The Blood Queen shall rue the day she dared to challenge the indomitable spirit of Eternitie!"

My muscles shake uncontrollably as I try to keep my nerves under control. I shouldn't have come here. This was a mistake.

The soldier behind me presses his elbow into my back, and I stumble forward, following the army.

If Queen Synadena and Queen Caecilia don't hold to their words of rescuing my father and friends, those machines won't stop from taking everything down in their path. When I came to ask for help, I didn't mean to start a war against an entire kingdom.

Tailing Eternitie's army, I try to find a way to stop this madness. I thought Monsteress was our enemy all this time, but the King's hunger to destroy her is even more terrifying.

I need to do something.

TWENTY-TWO

KHAOS

Panting, my senses slowly return to me. This wasn't supposed to be the way we connected again. On top of that, it was totally out of line. I should be searching for my father and not succumb to my irrational needs.

"We have to stop doing this," I say, pulling my pants up to tighten it.

"Doing what?"

"You know exactly what I mean. We can't just throw ourselves at each other every time to avoid a confrontation."

"I avoid nothing."

"Then tell me: what happened to the kingdom?" I can't take this damn silence anymore. She has to break down this barrier between us at some point. "This isn't going to work," I say, straightening my pants while she stares at me. "I'm done."

Feelings overwhelm me—mine and hers—but I keep my head high, ignoring them. I feel dumb for wanting to return to Crymzon. Somehow, I thought I could coax some parts of the old Soulin out of her. Just a fraction would be a big step in the right direction. It's one thing to have a traumatic past and be a hellcat for a certain amount of time to deal with it. But Soulin has no reason to be this ferocious *all the damn time.*

This isn't a trauma response anymore; it's her way of living, and I won't support it any longer. If she doesn't see it as a problem, I can't help her.

"Where are you going?"

"Why do you care?" I snap back, marching out of the throne room.

As I round the corner to ascend the steps to my room, a man follows me, his footsteps heavy but slow. I speed up, and to my surprise, so does he.

"What do you want?" I growl, spinning around, and my irritation subsides when I face him.

"Khaos Zedohr?" the old man asks, a broad smile plastered on his face. "I'm friends with your father."

His hair is white as sea foam, his skin wrinkled and weathered, but his eyes are sharp.

"I didn't mean to spy on your conversation, but I heard you're searching for him. Have you looked inside the prison yet?"

My heart skips a beat. Why would my father be in prison? And who is this man?

"I'm Conrad, King Obsidian's former trustee," he says as if he just read my mind. "Again, I'm very sorry about sticking my nose into your business."

"You're mistaken. I won't find my father there. He has done nothing wrong."

"The prison might not be what you think it is," he says, his eyes gleaming with mischief.

"What's that supposed to mean?" I ask, but the doors to the throne room swing open again. I can't be here when Soulin gets out. If I lay eyes on her, I might cave again, and whatever my Connection desires is far from what my head wants.

"Tell him I said *hi*," Conrad adds before he takes a few steps down to walk back to where I came from.

What a meddlesome old man. I notice something I haven't before when he slips out of my view. Conrad wore armor just like every other soldier in Crymzon. How come I've never seen him before?

Shaking my head, I change my destination and head to the secret passage from the palace to the outside of the Crymzon Wall. His idea of where I can find my father might be far-fetched, but it's my only lead. I need to check it.

I wearily approach the entrance to the prison. As I reach the narrow bridge leading from the Crymzon Wall to the prison's imposing gate, I feel a knot tighten in my stomach.

The bridge, constructed from weathered red sandstone, stretches endlessly across a chasm of uncertainty. Its narrow width allows only one person to pass at a time, demanding balance and focus. My legs shake with each step in the stale midnight air as I venture forth, one foot at a time.

The red sandstone beneath my boots radiates heat, intensifying the sweltering environment. The air is heavy as if carrying the weight of countless stories of despair and anguish brushing over me from the prison. Beads of sweat trickled down my forehead, the moisture constantly reminding me of the oppressive conditions I was about to witness.

As I make my way across the bridge into the doors, held open by the guards, my gaze wanders towards the rows of cells lining the perimeter. Eyes filled with sorrow, anger, and desperation follow my every move. The prisoners, clad in tattered clothing, press against the iron bars, their faces etched with the marks of a life behind bars. Some whisper words of hope, while others wear expressions of resignation.

Each step I take deepens my understanding of the suffering within these walls. The bridge, in all its narrowness, seems to symbolize the division between freedom and captivity, a threshold that separates me from the world I once knew.

With a heavy heart, I press forward, counting the cells as I pass them, spiraling down the corridor to reach the bottom of the prison.

He has to be here somewhere.

But I haven't come across a single Crymzonian so far. All the cells are filled with prisoners of other kingdoms. Yet, my mouth dries every time I look at an older man.

Holding my head high, I push forward, and when I reach the bottom of the building, my muscles relax, but my fury returns.

He's not here.

The last cells are empty, and this part of the prison is unguarded, so I lean against the wall before breathing in deeply with no one seeing me.

In and out. That's what I promised myself. I would go in and leave as fast as I could.

If my father is not here, where is he?

I'm about to push myself off the wall and storm back to Soulin when I notice the crackling sparks beneath my hand.

A tingling sensation catches my attention as I press my palms against the rough surface harder. I furrow my brow, perplexed by the sudden surge of magic emanating from my hands. The faint sparks flicker beneath my touch, dancing like tiny stars against my skin.

My heart skips a beat as a realization dawns upon me.

My magic isn't causing this.

Could it be some long-dormant magic awakening, or is it a spell intricately woven into the very fabric of the prison walls? Determined to uncover the truth, I withdraw my hands and examine them intently. The sparks persist, growing brighter and more vibrant with each stroke of my fingers.

Curiosity mingles with caution as I tentatively place my palms against the wall once more, eyes fixated on the dancing sparks. The energy surges within me, an undeniable connection springing to life.

This might not be my doing, but the power is close to mine, which means...this is Soulin's.

In a moment of clarity, I grasp the essence of the spell, its purpose, and its hidden design. Focusing on my will, I channel my magic, allowing it to merge and unravel. The air crackles with energy as I push against it.

A hidden mechanism whirs to life, and the solid prison wall yields to my command. A concealed door materializes before me, its outline shimmering with the faint glow of enchantment.

With a deep breath, I step into the newfound passage, descending into the depths below.

The temperature immediately drops, and the air becomes less pressing and hot. As I venture further into the underground labyrinth, my eyes widen. A vast cave stretches before me, illuminated by the soft glow of innumerable small fires. Laughter and mumbling fill my ears, resonating with a joyous symphony. There, amidst the flickering light, I behold the faces of my people—my fellow citizens of Crymzon—forgotten souls whom Soulin has unjustly imprisoned.

When I step forward, the light of my magic mingles with the fires, creating a vibrant aura that illuminates the cavern. Tears well in my eyes as I absorb the beauty of this hidden place.

What is this?

Carefully, I adjust my position, not knowing if someone has seen me enter.

How did I not know about this place? I've watched the prison being built and extended over the last decade and never considered visiting it because most prisoners are here because of me.

"Khaos!" a small voice yells as something wraps around my legs.

My first instinct is to pull away and grab for my sword, but when I look down, sparkling blue eyes stare up at me, and I realize it's my neighbor's youngest daughter. Without thinking, I grab her under her arms and hoist her into mine. She throws her short limbs around my neck and giggles into my shoulder as I spin her around like I always do when I see her.

Her laugh is enough to heal every broken part inside me. Her carefree giggles remind me of how beautiful the world can be when unaware of its dangers.

As my head spins from turning so fast around my axis, I slowly come to a halt and let her down gently. Usually, I would let her stumble away while following her to catch her fall. This time, I hold on to her little fingers as if my life depended on it.

If I let go, she might vanish. I can't risk that.

"Khaos?" another voice asks, and it almost breaks my willpower to hold on to Vinera.

"Myra?" I call back, searching the cave for her long silver hair and green dress.

I must be dreaming. She can't be here. I spoke to her just minutes before she left Crymzon for good.

When I scan the faces looking in my direction, some familiar, some not, I see her. She marches in my direction, her arms wide outstretched, and I guide Vinera in her direction. When I'm sure Vinera won't crash to the ground, I release her just in time to close my arms around Myra.

"You're hurting me," she giggles, wiggling in my embrace.

"I'm sorry. I'm still trying to get my powers under control," I answer, out of breath.

"I'm so relieved you're well. I was worried about you," she says, holding me away from her to take me in. "You look so...well."

"Then I look better than I feel," I answer, smirking. "How are you here? Why—"

"When you told me to leave, I went to grab as many Crymzonians as I could and brought them to the only place I know is safe."

I look at the cave again, noticing all the tunnels leading away from the central void, like a spiderweb.

"You created this?" I ask, taking in all the people surrounding us.

"No," she says, her brows almost touching each other. "Soulin did. You didn't know?"

"There's so much she keeps from me," I whisper, trying to understand what's happening. "Does she know you're hiding here?"

"I'm sure she does. I mean, that's why she built this cave."

I shake my head over and over again. Nothing makes sense anymore.

"I can't believe she didn't tell you."

"I can."

"Soulin has been planning this kingdom beneath the prison since the first speculations of King Keres' arrival. Her mission was to build a safe place for her entire kingdom to shield them in times of war."

"What are you talking about?"

"The prison is her greatest scheme. From the outside, it looks like it wasn't even worth being located in the kingdom. But if Soulin dies, everything *inside* the Crymzon Wall will be sucked into an abyss. Did you ever wonder why the prison bridge is so narrow?" She doesn't give me any time to think about it. "It's not to make it impossible to leave or storm. If the Wall collapses, taking the bridge with it, it would cause the least amount of damage to the prison. And with the prison being located outside the kingdom, it will stand even after Crymzon falls. Plus, it's the only building in Crymzon that attackers won't pay attention to. It's the perfect cover-up."

I can't believe I've been so blind. Through the years, I ignored her obsession with the creation of the prison. It was easier to ignore it than to think about all the suffering and death the building would bring to Crymzon.

I was wrong.

"Everything is a lie," I mumble, thinking about all the older adults and children she ordered to be sent to work in the prison who never returned. My mind wanders to all the angry soldiers, thinking their family members are rotting inside cells above me.

None of it is true...and I believed it.

"Why would she—"

"Take the blame for all of it? Play the cruel ruler so everyone hates her?"

"Yes, it makes no sense. None of this is needed if Soulin hadn't provoked the Gods with her ways of running Crymzon."

"I don't think it would have made a difference. Otyx would probably have targeted Crymzon anyway because of our magic. We're the strongest kingdom in Escela. He doesn't play by the rules of the other Gods, which makes him as unpredictable as Soulin."

My head spins. I've been searching for Soulin's innocence for so long that I feel overwhelmed to find it. Everything Myra says sounds plausible, yet it sounds too good to be true. It's the best news I've heard in almost fifteen years, but somehow, it feels like a betrayal.

What if all of this is just a coincidence, and it looks like she plotted it? What—

Stop thinking like that, Khaos. I'm on her side. I should be relieved.

"Why didn't you tell me earlier?" I ask, scanning my surroundings again. "Knowing about this place would have spared me so much heartache."

Sadness clouds Myra's eyes, and it's hard to hold her gaze. "I thought you knew. You both were so close. I thought she trusted you."

"I knew she had her secrets, but I didn't know how deep they run," I answer, grabbing my sword. "Have you seen my father?"

Myra smiles. "I can bring you to him."

I shake my head. "Thank you, but there's something I need to do. Please tell him I will find him when I'm ready."

Myra nods. There's nothing she can say or do to stop me from seeking Soulin. I've been following her mindlessly since I saw her for the first time. But now, I need her to come clean, trust me, and let me share the responsibility of leading a kingdom, or I will turn my back on her like she's done to me so many times.

I might be drunk in love and marked by a Soulmate Connection, but I'm still sane enough to understand that if our relationship is built on mistrust and lies. It will disintegrate eventually. I might as well get it over with before I get too attached—if that is still possible.

TWENTY-THREE

CYRUS

Nervously, I look over my shoulder to see if someone is following me. Somehow, I can't imagine Monsteress allowing me to roam through her palace and kingdom without monitoring me. After all, I spent quite some time being her prisoner.

Either she lost interest in me because she didn't need me anymore to lure my father out of Eternitie, or because she got bored with me. Whatever the reason is, I'm totally fine with it.

Wayne. I need to find Wayne. If I see him, I will find the other villagers, and somehow, I will free them before my father arrives. Devana would never leave without him. Wayne must be still here if she stood up against King Citeus alone.

What started as a stroll through the Crymzon Palace turns into a trot. I need to search as much ground as I can before Eternitie arrives.

Nervously, I rub the red crescent moon on the back of my hand before pulling my shirt sleeve over it. Great. I really needed another thing to worry about. While I might be able to cover the mark from curious eyes, how am I supposed to leave Crymzon now?

Guards and servants look at me in surprise as I rip open doors and slam them shut as I make my way through the palace. My heart pumps faster when I see the door that used to hold me prisoner. I don't want to open it, but I have to.

My mouth goes dry when I find it empty.

Thank Odione that Monsteress hasn't been able to replace me with another poor soul.

The closer I come to finding out that she's holding none of the other villagers in her palace, the more my anxiety grows. It might not have been ideal to be held in a windowless room, but it seems like a luxury when I think about the dungeon and prison.

"What are you doing here?" a guard yells at me when I slam another door shut.

Somehow, I thought I would be stopped sooner. What's more suspicious than a stranger storming past guards and servants?

"I'm looking for a friend," I say, trotting to the next door.

"You won't find your friend here," he says, grabbing for his sword.

I hold my hands up and look at him. "I'm not here to cause any trouble. I'm unarmed."

He studies me for a moment and then relaxes. "Are you Queen Soulin's pet?"

Ugh. Really?

"I used to be her prisoner, yes. But now she's granting me to search her kingdom in return for wrongly incarcerating me."

Silence forms between us.

"If I were you, I would search the prison," he says, looking over his shoulder to see if someone is watching us.

I cock my head. "Are you helping me?"

"I'm just saying, if you are looking for your fellow Ordinaries, they are all held in the prison," he whispers before walking off.

He either is trying to lead me in the wrong direction, or he's giving me a clue. It's foolish to believe that a Crymzonian is helping me. But what if he's right?

I'm unsure if I should follow his hint or continue searching the palace until I run out of options. Looking after him, I decide to believe him. The way he checked if someone overheard his words didn't seem like a deception.

And with that, I follow the map of the Crymzon Palace I've built inside my head to find my way out.

TWENTY-FOUR

Queen Soulin

Outside, the setting sun paints the sky in hues of crimson and gold, mirroring the bloodshed Cyrus tried to warn me about.

I've been patient, waiting for any signs of battle. Any changes in the air. The sounds of Eternitie drawing closer to Crymzon. But so far, he's just delivered another lie.

While waiting, I send my Connection out to feel how Khaos is doing. I shouldn't be doing this. I should let him go. He has every right to hate me. By now, he must have discovered that his father isn't being held in my prison—at least not the part he can reach.

It crossed my mind to tell him where he and the rest of the Crymzonians are, but what's the point? We're not in the years of Obsidian anymore. Someone tried to assassinate me before I could even reach the Crymzon Throne. Escela isn't the same place it used to be when I was a careless young Princess.

Playing the role everyone expected of me after they heard about my outburst in the throne room was the easiest way to rule a kingdom alone. No one questioned my abilities, willpower, or authority as a thirteen-year-old child as their Queen.

If I die, I'm the only one knowing that everything I've done after my accidental magical super surge was rightful—well, besides the Lady of Fate. But I couldn't risk her telling my secrets to Queen Caecilia. Holding her in the windowless cell is the most cruel thing I've ever done.

Back then, it was the only solution I could think of to keep her hidden. What if the stars can see her and whisper her location to her ruler? What if the clouds serve as extended eyes, searching every part of my palace for her?

Ok, I must admit, I hate her. She could have helped me figure out what my fate meant when she showed it to me as a child. All of this wouldn't have happened if she had taken the time to make me understand.

Besides her, I've been somewhat good.

I built the cave and tunnels beneath the prison, hoping never to use them. Once I'm done with Keres and Otyx—and apparently King Citeus—I have to release my citizens eventually, which means everyone will know what I've done.

Maybe it's for the better. Or perhaps I can erase their memories and replace them with other images to keep my reign going.

No matter what happens, I need to get Otyx off my back. He's the one who started all of this. If he hadn't created Keres just to fuck with our world, I would have never chosen the role of Monsteress.

He forced me into sending my soldiers to the Confines to rescue as many Ordinaries as possible before he killed them and turned them into his undead henchmen. Otyx forced me to fill my prison with people who want me dead because they think I'm raiding their villages out of sport.

Is the prison the ideal solution to keep the villagers alive?

No, certainly not.

But it keeps them far enough away from me so I don't have to worry about another attack, and if Crymzon falls, the prison will stay intact.

I keep trying to sense Khaos through our Connection. The last time I felt him, he was livid, distancing himself from me. The knowledge of causing him so much pain is almost unbearable, but I need him to believe it. If he knows how pathetic I really am, I will give him the upper hand, and I can't jeopardize the plan I've been devising for over a decade.

Besides the gods, Khaos is the closest threat to my being. Not only does his magic almost match mine, but he's the reason that kept me going all these years. Even when I used my magic to block out all my emotions to be the person Crymzon needed me to be, he was my soft spot.

But no one knows about that. Not only would it put him in great danger inside the Crymzon Wall, but it would also put a giant target on his back for everyone beyond the desert. If something happens to him, nothing will stand in my way to become the person everyone thinks I am.

Through our Connection, I can't feel a thing. It's like the earth swallowed him, shielding him from me. What is he doing?

When I recheck the desert through my open windows, I notice a faint line on the horizon. It's so tiny that I need to squint my eyes.

"The bastard didn't lie," I whisper, watching the line thicken.

The sound of flapping wings makes me break eye contact, and I step back to let Adira fly through my window into my room. She vibrates her wings, nudging her head into me over and over again.

"Calm down," I whisper, touching her body to use my magic. Immediately, her wings relax, and I force more of my power into her to retrieve the images in Adria's mind. The elevated view from the sky shows me that Eternitie is indeed invading my desert. I stop counting the rows of soldiers when my eyes fall on the weird moving contraptions between the marching soldiers.

They look like metal rectangles from above. Some are small, with a metal tube attached to the front, while others are tall, almost resembling driving ladders.

A chuckle escapes my throat, and I release Adira, whose round black eyes stare at me.

I'm not the only one preparing for the worst-case scenarios. While I was trying to put a God back into his place, Eternitie's ruler has been weaponizing himself to strike me.

If he would put as much effort into fighting alongside me, Otyx would be a thing of the past.

The sound of clinking boots rushing down my corridor and a bell chiming outside, shaking the entire kingdom, are just what I have been waiting for. I'm not the only one who noticed the invasion; now, it's time to go to war.

I look into the darkened corner of my room. Glowing eyes meet my gaze, and I release the darkness holding on to the creatures meant to harm me.

"It's time to meet your captors," I say, stepping closer to the monstrous yet beautiful creatures stalking in my direction.

TWENTY-FIVE

Devana

I can't believe my eyes. Through the open Crymzon gates steps Monsteress, a burgundy dress flowing around her.

There's no way she could have gotten out of that room alive. I saw the creatures emerging from thin air. One of them buried its talons into her chest like a knife slicing paper.

But she's alive. Somehow.

When I look behind her, I choke on my spit. My eyes fall on the same vine-covered feline creature with red eyes that I saw inside the palace. Besides, it marches a beast. I'm not sure what it's supposed to be. It towers over Monsteress and resembles a giant bird-like figure with black feathers and scales. The massive wings are untucked, spanning at least eight feet, maybe more. But the woman walking right beside Monsteress brings my heart almost to a stop.

How did the Crymzon Queen get Sylvora to join her ranks? The silver-skinned woman with blue silver hair and two horns protruding behind her ears is one of the deadliest creatures known in Escela. Every word that comes out of her mouth is the sweetest lie you will ever hear and is as fatal as venom. Her whisper can make even the sanest person commit the most violent crimes.

It took me a few deep breaths to bring my heart rate back to normal, and in that time, King Citeus brought his army to a standstill. Monsteress keeps marching our way, her steps graceful yet dominant. Dismounting his horse, King Citeus closes in on her over the outstretched desert to meet the Crymzon Queen halfway.

Shit. This can't be happening. I need to stop this war before it begins.

I stumble forward, my legs faltering every other step. I curse. It's the worst time for my muscles to protest. With clenched teeth, I press forward, watching them exchange words.

So far, everything seems fine. Maybe the ruler can agree, and my panic is uncalled for.

But whom am I kidding? I'm talking about Monsteress.

I scan the open stretch of desert as I seek a path through the soldiers' formation, standing as an impenetrable wall between me and the two rulers at a distance. With every step, my fatigue worsens as my body trembles from the weight of my condition.

Quickly, I push forward, my breath growing shallow and rapid. Beads of sweat form on my brow, mingling with the dirt and grime that covers my face. I pay it no mind. How can I knowing what's about to unfold?

My legs feel heavy as if dragging through quicksand, and my vision blurs occasionally. The sheer exhaustion from the march threatens to overwhelm me, but my resolve burns bright, igniting a flicker of strength that pushes me onward.

My father is in that damn palace. If King Citeus attacks before the other kingdoms get here, his chance of survival is slim.

My goal remains fixed in my mind's eye: to reach the two titans engaged in conversation, their decisions holding the power to stop the destructive tide of war. With every stride, I draw closer to my destination, my body fueled by a conviction surpassing my physical state's limitations.

As I near the two rulers, my voice rises above the howling wind. "Please, stop this madness!" My plea echoes through the air, and King Citeus turns around, interrupting their conversation for a brief moment.

My trembling hand stretches out, extended in a gesture of desperate hope. I've come so far, overcome so much, to bridge the chasm between the two leaders and halt the ravages of war. It's going to be enough. It has to.

In that charged moment, my surroundings fall silent. The fate of countless lives hinges on the response of Queen Soulin and King Citeus.

Breathless and trembling, I raise my voice again. My words carry the weight of my struggle and the collective hope of those affected by the impending conflict. "I'm begging you. Don't start a war."

Monsteress' eyes wander over me before she dismisses my plea. She turns her head back to the King, and I watch his hand signaling a command to his army at the exact moment. Before I can decipher what it means, I hear an ear-ripping sound, followed by glowing rocks shooting down from the sky at us. I cover my head but keep my eyes on them.

Monsteress stretches out her hands and creates a barrier between her and the falling gems, but they effortlessly slice through her magic. I see the terror in her eyes as one of the glowing pieces shoots through it and hits her shoulder. Immediately, the surrounding barrier dissolves, and she hunches forward, holding her shoulder while more of the unknown substance rains down on her, embedding itself into her body.

I scream as a sharp throbbing erupts in my shoulder blade. No, it's not just there. I can also feel it in other body parts. My knees cave under the pain, and I tap my shoulder with my hands to find the cause of my discomfort.

Whatever struck me, I need to remove it. Now!

My fingers search for the entrance wound, and when I don't find one, I look up at Monsteress kneeling on the ground before King Citeus, holding the same spot on her body as I do.

Tears stream down my face, and I wipe them away to clear my vision.

Another glowing rock piece hits her neck, and I don't have to imagine how much pain she must feel because I feel it, too—I feel her pain rippling through me like the fragment hit my own body. I grab my neck and scream in agony.

What the fuck is happening?

TWENTY-SIX

Queen Soulin

One second, I'm asking King Citeus to aid my cause to bring down Otyx, and in the next, I see one of his massive contraptions moving forward.

It positions itself at the forefront of his army, and the hatch atop opens, revealing a team of skilled operators, their faces etched with hatred toward me.

I wait patiently for King Citeus' response when my attention zooms in on a screaming woman running in our direction. Her long brown hair is a braided mess, her face is covered in dirt, and her unnatural light brown eyes are fixed on me.

I've never seen her before, but somehow, it's hard to break her eye contact. It's like she's looking straight into my soul.

I'm about to ask the King about the unusual soldier falling out of this line when metallic capsules are ejected with a resounding clang from compartments within the gadget's hull. The capsules burst open mid-air, and my ears ring when they explode above me. Shards of some rock, each one pulsating with suppressed magic, soar into the sky like a flurry of dark, angular projectiles.

The shards arc high above, glinting ominously as they reach their apex. Then, as if guided by an unseen force, they descend towards me.

The shards hurtle downward with incredible speed, leaving trails of a faint glow in their wake as I lift my hands to shield myself from them. As the fragments make contact with my spell, a horrifying display of power unfolds. Upon impact, each shard erupts in a brilliant burst of energy, creating shockwaves that ripple through my barrier like it's nothing.

This isn't supposed to happen. Nothing Eternitie has is strong enough to break through magic.

And yet it does.

The first shard hits my shoulder, and I gasp when I feel my magic being sucked out of me, like pulling the guts out of an animal.

I search for my power, but the pain in my shoulder blade forces me to my knees. I don't have enough time to yell at my army hiding behind the Crymzon Wall to let them know what's happening. But they must have sensed it, and I can feel the ground shaking beneath my kneecaps.

Leave you fools, I scream, but it doesn't reach my mouth.

Another round of shards rains down on me, and each of them feels like it's burning through my skin into my flesh.

It fucking hurts so much!

Somehow, I lift my head, and my gaze falls on the woman close to me. She's almost in the same position I'm in, and I watch her wipe her tears away as she tries to press her other hand against her shoulder to ease the pain from the shards that must have hit her.

Bile rises in my throat when she rubs her face, repeatedly. That's when I notice the silver freckles shining through the dirt and the tears she just cleaned off. Her golden-brown skin can only mean she's from Tenacoro, yet the freckles on her face show that the Goddess of the Moon blessed her.

How is that possible?

She has the same silver markings on her face that I received when I was born, and my father insisted that I'm the only one Lunra bestowed her grace on.

Another shard hits my neck, and I'm about to lose consciousness from their overwhelming effect on me.

I need to warn my people. Somehow, I have to tell them to run. If King Citeus' creation is strong enough to render my magic null, taking out my entire army will take less.

The air fills with the gut-wrenching screams of my soldiers and the metallic boots hitting the ground hard.

No.

No!

In the distance, another contraption of King Citeus releases another wave of shards into the air. And it takes less than a heartbeat to hear my soldiers falling around me like sacks of potatoes.

TWENTY-SEVEN

Cyrus

When panic broke out inside Crymzon as I made my way back from the prison to the palace, I hid in an alley to avoid being spotted by the soldiers. I'll not throw myself into whatever is going on.

My rescue mission has already been as successful as me trying to stay away from Crymzon. I could find a handful of my villagers, but Wayne wasn't one of them, and I'm still missing about a hundred more.

The frantic boot thuds ring in my ears as I press against the wall to make myself as unnoticeable as possible.

"Eternitie is attacking us," someone yells on the streets, and my stomach bottoms out.

My father is here.

I warned Soulin to take me seriously. I told her he was out for blood.

Even though I told myself I would find the Lady of Fate, Devana's father, and my villagers, and get them out of here without getting involved, somehow, this feels like it's all my fault.

I have no desire to present myself to my father. If my brother is with him, one of them will make it their mission to take me out.

The sound of metal hitting the sandstone ground slowly subsides, and I exhale sharply. I need to search the palace again. Besides the villagers, I still haven't found the two most important people I need to retrieve.

Sprinting from shadow to shadow, I make my way in zigzags through the kingdom until a loud bang and screams shatter the silent air around me.

I know the sound and the agony that follows. My brother and father have managed to turn my drawings into reality.

Cold sweat forms beneath my clothes when I think about the damage my inventions are about to unfold. But they were never meant to be used in war. They were never meant to cause any harm to people.

When I searched for an invention to earn my place in the palace, I came up with many ideas. The Soulkeeper was only one of the many unique gadgets I created to make my life easier. While I used the Soulkeeper to trap new friends inside, it was initially designed to capture dying souls. With that invention, I could have saved people the heartache of saying goodbye to their loved ones on the deathbed, and instead, they could keep them alive inside the Soulkeeper to talk to them.

But the thought of carrying a dying soul inside a gadget was too much, so I kept working on it for personal use only.

My next idea was to help my people to capture prey, but a simple trap wasn't enough. Eternitie isn't known for its hunting and fighting abilities, so I needed to create something easy to use yet strong enough to simplify our ways of hunting.

That's how the Steamspitter was created. I designed a weapon that forcefully spits out steam at a target. When I showed my prototype to my brother, Cyprian, he suggested using another projectile instead of water vapor. He called it Gearshot because it propels projectiles with the force of gears.

When he tested my Steamspitter filled with a round metal ball, I should have known the damage it could cause. When Cyprian aimed at the target one of our servants held, I watched as the metal projectile split through the wooden board and directly into the man's chest behind it.

My stomach emptied when I watched the blood spraying out of the wound my invention had left in the man's chest. On the other hand, my brother jumped in the air as he screamed in excitement.

"You're a fucking genius!" he yelled at me, dropping the Gearshot, and pulling me off the ground to hug me.

"This...this is...no. This thing can't leave our hands," I mumbled. My stomach was empty then, but my body kept forcing nauseating pain through my abdomen.

"What are you talking about? This Gearshot will change everything!"

And indeed, it did.

I thought I burned all my drawings to make my mistakes disappear. But somehow, my brother found a way to duplicate my invention and claim it as his own. He even presented my other drawings to my father, reassuring him that everything could be used against an enemy if the time ever came.

That night, I packed a few of my belongings and fled after my brother threatened me, he would do everything in his power to shut me up from telling on him.

Another shot splits the air, and nausea takes over.

As much as I want to turn my back on my family and Monsteress, I'm the one who gave my brother the tools to build his Gearshot, and it's my responsibility to stop running and correct what I've done—if it's not too late already.

Thick smoke billows across the landscape, obscuring the horizon and casting an eerie haze over the scene. As I run out of the gate, I spot one of my Arcanes before anything else.

The hunting engine I created to shoot large birds out of the sky has been modified with a unique and fearsome arsenal. A large launcher stands ready to unleash its deadly payload atop its armored turret. This launcher, designed for shard deployment, houses a stockpile of shattered rock fragments I've only heard about but never seen—Nullstone.

At this point, it doesn't surprise me that my father got his hands on the only substance designed to combat magic.

The glowing, anti-magic rock only serves to counter mystical forces while capturing the essence of it to destroy or remove magical abilities.

As an Arcane rolls forward, its massive treads pushing away the sandy ground, the crew inside works in tandem to unleash the power of the Nullstone shards. A metallic clang echoes through the machine as the team loads the fragments into the launcher, their expressions focused on one person in particular—Monsteress.

With a resounding blast, the launcher roars to life, propelling the shards of Nullstone into the air with incredible force. The bits soar, glinting ominously as they streak across the battlefield. Each shard is a concentrated reservoir of anti-magic potential, ready to neutralize the mystical powers of the enemy.

My muscles tense as the rock fragments rain down upon Crymzon's ranks like malevolent meteors. Upon impact, the Nullstone shards explode into dazzling bursts of energy, releasing waves of magic-nullifying force. They shatter upon contact, dispersing their power in a chaotic and destructive display.

With each explosion, magical energies are disrupted and snuffed out. Spells fizzle and fail, leaving every struck Crymzonian powerless. The soldiers who rely on magical weapons find their blades rendered mundane, while magical barriers crumble under the onslaught of the Nullstone.

No, it can't be.

The Crymzon Army, once the most formidable force in Escela, now falters and stumbles, their magical advantage stripped away in mere minutes. Chaos and confusion spread among their ranks as the Arcanes continue their assault, launching shard after shard, decimating their ability to wield magic.

While it's painful to be hit by a shard as I cut through the mingling mess of soldiers, it's still nothing compared to what the Crymzonians must feel. It will only leave a bruise on my skin while it drains their magic for an unforeseen time because I don't have any powers that could be affected by it.

The closer I get to the central battle zone, the more fear creeps up on me. What if my father or brother have already spotted me? At least one has to be here leading the army, and I'm unsure which one I would rather encounter.

My questions are being answered when my eyes lock on a figure in the distance, stepping into a small clearing. It's my father, the King of Eternitie, a ruler whose once-proud demeanor is now distorted by the ravages of war.

I maneuver my way through the maze of combatants, ignoring the faces that whip around to throw a second glance at me. As I draw closer, I see the Queen, Monsteress, who's on her knees before him. Her curvy form trembles with pain and despair, but her eyes are filled with fire and hate.

I know my father expects her to plead for her life, and for the first time since encountering Monsteress, I'm relieved to see her salty ass throwing shade at him. It would be easier to tame a wild desert lion than break Monsteress' cruel spirit.

Just as I near my father, my heart wrenches with anguish as I witness the king raising a Gearshot, his face contorted with a ruthless determination. My gaze falls on my father, and a flood of emotions surges within me. I see the weariness etched upon his face, the weight of the crown upon his brow, and the determination that has driven him to lead his forces into this brutal conflict. But now, I see something else—an unfamiliar glint in my father's eyes, clouded by the maelstrom of battle.

My breath catches in my throat, my mind racing for a solution to prevent the impending tragedy.

I dreamed of so many ways I could kill Monsteress. Every death I imagined wasn't enough to make her pay for her crimes, and yet, seeing my father so close to using my invention to take her life is gut-wrenching.

I never thought I would find myself in this position. Taking Monsteress' side is not where I saw myself once all this started, but she's done nothing to provoke him. Her ways of running her kingdom never interfered with Eternitie. My grudge against her for incarcerating me and whipping Liza should be unknown to him.

So why is he doing this?

He points the Gearshot right at her face.

"You make me sick," my father yells at Monsteress, his hand steady as he points the Gearshot at her. "Did you really think your kingdom is stronger than the others?"

Her lips curve into a smile as she studies the weapon pointed at her. "Apparently, you think I'm threatening enough to come all this way," she says, her voice unwavering. "I've done nothing to break our treaty."

"Your presence alone is enough to violate the treaty. Before you claimed the Crymzon Throne, there was peace. And look at Escela now. But don't worry. I will even the scales and return my land to its former glory."

My father cocks back the mechanism to ready his weapon.

Then, in a moment of uncertainty, my eyes catch a glint of steel on the ground. With desperation, I snatch it up, the cold metal fitting perfectly into my grasp. The Gearshot trembles slightly in my hand, its weight a stark reminder of the gravity of the situation.

I witnessed what this thing can do. I tried to make it disappear. But here it is, in my hand.

Summoning my courage, I step forward, closing the distance between me and my father. My voice emerges, a blend of anguish and resolve, as I cry, "Father, stop! Please, I beg you!"

The king's eyes, momentarily torn from his intended target, dart towards me. Recognition and a flicker of something deeper pass across his weathered face. But the rage that consumes him, fueled by the relentless chaos of battle around us, still burns in his eyes.

With trembling hands, I lift the Gearshot I seized, pointing it directly at my father. The weight of the decision hangs heavily upon me, yet I stand straight, driven by the belief that this is the only way to protect everyone I hold dear.

Silence descends upon the battlefield, starkly contrasting the relentless clash of steel and the cries of agony. The surrounding combatants seem to fade into the background, the world narrowing down to this pivotal moment between my father and me.

Time stands still as I hold my breath, hoping that my plea and the weapon in my hand will be enough to break the grip of violence that holds my father captive. In that suspended moment, the fate of my family, Monsteress, and the course of history hangs precariously in the balance between two irreconcilable choices.

"We cannot lose ourselves in this darkness. Remember who we are; who you are!" the king says, eyes narrowing on me.

With the threat temporarily diffused, my weapon wavers, and I slowly lower it to the ground. My father's gaze remains fixed on me, the depth of our connection and the significance of our choices interwoven in the shared silence.

At that moment, a fragile semblance of hope flickers within my heart, and after all this time of hiding, I might have done the right thing to face him.

TWENTY-EIGHT

KHAOS

Soulin is in pain. I can hear her screams through the Soulmate Connection, and a sharp discomfort aches in more places than I can count. But it's not my pain. I know for sure because I checked. This phantom pain seems to leak through our connection.

Something is very wrong.

I bolt through the hidden door and push a guard out of my way, which must have come looking for me.

"The Queen," I scream, catapulting him against the wall as I make my way up the spiraling corridor into the open air.

The night sky is filled with screams and lightning explosions on the horizon. My heart tells me to run into her chambers and look for her, but the tugging sensation in my chest pulls me to the tumult outside the gate.

I don't even look down when I sprint over the narrow bridge, not even a little concerned that one misstep could lead to my death. Like in a trance, my boots hit the Wall, and I run as fast as my magic allows me from the south side of the kingdom to the north part.

That's when I see it.

A chaotic scene unfolds beneath me, with smoke and dust filling the air as the opposing forces clash. Amidst the sounds of swords meeting metal on metal, the rumble of war machines, and the cries of soldiers, a massive metallic moving invention emerges.

What in Lunra's name is that?

My eyes scan the battlefield, and I notice the crimson armor of our kingdom and brown leather mixed with brass and steel.

Frantically, I search the ground for my Soulmate. She has to be here. I can feel her.

The ground is already littered with fallen comrades, and my heart stops when I see the blood-red dress among it. Before her stands a man I know too well. He's been in and out of Crymzon for Council meetings...

King Citeus.

How long was I down there in the prison? How did I not notice Eternitie marching against our kingdom?

I don't have enough time to take the steps and reach Soulin. Instead, I jump.

My feet collide with the rock-hard desert ground beneath me as I land. Without using my magic to dampen the impact, my legs would be broken in more than one place right now. I wasn't thinking when I took the leap, and even if my power wasn't enough to let me walk away from such a fall, I would have found a way to get to Soulin, broken bones and all.

But I can walk, and I use my unscathed legs to navigate through the chaos, expertly ducking beneath swinging weapons and narrowly avoiding the impact of flying shards raining from the sky.

"Don't let them touch you," a female soldier gasps as I pass her, and my eyes widen when I watch her being hit by a piece of rock as she speaks. The glow surrounding her flickers, and her magic seems to be gone within the next breath.

I look up at the sky, and to my horror, more glowing rocks race towards us.

Don't let them touch you.

I don't need to be a genius to figure out that the little gem pieces have the power to drain our magic. I dodge through the fighting soldiers and jump over unmoving bodies while keeping my eyes on the sky and the direction in which I saw Soulin last.

The shards continue to rain down upon the Crymzon Army, tearing through ranks, causing chaos, and spreading fear among my soldiers. I can practically feel our morale shatter under the weight of the attack.

Has a piece struck Soulin? And if so, was her magic strong enough to withstand the draining?

Pushing people out of my way left and right, I practically bulldoze through the battlefield, searching for Soulin. I have to be close by now. The screams inside my head get more louder, and the tugging inside my heart turns from a soft pull into a painful hammering sensation.

When I finally see her, I use my magic to clear the way. I should have used this spell when I entered the battlefield. But the thought of drawing everyone's attention to me and risking getting involved in one-on-one combat that would have taken precious seconds from me was enough to dampen that idea.

My heart stops when I see Soulin kneeling before King Citeus. Even though she looks unscathed, she shakes violently but holds her head high.

What did he do to her?

Jolting forward, I notice King Citeus' outstretched arm gripping a peculiar object. The object emits a dangerous aura unlike anything I ever felt before. Its sleek design contrasts with what I've seen in Eternitie on my journey to Terminus as a young lad.

He points the opening of the gadget at her face, and without a doubt, I can tell that nothing good will leave its narrow end.

I'm about to scream her name to let her know I'm coming for her when I see another man step into the clearing. I can't see his face, but he knows him from what King Citeus' facial expressions are giving away. The stranger lifts his arm, and I press forward to reach the men before something terrible happens.

"Soulin!" I yell, just a few steps away from her, and that's when a loud bang fires, and her body hits the ground.

TWENTY-NINE

Devana

The pain surging through my body gets stronger with every minute, but that's something I'm used to. While my muscles still ache from the treacherous march and the pain from my invisible wounds presses me down to the ground, I bite my lip and breathe through it.

I can do this.

I lived this long dealing with daily aches that would bring most people to the edge of insanity. For so long, I've mastered hiding my discomfort from the villagers and my father.

It's just pain—excruciating, endless pain—but I have experience with it.

The sounds of the battle fade in and out, and occasionally, I hear those deadly contraptions spit out more stone shards. So far, I haven't been hit, but it's just a matter of time.

With a trembling hand, I reach up to clasp the feather around my neck, my fingers tracing the contours of its soft quill. As I do, a surge of pain shoots through my body, an agonizing reminder of the wounds

I don't carry and yet somehow feel. But I don't falter. I'm no stranger to pain; it is a companion that has accompanied me since birth.

Summoning every ounce of strength, I raise the feather to my lips, pressing it firmly against them. My breath, ragged and strained, fills the air as I exhale. Then, an inaudible whistle escapes my lips. It's a sound only I can hear, a signal unique to an unbreakable bond I've sworn never to use again.

The pain intensifies, threatening to overwhelm me, but I grit my teeth and push through it. My mind focuses solely on the purpose at hand: the summoning of Erinna. I've always known that my Glimmarum will answer my call in the moment of need, soaring through the skies with wings of comfort and protection.

As I blow into the feather again, a surge of energy courses through my body, mingling with my discomfort. I feel our connection, a lifeline forged so strong that only death can separate us. And in that moment, I know Erinna is near, racing against time to reach my side.

My eyes scan the horizon for any signs of her, and before I can spot her, a powerful gust of wind whips around me, swirling my hair and billowing my baggy armor. The air trembles as I close my eyes, listening for the telltale beat of mighty wings. And then, like a thunderclap, it comes.

A griffin descends from the heavens, its majestic form cutting through the sky with effortless grace—brown feathers shimmer in the moonlight, glinting like shards of precious gemstones. With a thunderous thud, she lands beside me, her eyes searching my body for injuries.

"I'm okay, but I need you to get me out of here," I whisper, pushing myself off the ground.

With a surge of strength, I hoist myself onto Erinna's back, my pain momentarily forgotten. Together, we rise into the sky, leaving the massacre behind us. Unsteady, I gaze down at the world beneath us, and when I see the green colors of Tenacoro closing in on Crymzon from the east, I know exactly what to do next.

THIRTY

Cyrus

No, he didn't.

Please tell me I got it all wrong.

My hand shakes so uncontrollably that the Gearshot flies out of my hand. The world around me spins, and the contents of my stomach fly out.

This is what I tried to prevent. My inventions were the reason I left. Maybe if I hadn't been such a coward, I could have made a difference; I could have talked sense into my father.

If my brother hadn't stolen my drawings, I would still be the Prince of Eternitie, living a luxurious life alone.

Everything happened so fast that I must look up again to verify what I've done.

Monsteress' body lay sprawled out before me. Her red dress clings to her as the pool of blood seeps into the fabric, weighing it down.

What have I done?

My eyes wander over her body, searching for any movement.

Shit! Do something!

Her fingers twitch, and a man pushes me out of the way, throwing himself to his knees to get to her.

Another load of vomit finds its way up my throat. I can't stop my body from shivering.

Slowly, I turn my head. When I see the cold eyes of my father, I freeze.

This is all my doing. I had a choice, and my father forced my hand when he cocked the Gearshot.

The perfectly round entrance wound between his brows makes my stomach turn again. My father wasn't supposed to die like this. No one deserves to end this way.

I can't believe I really did it. I shot my father, knowing it would kill him, just like my brother pointed the Gearshot at that poor servant.

I should have aimed for his leg or stomach. Maybe that would have spared his life. But to what good? Could I say with certainty that he would have left Crymzon alone after his recovery?

No.

The path of rage he was spiraling down isn't something new. I've felt his hatred towards me and my sister every moment I stood before him. There's no one as amazing as Cyprian in his eyes, especially after he stole my drawings.

When I squeezed the trigger, all I thought of was my sister. As the rightful heir, she's the next in line to climb the Brass Throne. Knowing that made my decision to act on my father's intentions not easier, but it made my conscience feel better.

Catalina will lead our people back to the right path, but I'm unsure if she can ever forgive me for what I've done—abandoning her and killing our father.

The blood pooling from the exit wounds keeps flowing, creating a little stream that leads right to the woman lying next to him.

Monsteress moves her hands, pressing herself off the ground, and the man beside her pulls her up and lifts her in the air.

"What hurts?" he asks. When he turns around, I see the scar on his left cheek.

The veil of silence around me lifts, and the sounds of war and dismay return as the world around me spins again.

The moon hangs low in the blood-streaked sky, casting a haunting glow across the desolate battlefield. Smoke billows from the charred remains of fallen soldiers, while the air is heavy with the stench of blood and sweat. Amidst this grim tableau, I stand hunched over, my eyes surveying the chaos surrounding me.

My heart sinks as I watch my comrades, once filled with courage and determination, retreating in disarray.

They must know.

Fear must have gripped their souls when they heard the news of my father's passing, prompting them to abandon the fight and seek solace in the safety of home. A bitter taste of disappointment and shame mingles with the metallic tang of desperation on my tongue.

"You," I say, pointing my finger at the man holding Monsteress. "You're the one who brought me here."

And the one who also knocked me out when I tried to escape from the throne room right after he seized my village.

His dark curly hair is longer, almost reaching his shoulders, and the stubbles on his face have grown quite a lot, but it's him; I know it.

His face etches with confusion and utter annoyance as he holds Monsteress against his chest, covering most of her body with his. "Step aside. I don't need my hands to crush you," he growls, stepping past me.

"I'm not an Eternian," I say, shaking my head. "I mean, I am, but I'm on your side."

"I don't care who you are. Go run back home with your comrades," he says without looking at me.

I don't have a home anymore. After what I've done, I'm a traitor. There's no need to contemplate if someone saw me shoot my father—I know at least one of the Eternians must have watched me pull the trigger. I'm no stranger in Eternitie, and even if that person doesn't realize I'm the *deceased* prince, a few people already recognized me.

I can't go back to Eternitie ever again.

"She promised me to release two prisoners," I say, holding on to the only thing that can save my neck.

"What do you still want from us?" he yells, marching against the stream of running Eternians.

I keep my head low to conceal my face. "I saved her *twice!*"

Those words make him stop. He whips around, and when his eyes search my face, I know he recognizes me.

"You're the villager who hid that woman inside his hut," he says, eyes narrowing on me. "That damned gadget was yours."

"You found it?"

"I confiscated it. I hate to break it to you, but it's a bad time for small talk and promises."

No shit.

"I'm not leaving without the prisoners," I say, standing my ground.

"And I'm not—"

A scream shatters through the air, and when my eyes follow the sound, my legs root to the ground.

Amid the fleeing soldiers, my gaze falls upon a figure that sends a chill down my spine. It's my brother, Cyprian, his face contorted with rage and vengeance. Consumed by a newfound anger, he charges toward me with unrestrained fury.

Time slows again as my heart pounds in my chest. The ground beneath my boots feels heavy, mirroring the weight of the choices that led me to this moment.

As Cyprian closes the distance, his sword gleaming in the light, a glimpse of our shared past dances before my eyes. A flicker of pain and sadness mixes within the depths of his gaze, battling against the overwhelming rage.

He never used to be this...hateful. I remember when we used to play games together and laugh until the crown's weight made him bitter. He wants it—the crown—for himself. Seeing Catalina on the dais is something he will never support.

I yearn for the connection we once shared, all three of us, a bond that weathered countless storms before we learned about our future. But the tempest of the Brass Throne has driven us apart, molding our souls into different shapes.

With a deafening cry, my brother lunges, fueled by a maelstrom of emotions. My instincts take hold, and I sidestep the onslaught just in time. I feel the rush of air as my brother's sword swipes through empty space.

Caught off balance, my brother stumbles, momentarily vulnerable. I hesitate, my heart heavy. In the fleeting moment, I see an opportunity to bridge the gap that has grown between us. I reach out, my hand extending toward my brother, a silent plea for reconciliation amidst the chaos.

But as our eyes meet, the anger that blazes in my brother's gaze remains unyielding. The plea for peace is met with defiance, and my brother's resolve solidifies. He rises to his feet with renewed vigor, ready to unleash his wrath upon me.

There's no saving us. What started as an attack on Monsteress will end as bloodshed for the Brass Throne.

But I don't want it—I never did.

Grief and regret well within my chest, intertwining with the strength that propels me forward. I brace myself for the clash that awaits. As our fates collide amidst the scorching landscape, I prepare to confront the horrors of my past, not only by combat, but within the depths of my fractured bond with my brother.

One of us is going to be buried with our father today. As long as I breathe, Cyprian won't stop hunting me.

Cyprian lifts his sword again, and I have nothing to defend myself with. All I can do is stand here, close my eyes, and hope it's a swift end.

I wait for a few breaths. It should be over by now.

When I open my eyes, I see Monsteress' savior standing between me and Cyprian. He has her hoisted over his shoulder, one arm outstretched, pointing at him.

"I give you one minute to clear my kingdom and take your fight there before I change my mind and crush you like a brittle rock," the soldier says, covering my view.

"You don't know whom you're talking to," Cyprian yells, his teeth clenched. "I'm the new King of Eternitie."

My heart stops.

He knows.

My brother already knows that our father is dead.

Still, he's wrong. Catalina is the next in line, not him.

The man chuckles, his chest rattling as he takes my brother in. "You're just the Crown Prince," he says, and Cyprian's face contorts with hate. "I don't want to be responsible for killing Eternitie's last male heir."

Cyprian smirks as he looks past him to glimpse at me. "I see you have been keeping everyone in the dark, dear brother," he says, directed at me, and I see the man shift his weight to look over his shoulder.

His eyes darken. I see the exact moment he realizes who I am. That minor distraction is enough for my brother to bolt past him and bring his sword down on me.

THIRTY-ONE

KHAOS

From the first moment I saw him, I should have known. He looks so much like his father, yet I didn't connect the dots when I tranquilized him and hauled him back to Crymzon.

All this time, Soulin knew and let me believe he was no one. Well, the moment she locked him in a windowless chamber, I realized he was more than the regular prisoner, and because of that, I should have seen it.

If Soulin were awake, I would ask her why she kept such vital information from me. I would also kiss her for being alive. But she's dead weight right now, driving in and out of consciousness.

In a split second, I look over my shoulder. I watch as Cyprian lifts his sword in the air and tries to outmaneuver me. With my free hand, I reach for the sword, channeling magic into it, and when the metal collides with my flesh, the blade splinters into little fragments before the wind blows it away.

"What did you not understand when I told you to leave?" I ask, grabbing Cyrus by the neck to pull him behind me and out of his way.

I'm still upset about all the secrets Soulin has kept from me, but somehow, she thinks Cyrus is important. If he's important to her, I need to accept that he's somehow important to me.

While Cyprian searches the ground for a weapon, I whirl around and gently press Soulin into his arms. "Take her to the throne room. Behind the dais, you will find a tapestry. Hide there. I will find you."

My stomach clenches when I hand Soulin over to him, and I'm sure he will collapse under her weight. In an instant, he takes her and starts running.

I have little time to watch them disappear into the crowd surrounding us. If he cannot keep her safe, I will never forgive myself. But I can't hold on to her and fight at the same time.

Another growl behind me makes me aware that Cyprian must have found something to attack me with. Ripping my eyes away from Soulin, I spin around, and my eyes widen when I see Cyprian so close to me. His arm swings down on me, and before I can concentrate on my magic, something sharp pierces through the fabric of my armor. The pain rushing through my arm into my heart takes my breath away. My eyes land on the gleaming rock shard sticking out of my left bicep, and I look up to see Cyprian's amused smile.

"You're not as invincible as you think," he laughs, pointing at my wound. "Just a little piece of Nullstone is enough to drain your magic."

Until now, I've never heard of a Nullstone before. It's the same rock I saw flying out of the gadgets when I searched the battlefield for Soulin.

I can feel the Nullstone pulsating beneath my skin, doing its absolute worst to work against me.

"What did you say again?" He rubs his chin and looks into the sky. "You're going to crush me like a brittle rock? I guess it's my turn now to do with you as I please."

Tears sting in my eyes as I try to keep myself upright. I couldn't figure out what brought Soulin to pass out, but if one shard alone feels this agonizing, she must have been hit by a lot.

Thinking about Soulin forces a rush of adrenaline through my veins. I can't let him beat me. I promised I would get to the throne room, and it's a promise I must keep.

Cyprian picks up another glowing shard off the ground, and I try to move, but my muscles won't budge. "You know, the funny thing is, for me, it's just an ugly rock. I can touch it without feeling a thing. But for you," he builds himself up and rams another piece of Nullstone into my other arm, "it must be so painful to feel your magic being compromised."

I clench my jaw to muffle the scream that's building up inside my throat. There's no way I can take another Nullstone shard. My vision goes blurry as I watch him reach down for another splinter.

"I wonder if the stone is powerful enough to kill you. Do you need your magic to live? Is it like an engine that keeps you running, or can you stay alive without it?"

I lived almost fifteen years without magic. Since the day Soulin was attacked at her coronation, I have had none. If I had to use my power to save Soulin again, I would do it and live the rest of my life without it. But I can't tell him that.

He's serious. Juggling another Nullstone, he comes closer. And closer.

He reaches for me, and I do the only thing I can think of before my body goes numb and everything around me falls silent.

I open up my connection to my Soulmate and hope she can hear me.

Soulin! Get out!

THIRTY-TWO

Queen Soulin

My eyes flutter open, revealing a landscape of devastation that stretches as far as I can see. I move, my body aching and battered, but I'm not walking.

Confusion and disorientation grip my mind as I struggle to piece together what happened. Images and sounds flash through my memory like shattered fragments of a nightmare. The clash of swords, the cries of pain, and the thunderous roar of rocks hitting the ground echo in my ears.

But most haunting of all is the ghostly presence of a woman who passed away years ago.

I blink.

Red long hair flows over her crimson gown as she steps towards me.

I blink again.

I try to force all my magic into my heart to numb it, but my power doesn't respond to me. Bile rises in my throat. Forcefully, I swallow it down without breaking eye contact, and that's when I notice I'm being carried away from her.

"Let me down!" I croak out, kicking and scratching.

The person holding me drops me, and I land on my wobbly feet. Cyrus' face comes into my view, and I push him out of the way to look for the figure behind him.

She's closer now, her eyes black, her face pale and distorted as if she's crying.

My limbs shake.

No...not her.

If she comes a step closer, I will lose it right here, on the outskirts of my kingdom.

Struggling to stand by myself, I notice the devastation that surrounds me. The once serene landscape has transformed into a battlefield littered with broken weapons, torn banners, and lifeless bodies. My heart pounds in my chest as the reality of the situation seeps into my consciousness.

We're losing.

My mother takes one careful step after another. Cyrus turns around to see what I'm staring at, and before I can do anything, he grabs me by my hips and throws me over his shoulder.

"I got you!" he yells as his feet pound into the dusty ground. I push myself up, using my trembling arms to support my weight against his ass to look at her.

She's coming closer.

We can't outrun her.

My heart hammers in my chest, and that's when I hear a clear and strong voice in my head.

Soulin! Get out!

Khaos? Khaos! I send back through the Connection, but it's silent on the other end.

Grief twists within me, intertwining with a fierce anger that bubbles up from the depths of my being.

Why is Khaos telling me to leave? And how is my mother here? Is this some cruel illusion or a trick of my mind?

My breath catches in my throat as I struggle to comprehend the impossible.

Tears well up in my eyes, blurring my vision as Cyrus carries me away from my mother's apparition. The ground beneath us feels unstable, as if it bears the weight of countless fallen warriors.

"Run faster," I yell at Cyrus, watching my mother get closer with ease. Behind her, the dead twitch before they lift themselves off the ground.

Fuck.

It's not just Eternitie who came here to challenge me. With each rising Undead, my anger deepens.

Keres came out to play, too.

Just as I think Cyrus caught another wind and is strong enough to bring us to the Crymzon Wall, I'm tossed to the ground.

I hear one of my ribs crack as I land on a sandstone buried beneath the sand. I don't have time to tend to my fresh injury as my mother steps closer, her hair billowing in the wind.

It has been too long since I saw her last. Somehow, in my mind, I remember her differently. Besides the pale color and the black eyes, I thought her hair was longer and her body rounder.

This image of her will always stick with me.

My mother reaches out a trembling hand. Even though she's one of Keres' creations, she acts differently than the others. The way she walks and the gentleness in her movement make me believe she's still in there.

"Don't touch her," Cyrus yells from the distance, but I can't rip my eyes off her.

She's real. She's here. Maybe I can save her. Perhaps my magic is enough to bring her back.

"Move, damn it!" Cyrus screams, and the urgency in his voice is strong enough to break the surrounding haze.

Scrambling to my feet, I dodge my mother's hand. Her eyes narrow on me, and she tries to touch me again.

I reach inside me to pull on my magic. Maybe the undead version of my father is immune to it, but I could fight off his Undead creations with it.

Still, my body isn't reacting to my plea. I can feel my power flickering, but the shards in my skin render it useless.

Hastily, I back away and search for Cyrus. Why did he drop me?

When I finally find him just a few steps away from me, I realize how dire our situation is.

Before him stands his brother, Cyprian, equipped with not one but two swords as fallen soldiers swarm in our direction, enclosing us in a circle.

There's no way out.

I have no magic, Cyrus isn't an experienced warrior, and I can't reach Khaos.

Just as I thought it couldn't get any worse, I see the boulder of a man, his black armor absorbing the early sun while his red hair looks like fire, breaking through the Undead.

All I wanted was to see him again. But now that he's here and I cannot protect myself, I can feel my last minutes begin to count down.

The King of the North, my resurrected father sent by Otyx, stops beside my mother and smiles at me.

"Isn't she beautiful?" he asks, his eyes roaming over my mother's body. "I thought you would like to see her again."

My mouth is dry, and my body hurts, but somehow, I find the strength to straighten my shoulders and answer. "Why are you here?"

"I'm Death. Wherever a soul needs to be claimed, I'm there," he whispers, his blackened teeth showing through his cracked, pale lips. "You brought me to your doorstep with all the death following you."

His fingertips graze my mother's face, and her apparition fades, dissipating like smoke carried away by the wind.

As the grief washes over me, another emotion wells up from within my core—rage. It courses through my veins like wildfire, fueling my resolve to avenge the senseless destruction and lost lives. It burns so deeply within my chest that I clench my fists, my voice cracking as I cry out in anguish.

Keres just resurrected my mother to take her away from me again.

My heart shatters, yet it also hardens. The pain of loss is raw and unyielding, threatening to consume my entire being as I vow to seek justice for my mother and honor the memory of my fallen Crymzonians.

With each step, I move forward, my feet finding purpose amidst the carnage. I'm outnumbered and powerless, but for the first time in my life, I can feel the weight of my name, and I love it.

They wanted Monsteress, and that's who they will get.

THIRTY-THREE

DEVANA

I feel her pain. Whenever a shard hits her, it feels like my skin is ripped open and burned. Holding on to Erinna gets harder and harder.

Then, suddenly, the pain is gone.

Every aching part of my body feels numb besides my sore muscles.

Looking over my shoulder, I search for Monsteress. Something isn't right. Why did the pain stop so suddenly?

The entire time I wondered why my father had changed his mind about Monsteress, and it became apparent when I felt her agony like my own.

How long did he know? How long did he conceal the truth that not only is she my Soulmate since birth, but we're also somehow connected? Is the pain I've been experiencing since I was a child caused by her?

Erinna stretches her wings, and the wind whipping against my face makes me forget momentarily that I might be in danger. I have longed for this feeling since I left Tenacoro because I never got to experience it. While I could always feel Erinna close to me, we never got to have our first flight. Actually, we only met once before my father took me away from her.

I've dreamt of this moment for over twenty years since I first saw her soaring through the sky. The majestic creature with mighty wings, an eagle-like head, and a lion-like body has captivated my imagination. I've spent countless hours studying griffins behind closed doors, learning about their behavior, and dreaming of the day I would become one with my magnificent beast.

With trembling hands, I carefully reach out, my fingers brushing against Erinna's feathery mane, and a wave of connection passes between us. It's as if our souls recognize each other, bound by an unbreakable bond. The griffin's muscles tense beneath me, sensing the weight of this monumental moment. My heart pounds in my chest as I hold on to her mane, gripping it tightly but trustingly.

Erinna lets out a low rumble, a mixture of excitement and encouragement. She launches us higher into the air with a powerful beat of her wings.

I feel a rush of exhilaration as the ground falls away beneath us, my dreams coming true in a breathtaking flurry. The wind rushes through my hair, bringing tears to my eyes as Erinna and I dance through the sky.

From our elevated vantage point, I can see the world stretching before us—an expansive tapestry of the red desert, rolling hills, winding rivers, the ocean, and towering mountains.

The fear and nervousness that clung to my heart dissolve, replaced by an overwhelming sense of joy and wonder. I waited patiently for this moment, and now I'm soaring through the skies, riding my griffin with a freedom I've never known before.

We could leave right now, and no one would ever know. Together, we could start a new life away from everything and everyone.

The sharp pain returning to my shoulder and neck reminds me I won't be able to leave. For a few minutes, I forgot how it is to be in constant agony, and when it returned, the thought of my father and Monsteress came with it.

Below me, the sprawling red desert stretches out like a fiery tapestry, contrasting vividly against the cloudless sky. As I survey the arid landscape, I gaze upon an army clad in gleaming green, marching resolutely through the unforgiving terrain. It's the army of the kingdom I once called home—a kingdom I left behind but never honestly forgotten.

Among the marching warriors, my keen eyes see a figure standing out amidst the sea of uniforms. It's Synadena, Queen of Tenacoro, a ruler known for her fierce and committed leadership, renowned for her unwavering connection with the wild and the untamed.

A gentle touch is enough to make Erinna descend towards the Queen. With graceful flaps of her mighty wings, my griffin glides through the air, closing the distance between us.

As we approach, the rhythmic thumping of marching boots grows louder, blending with the steady beating of my heart. The dust stirred by the army's advance swirls around us, casting a nebulous aura upon them. I lock eyes with Queen Synadena, and for a brief moment, the world fades into the background.

With a swift landing, we touch down before the Queen, the gust of wind from Erinna's descent causing ripples in the Queen's regal green attire. Her piercing eyes show faint smile lines as she studies me.

Words escape me for a moment, the weight of the reunion overwhelming me. But then, after finding my voice, I speak. "Your Majesty. I chose to seek my own path, but I need your help. I'm asking for a bow to fight for what I believe in."

I should get more into detail. I should tell her how serious the war between the two kingdoms is.

But Queen Synadena nods, her gaze wandering to the next soldier beside her, and she takes the recurved bow and quiver filled with arrows off his back. "You've carved your destiny, and I honor your choice. Remember, the jungle and the sky have always been your domain. Soar freely, but never forget the home that shaped you, Hunteress."

With those words, a bittersweet understanding settles between us, and she hands me the bow and arrows.

I look up at her.

Hunteress.

Just like Monsteress, I've earned my new name through my choices. And to be quite honest, I like the sound of it.

Looking at her bright smile, I notice the Queen is everything I wanted my mother to be. Even though I abandoned my ruler, her love shines through everything she has done for me the last few days—from asking me to return home, to her now offering me a bow and arrows without questioning what it will be used for.

Somehow, I expected the Queen to be as disappointed in me as my mother was. It never crossed my mind that she might have been watching me my entire life, waiting for me to return home.

Home.

What a bittersweet word.

For years, my home was wherever my father was. I didn't need anyone or anything if he was there, tugging me into bed and telling me that someday I would change Escela's history. His confidence in me was enough to push me to my limits—every day, every training, every soaring arrow, and every slice of a sword.

Now, all I can think about is leading him *home* to the world he left behind because of me.

As I mount Erinna again and ascend back into the boundless sky, I cast one last glance at the army of my past, and Queen Synadena, standing tall amidst the green-clad warriors.

I will honor my roots and make my Queen proud.

Embracing the boundless horizon that awaits us, I let out the war cry my father taught me as a child. My voice vibrates in my throat as I release all the tension and emotions I've been holding in since leaving Tenacoro.

Soar freely, but never forget the home that shaped you.

It didn't take me long to retrieve a bow, yet the war had shifted from Eternitie attacking Crymzon to Crymzonian and Eternian soldiers attacking each other and their own. I watch a handful of fallen soldiers rise from the dead, and my muscles tense at the sight.

How is it possible that the dead resurrect? Is it Monsteress doing? Does she have the ability to breathe new life into them?

The thought of being linked to a monster sends a shiver down my spine. Still, I need her to find my father.

While I leave my Queen to rescue the prisoners outside the wall, my mission is to hunt Monsteress down. Maybe my father is in prison already, and the Tenacorians can free him. If not, I can't risk missing the only shot I have to locate him.

Besides being turned into a weapon, he also showed me what it means to have someone's back. He has always been in my corner, and I will show him I'm in his.

As my eyes sweep the ongoing battle, spotting her red dress doesn't take long.

No, wait...there's two of them.

I point at the female on the ground, and my hand shakes as Erinna draws closer, and I see the man standing beside her. I gasp.

His brown hair clings to his face, sweaty and dirty, and his clothes are ragged and ripped.

I expect him to pick up a sword and ram it into Monsteress' heart. Instead, he carries her on his shoulder, away from the mess enclosing them as if trying to protect her.

Oh, Aemilius. What have you gotten yourself into?

My adrenaline spikes when I observe his arms wrapped around her. I shouldn't feel this way, especially since I don't know if he's under a spell and involuntarily carrying her—but it hurts seeing him holding on to another woman.

Something stops me from diving to the ground and confronting Monsteress. Everything would be so much easier if Aemilius weren't there. His presence makes concentrating hard because I have to finish a task.

The other woman with the red dress follows Aemilius and Monsteress.

Why doesn't he drop her? He needs to let Monsteress go to outrun the woman.

I almost shout at him but close my mouth when I see another soldier entering the circle that's building around them. He wears the colors of Eternitie, and I need to blink a few times to ensure I'm not seeing double.

His brown hair is shorter than Aemilius', and he's taller than him and more muscular, but the resemblance between Aemilius and him is uncanny.

Aemilius never mentioned a brother. He actually never told me anything about his past.

I'm too slow to react when the soldier's intentions become clear. I watch as he lunges forward, tossing Monsteress to the ground as he tackles Aemilius.

My eyes dart between them—Monsteress staring at the other woman and Aemilius scrambling to his feet to hold his arms out to stop the lookalike soldier. From here, I can see Aemilius and Monsteress fight their own battle.

Taking a deep breath, I gently nudge Erinna to bring her to a hovering position. She holds herself steady, her wings beating with measured force. With practiced ease, I reach behind me and unsheathe the carved bow, crafted from the finest wood and enriched with delicate etchings. My fingers deftly grasp an arrow, its feather fletching quivering with anticipation. I pull back the bowstring, my muscles tensing, as I align my sights with the soldier attacking Aemilius.

I know Monsteress is my priority if I want to see my father again, but I can't let anything happen to Aemilius. While my brain tells me to redirect my aim, my heart yells to hold it steady and shoot.

I close one eye and inhale.

Slowly, I shift the bow to the left, pointing at Monsteress' forehead. I've trained for this. This is the mental image I've been carrying around since I last aimed at her. My arrow should have hit and killed her. She should be dead, and all of this would have been prevented. But I see her breathing. I see her scurrying away from the other woman.

I can end this—everything.

I'm aware of our connection now. But will I die if she does? Do I think she's going to give me an answer to where my father is?

What if he isn't in Crymzon anymore? What if he got out and walked away, and he's now looking for me? How can I think of him as weak, knowing the strength he has taught me? The thought of finally paying him back for raising me made me believe he could not save himself.

But what are the chances?

Really?

The quiver strapped to my back, a sturdy vessel for my arrows, gives way under the strain, and its leather bindings snap, causing the contents to spill into the air. Arrows cascade towards the earth like a fleeting constellation of steel and wood.

My heart skips a beat as I watch my precious arrows plummet, and I almost release the only one I have left.

As the quiver slips out of my reach, I swiftly glance at Erinna. Sensing my urgency, the griffin's amber eyes flicker with understanding.

One shot.

My aim switches back and forth between Monsteress and the soldier.

I either can end this entire war, or I can enable Aemilius' brother—I mean, he has to be his brother—and save him.

Slowly, I inhale again and let the arrow go.

THIRTY-FOUR

Cyrus

Cyprian lifts a sword, and I can only hold my arms out to shield my face from the blow. My brother was never much of a talker. Enraged, he's mute.

My last moments are filled with the images of Soulin watching her mother being taken away from her again.

Her mother.

Everyone in Escela knows the story. The Crymzon Queen died, and that was enough to unleash a magical outburst in her daughter that flattened an entire throne room with her brother and father inside.

I don't have to know Queen Ria to know that it's her. The red hair and demanding aura are more than convincing that only she can be Soulin's mother.

I'm taken aback when the person claiming her life *again* is the deceased Crymzon King.

Seeing his pale, fallen-in face, black teeth, and midnight eyes encourages me to understand why Soulin hates him so much. He looks terrifying and insane.

But that won't help me with my problem—my brother.

Fear and desperation etch across my face in the feeble attempt to shield myself from the impending attack. Through my arms, I see the deadly arc of the sword descending towards me. The sound of steel slicing through the air makes the hair on my arms spike up.

The atmosphere surrounding us transforms as a shroud of darkness envelopes the clearing. Shadows dance and twirl, swallowing the early sunlight.

Amid the encroaching darkness, a hissing sound pierces the air—an arrow whizzes past, finding its mark with chilling precision. It strikes my brother's chest with a sickening thud, burying itself deep into his flesh. His eyes widen with shock and pain, and the momentum of his attack disrupts as he staggers backward. A momentary flash of surprise and pain registers on his face before he crumples to the ground, his sword clattering beside him.

As the darkness recedes, three figures emerge from the gloom. These ethereal beings possess an otherworldly appearance, their forms a delicate blend of grotesque and beauty. Each holds a distinct aura, and I know them all too well.

Somehow, they must have found a way to escape, and now, after I thought I trapped them inside the Soulkeeper forever, they are here to claim me.

I swallow.

With solemn steps, the three creatures approach me, their eyes glowing with a hunting luminescence of red and silver.

I watch them in fear as they walk past me and gently lift Cyprian from the ground. As they turn to leave, dragging my wounded brother away, the darkness seems to follow in their wake, swallowing the remaining traces of light.

Trembling and disoriented, I watch the scene unfold before me, my heart heavy with conflicting emotions.

I should save him. He's my brother!

But I don't move. I can't.

As my former prisoners and my brother vanish into the depths of the encroaching darkness, a haunting silence settles over the clearing, leaving only the lingering echoes of my brothers' shattered cries.

Left alone in the chilling aftermath, I stand there, still shielding my face with one trembling arm. I survey the desolate battlefield, my heart heavy with grief and confusion. Having accomplished its sinister purpose, the darkness slowly dissipates, revealing the devastation before me.

THIRTY-FIVE

Devana

I couldn't do it.

I couldn't kill the Queen, knowing that Aemilius might not walk away from the duel between the soldier and him.

My choices were simple—do the only thing you have been training for your entire life. Yet, I failed.

But my arrow was meant to miss all his vital organs and only impair him from using the sword. What happened after wasn't my doing. At least, I don't think so.

Sylvora was standing right next to Monsteress when I saw her before the battle began. But in the heat of the moment, I forgot to look for the three creatures. Maybe they were in the background when I aimed. Or perhaps Monsteress sent them because she's working with Aemilius together if he decided to save her. It had to be a payback.

My mouth goes dry as I watch Aemilius look after the soldier, his feet glued to the ground. Why isn't he doing anything? Why isn't he trying to save him?

But I have little time to think about it because my body floods with anger that isn't mine. The heat surging through my veins is all-consuming and endless, and when my eyes fall on Monsteress, I know she's just feet away from getting ripped apart.

I need an arrow. I need it *now.*

Searching my body for anything I can use to join the fight, I'm startled when Erinna shifts her weight under me.

With a graceful sweep of her beak, the griffin snatches one of its magnificent feathers from its wing and grabs it with her claws. Gently holding it between her powerful talons, Erinna extends her majestic nails toward me. A look of astonishment and gratitude spreads across my face as I recognize her offering.

The last time I shot at Soulin, I used Erinna's feather. When we left Tenacoro, my father handed me two of Erinna's—one as a keepsake to remember her because taking her with us wasn't an option. And the second to increase my chance to deliver the deadly shot at the coronation. At the same time, the other was tightly pressed to my chest with a string.

I still remember inhaling the sweet scent of it when I aimed, and apparently, Erinna remembers giving it to my father, too.

I reach out, my slender hand taking hold of the feather, marveling at its beauty. The downy quill feels both weightless and resilient beneath my touch. Without hesitation, I swiftly notch the feather-arrow onto the bowstring.

A griffin's feather always hits true.

Always.

My grip tightens around the bow, my touch finding solace in the familiar embrace. Drawing back again with measured strength, my muscles regain their unwavering focus. With unshakable resolve, I steady my aim. In one fluid motion, I release the bowstring, and the feather-arrow slices through the air. It soars towards its intended target, cutting through the intensifying sunlight.

As the arrow shoots through the sky, I watch with bated breath.

It's going to work this time.

It must!

As the feathered projectile finds its mark, hitting its intended destination with unerring precision, I let out my breath, and an excruciating pain shatters my body.

THIRTY-SIX

Khaos

All I can think about is Soulin when I hear Prince Cyprian laugh as I crumble to the ground. The Nullstone shards sticking out of my skin absorb all of my magic and energy. It isn't enough to make me blackout, but it paralyzes me, leaving me vulnerable and unable to move. All he has to do is to pick up a sword and slice my throat. But he doesn't.

That's his mistake because the moment he sprints away, my muscles begin to tingle, and slowly, I regain my strength. Rushing after him, my body burns, trying to rid itself of the anti-magic rock, but I press through it.

He's only a couple hundred yards away as I chase after him, cutting everyone that looks like an Eternian out of my way with the sword I found on the ground. My magic might not be back, but I'm good at kicking ass without it. He's going to regret trailing my Soulmate. I'm going to crush his fucking bones.

Amid a battlefield clearing, more and more soldiers seem to join, even though I know that most Eternians are running back to the hills they came from. King Citeus' death spreads like wildfire through the desert, and most soldiers are smart enough to follow the hint that they lost.

But not that big dude I'm trailing. He's going straight for his brother.

I quicken my steps when Cyprian tackles his brother. Both crash to the ground, and Soulin, who's hanging over Cyrus' shoulder like an oversized tapestry, gets tossed to the ground.

I can feel her pain, and it ignites the fire in me.

He will pay for this.

Each step brings me closer, and my eyes are solely on the man leading his army right to my gate. I'm just a few feet away when darkness swallows me, followed by a noise I will never forget. The high-pitched whistle fills my ears, and instinctively, I want to use my magic to guard Soulin. Through the thick curtain of darkness, I can't see her. The only semi-sharp people in my vision are the Matrus brothers, and my lips curl into a smile when I watch the arrow find its way into Cyprian's chest.

What follows next, I'm not prepared for. Soulin's creatures burst through the dark veil and drag him away from me while his brother watches.

For a moment, I consider fighting the beasts to get to him, but when I see the darkness following them, I shake my head and decide to let them handle it. If they want him so badly, they can have him.

The air clears around me, and the sunlight returns after the creatures claim their victim. That's when I hear a second whistling noise.

I bolt forward to cover Soulin with my body. I'm still so far away, but I'll make it. I must!

My heart stops when I see that Soulin's face is already sprayed with blood, painting it almost unrecognizable. I was too slow. The blood sprinkled over her face should have been mine.

Frozen in horror, I stand there, unable to move a single muscle.

It should have been me. I should be standing right before her and not a few feet away.

Breathing heavily, I look around, and my eyes fall on the brown arrow. It's the simplest arrow that I recognize immediately. A thin shaft and only two fletchings instead of three.

Memories of the coronation night when I saved Soulin from an attacker flashback into my head. It's the same arrow that was used that night.

A scream shatters the air, and my eyes lift to the sky as something flickers in my vision, forcing my attention upwards. Without a moment's hesitation, I lunge towards a woman in free fall, instincts taking over as I reach out to catch her mid-air. She would have hit and crushed me if I hadn't done so.

I cradle her unconscious form in my arms, her raven hair cascading over my blood-stained armor. Silver freckles shine on her golden-brown face, her hair is a braided, matted mess, and she feels like a boulder unconscious.

Where did she come from?

I look up and watch as a giant winged creature lands before us. Its beak opens, and the screech reverberating out of it pierces my eardrums. I drop the woman to cover my ears and step back before its long talons swiping in my direction can dig into me.

"You can have her," I yell, raising my hands to signal the beast that I won't harm her.

I don't give two shits about that woman. All I want is to reach Soulin's body and enclose her in my arms.

Hissing, the creature steps forward to sniff on the woman, and I take that moment to rush past it. My legs and heart stop when I see Soulin on the ground, covered in blood.

Her lifeless eyes are directed at me, and when I see the smile forming on her lips, my heart pounds again.

That's when I notice the arrow isn't embedded in her flesh.

She's alive—but something changed.

Her usually bright green eyes have darkened, and her silver freckles are obscured by sprinkles of blood.

Slowly, she pushes herself off the ground, and her eyes wander to a man lying before her.

It feels like a déjà-vu. Just a few minutes ago—or maybe it was already hours—King Citeus lay sprawled out before her, unmoving and with a hole in his head.

Now, an unknown man covers the ground, an arrow sticking out of his shoulder blade.

My eyes wander over the man, and bile rises up my throat when I recognize the red hair.

It's my deceased King.

"He's dead," Soulin says, her smile widening.

I open my mouth and close it again.

Of course, he's dead. Or at least that's what everyone believes he is.

When I saw him in Terminus, I thought being so close to death played tricks on me. King Obsidian was also there.

My head spins, thinking about what must have unfolded while I tried to reach Soulin, and I don't have enough imagination to color the picture in. How is he here—again? And who shot him?

I need to know because that arrow is the answer to a question I've been asking myself for too long.

If I find the owner, I find the person who tried to end Soulin's reign before it even began.

The battlefield is strewn with the aftermath of a fierce and brutal conflict. Smoke lingers in the air, and the ground is stained with blood.

A worn-out soldier, his armor dented and dirtied, approaches Soulin, bowing respectfully. Breathing heavily, he straightens up. "Your Majesty, the battle is won. The enemy has been defeated."

Soulin's face remains impassive, her eyes reflecting the weight of the loss and suffering. "Behead them and burn them all. Let the flames bear witness to the cost of war."

The Soldier looks taken aback by her order, the gravity of it settling heavily on his shoulders. "Your Majesty, are you certain?"

Soulin looks at him, and he shivers under her icy stare. "Yes. Let it be a stark reminder to anyone who dares threaten my kingdom."

As the Soldier departs to carry out her cruel command, she turns her attention to me, grief-stricken but resolute. Her eyes find mine, and with a determined expression, she strides towards me, my hand tightly gripping the hilt of my sword. She takes my other hand in hers and firmly pulls me to her. "My love, it is time to go back to our kingdom."

What the fuck is going on?

Swiftly, my eyes scan the rest of her body. She's injured. Gaping wounds with Nullstone stick out of her like thorns, and her face is stained with blood. There has to be something wrong with her I can't see because otherwise, she wouldn't grab me by the hand and use the words *our kingdom.*

The way she said *our kingdom,* it sounded like it's ours—ours alone. Like she's *the* Queen and I'm *the* King.

Until now, I haven't even thought about what it would mean to take my place by her side.

Of course, Crymzon is my kingdom. I was born and raised here, pledged my life to the Crymzon Crown, and would do anything for the sovereign.

But that's not what's clouding my mind. It's the way she looks at me, her eyes filled with emptiness and longing all at once. Where her soul used to spark a light in her irises is now dimmed. But that tiny flicker used to be enough to make me believe I could bring the Soulin I fell in love with back.

What do I do now that it's extinguished? And the better question is, what made the fire burn out in her? Seeing her father again?

I mean, I can't believe he's real.

"Did you hear me?"

I look up at her, and my stomach clenches. "I'm sorry."

"There's something I need to show you," Soulin says, pulling me by the hand into the direction of the Crymzon Wall.

I should be relieved that she's finally touching me. It's her who grabbed my hand and holds onto it like I'm her lifeline. There's nothing more I want than to keep her safe and feel her skin on mine.

It's the look in her eyes that makes me shiver.

"I can't. I'm needed here," I say, trying to wiggle my hand out of hers.

Soulin realizes my attempt to escape and strengthens her grip. "You're not a soldier anymore. Let them do the dirty work."

My words get stuck in my throat.

I am a soldier. Even after she stripped me of my title, I couldn't help but follow my instinct of protecting my kingdom and my Queen. Now, even more than ever, because I've seen that the dead aren't really dead. Of course, I knew that because I already saved Soulin from her undead brother. But what if he came back again like his father?

Repeating her words in my mind, I hear the silent insult. Soulin thinks I'm too good for the dirty work now that I'm *her* equal. But without surrounding herself with soldiers, Soulin would have died at her coronation; she would have died during this battle.

"You can't take that from me," I say, pulling my hand away. "I might be your Soulmate, but I'm loyal to my kingdom first. Whatever needs to be done, I won't shy away from it."

Soulin narrows her eyes and circles the hand I escaped. "Fine. But if you're not inside the palace by mid-sun, I will come to collect you."

My heart hammers in my chest when I watch Soulin step over dead bodies and stroll through pools of blood to get to the gate.

I want to follow her. Wherever she goes, I want to go.

Yet I'm frozen in place.

If I walk away now, I might never figure out who used the arrow. Without the answer, I will never find out who tried to kill a child on her coronation day and who is responsible for me losing all my magic to defend the attack.

Fourteen years. I spent fourteen fucking years without magic because of that arrow!

My eyes roam over the massacre enclosing me. As far as my eyes can see, I gape at the carnage King Citeus brought to Escela until my gaze rests on the arrow sticking out of the former king's back.

It might not look like much, but as a trained soldier, I see the precision in the shot. The archer knew what he was doing. It's difficult to locate the heart through the shoulder. Only experienced archers have the sense to find the organs inside the body with such accuracy.

How was an arrow able to kill a man who was already dead?

A screeching noise rips me away from the brown fletchings of the arrow, and my eyes land on the griffin lying beside the unconscious woman I snatched out of the air.

My eyes dart back and forth between the arrow and the creature.

No. It can't be a coincidence that the griffin's feathers look identical to the fletchings.

I take a step closer, and the beast raises its head, its beak jumping open to unleash another screeching sound.

"I won't hurt you," I say, lifting my arms into the air after dropping the sword. "I'm just admiring your beautiful feathers."

"Step away from my griffin," the woman says, moving into a sitting position. "One step closer, and you'll regret it."

I noticed her freckles before. Besides Soulin, I know no one with silver freckles covering their skin, and that fact makes her even more interesting.

Something about her feels off. Maybe it's because her creature's feathers match the weapon or because even though she looks nothing like Soulin, something reminds me of her. Is it the freckles? Or the coldness in her voice?

I'm not sure what it is, but I will get to the bottom of it.

THIRTY-SEVEN

QUEEN SOULIN

"Magic doesn't touch it," the healer says, her skillful hands holding delicate tools, her eyes reflecting concern and determination. "Just a few more."

The atmosphere hangs heavy in my chamber as the healer pulls out shard by shard. My legs shiver as she digs out another one. I pull away and bite into my arm to ease the burning sensation.

"Your Majesty," the healer says softly, her eyes laced with empathy, "I know this is difficult, but we must remove these rock shards to restore your magic."

I nod, clenching my fists to endure the pain. The shards have lodged deep into my skin, causing immense discomfort and disabling my once-potent magic. As the healer approaches, I brace myself for the painful process to continue.

The room falls silent save for the occasional soft gasp I let out as each shard is extracted. The healer works diligently, mindful of every movement. "Breathe, Your Majesty," she reminds me.

My magic has always been a double-edged sword, capable of great power yet a burden to bear. It allows me to suppress my emotions, safeguarding my kingdom from the vulnerability that comes with it. Now, deprived of this ability, I feel exposed again, my feelings threatening to resurface like an unleashed storm.

But I know what this can lead to. I know how it feels not to have any magic or have so much that I explode.

As the healer's efforts continue, my façade cracks, my stoic demeanor giving way to emotions long suppressed. Tears well up in my eyes, and my grip on the chair tightens as pain mixes with the emotional burden I have carried for so long.

Why did Khaos reject me? I thought he would be thrilled to have me lead the way, to have me open up to him.

Now that my father is dead again, nothing stops me from finally accepting the Connection that was written in the stars. Yet, he looked terrified when I tried to pull him back to the Crymzon Palace. It's like he feared me.

But that can't be.

"Please, hurry," I whisper, my voice choking with anguish.

The healer nods, her hands never wavering, showing both skill and compassion in equal measure. "I'm doing my best, Your Majesty. I'll make you feel better soon."

As the last shard is removed, my body slumps slightly as relief and exhaustion overwhelm me. The healer carefully cleans and dresses my wounds, then offers a soothing salve to ease the pain for later use.

"Your magic may take some time to return fully," she explains, "but with some rest and good care, you'll recover."

I shake my head weakly, my eyes still glistening with unshed tears. "I don't have time," I croak, pressing my hand to the wound on my neck.

I realized that suppressing my emotions hasn't strengthened me; it only prolonged my pain. At that moment, vulnerability feels liberating, and I allow myself to express my gratitude to the healer.

"Thank you," I say, my voice soft and sincere. "You have my deepest appreciation for your skill and understanding."

The healer smiles gently, bowing respectfully. "It was my duty, Your Majesty. I'm glad I could be of service."

"If any of this ever leaves this room, I will hang you," I add to ensure that this doesn't become the next gossip spreading through the kingdom.

She nods, but her smile doesn't falter, as if she knows about my empty threat. "There's one more thing, my Queen," she says as she stalls at the door. "I was informed that the prisoners have been free during the attack."

Slowly, I look at her. "And?"

"I thought you would like to know," she answers in a hushed voice. "Also, it wasn't Eternities' doing. Starstrand and Tenacoro were also involved."

Interesting.

"There's a reason I kept them outside my Wall. If they were important, they wouldn't rot in prison," I say, not taking the bait.

Even though I want to ask more questions, I can't sound interested. I can't draw any attention to the most crucial place in Crymzon.

If Queen Synadena and Caecilia think it's best to rescue those poor souls, they can have them. Even after I saved them from Keres' soldiers—who attacked their village in the first place—they still showed aggressive behavior towards my people, and that's how they ended up in those cells.

Most of the 'prisoners' I took who behaved accordingly to keep my kingdom safe are now in the tunnels below Crymzon in safety with my Crymzonians.

Someday, I will give them the choice to leave, but right now, every fallen soul is just expanding Otyx's playground to do with their dead bodies as he pleases.

I can't support that.

As the healer leaves the chamber, I remain seated, taking a moment to collect myself. Realizing that I can no longer rely solely on my magic to shield my emotions has brought a newfound understanding of my strength. Facing my feelings, no matter how difficult, is crucial to make the Connection with Khaos work, and I need to feel more than rage when I face Otyx again.

A tear rolls over my cheek, and I lick it away before it can slip off my face.

Is this what sadness feels like? Does it always require such a strong physical toll?

Another tear escapes my eye, and I allow myself to cry, releasing the pent-up emotions that have burdened me for far too long. As the tears fall, I feel a sense of relief wash over me, knowing that in my vulnerability lies true power—the power to heal, grow, and lead my kingdom with a renewed force to stop the God of the Underworld from messing with me.

I stare at the shards lying before me. They're unlike any ordinary stones; they possess an otherworldly appearance that seem to trap light within their depths. Each fragment is jagged and sharp, a stark contrast to the elegance of my surroundings.

As I gaze at the broken stone, my thoughts swirl back to the Lady of Fate's words.

But beware, dearest Queen. For these stones are both a gift and a burden. There are so many more powerful gems you don't even know of. They hold the power to heal and to harm, to empower and to ensnare. It is the path of the wise to wield them with care and respect.

You're about to find out how much damage they can do.

She knew. She fucking knew King Citeus would attack me with those shards.

These innocent pieces of rock hold a malevolent power capable of robbing me of my magic and bringing out my emotions, two pillars that have supported me throughout my reign. The revelation of their existence has left me feeling vulnerable and exposed.

I reach out and gingerly pick up one shard, feeling an unnatural coldness seeping into my fingertips. Its surface is smooth to the touch, but beneath the surface lies an intangible aura of suppression. It's as if the stone itself holds a dark consciousness, seeking to quell any source of mystical energy it encounters.

In my mind, I can almost hear the whispers of ancient tales warning of the stone's power.

My thoughts shift to the battlefield when my magic faltered, leaving me bewildered and useless. King Citeus' attack with those shards took me by surprise, and the repercussions were profound. My magical abilities allowed me to lead my kingdom with a sense of control and detachment for years. But now, without that barrier, I feel raw.

As I hold the fragment, I feel its malice, unyielding force that diminished my magic. This stone may disrupt my control but hasn't robbed me of my core virtues.

Rising from my chair, I set the shard down and glance at it.

Asking the Lady of Fate for any information regarding this gem will be another riddle-heavy conversation I'm not ready to have. Even if she gives me the answer, it won't be easy to put all the pieces together. So far, she has always been right without giving it away.

That alone leaves one place I can go to seek the answer: the Librascendia.

But even if I can open the forbidden library my father sealed off just before his unfortunate death, I'm unsure where to look.

As the Princess, I was never allowed inside the library filled with forbidden grimoires, arcane artifacts, and timeless scrolls, to name a few. I'm not even supposed to know about it, but luckily, my father grew careless with his trustees when he thought I was already in my chamber.

If I can break the seal, I'm confident I will find the answer to what this stone is called and everything that comes with it. Because what's a better place to hide a secret than a forbidden library?

THIRTY-EIGHT

DEVANA

Amidst the blue-hued clouds, my mind dances between lucidity and the haziness of memories. My heart pounds as fragmented images flood my consciousness. The wind's embrace. The rhythmic beating of wings. The gentle touch of my loyal griffin's feathers against my skin. And a sudden jolt, a jarring impact of pain that shook me to my core.

I recall slipping into unconsciousness, my body losing its grip on Erinna's back. Time suspended as I fell through the sky, a heavenly dance of descent. The world whirled around me, a kaleidoscope of colors and shapes before darkness enveloped me completely.

As I stir, my eyes flutter open to a cacophony of sounds. Erinna stands nearby, her massive wings spread wide, screeching in distress. Her eyes are filled with concern.

Somehow, she saved me. Not only did she show up when I needed her the most, but she also stopped my fall and brought me back to solid ground.

Pain pulses through my body as I try to move, my muscles protesting against the effort.

My gaze turns to the soldier approaching me, his figure silhouetted against the backdrop of the crimson sun dipping toward the horizon. Recognition strikes me like a lightning bolt as I squint to see clearer. It's him—the soldier who stood beside Monsteress on the day of her coronation, now aged and weathered by time. Khaos.

Long brown hair cascades down to his shoulders, flowing like a river of chocolate silk, starkly contrasting with his youth's short, tousled locks.

His brown eyes, once filled with the innocence of adolescence, now hold the weight of countless memories. They sparkle with an inner fire, revealing the change that must have happened after I saw him last.

As the man turns, the sun's rays caress his muscular frame, sculpted through years of sweat, training, and maybe a touch of magic. Once slender and unassuming, broad shoulders now bear the mark of a man who has honed his body through discipline and effort.

Yet, the scar on his left cheek captivates me. It's a thin line etched into his skin like a warrior's badge of honor. A beard he didn't have back then covers it partially. Or did he always have it and I didn't notice?

The last time I saw him, he was a teenage boy beaming with youthful exuberance, his short hair ruffled by the wind and his eyes filled with dreams of the future.

Fear and confusion intertwine within me as I wonder how Khaos can be here so close to me. Have I traversed into the Crymzon territory during my unconsciousness? It seems plausible, yet the memories feel tangible and unrefined.

Am I a prisoner?

As Khaos draws closer, I notice a sense of hesitance in his movements. He carries himself with the weight of experience, wariness etched into the lines on his face. My mind struggles to reconcile the youthful soldier from the past with this seasoned veteran before me.

As handsome as he is, he reminds me of Aemilius, and my stomach turns.

I need to find him.

"Are you alright?" he asks, his voice gruff but tinged with a hint of familiarity. "You took quite a fall, but you're lucky I caught you. Your beast is quite possessive of you."

Caught me? He's the one that saved me from plunging to my death?

I wince as pain shoots through my limbs, my memory slowly returning in fragmented bursts. "I... I'm fine," I say, my voice weak and trembling.

I can't tell him I've seen him before. Hopefully, my face doesn't give me away because if he finds out I'm the one who shot the arrow that night, I'm as good as dead.

"Where is she?" I ask, biting my lip to restrain myself from crying out as I move my legs again.

A flicker of surprise crosses the Khaos' face, quickly replaced by a reassuring smile. "She's alright. But you should rest now. We'll get you back to the palace, and a healer will tend to your injuries."

That's it.

There's my invitation into Crymzon. I must go because if Queen Synadena couldn't find my father in prison and free him, he's still in Monsteress' kingdom.

If he hasn't figured out by now who I am, it should be safe to go with him, right?

With his help, I rise unsteadily to my feet, my body protesting every movement. I lean on his arm for support, still grappling with the surreal nature of my situation. How has time played such a trick on me, pulling me into this moment where the past and present collide?

Erinna snarls beside me. I can feel that she disapproves of my decision, and if I had spent more time with her, I might have been able to interpret her behavior and sounds. But for now, I need to rely on my gut instinct, and every fiber in my body tells me to enter Crymzon.

As we make our way towards the palace, I can't help but feel a connection with Khaos. Perhaps fate has woven our lives together in ways I can't yet comprehend. I mean, how else can you explain crossing paths twice in our lifetime without even trying?

"Your beast's feathers are beautiful," he says as we reach the gate, and I break out in a cold sweat.

They are as beautiful as they are deadly. But I can't say that.

"Do you have more of those creatures in Tenacoro?"

I don't have to ask him how he knows I'm from Tenacoro. If my complexion hasn't given it away, having a Glimmarum totally did the job.

It would not be very smart to answer his question correctly. Apparently, he isn't aware that every animal living in Tenacoro blends in with the green backdrop. That's another reason my father loved Erinna so much.

Her brown colors make her look like the kingdom drained her vibrant emerald coloring that every other animal has. He always said that Erinna is unique, just like me.

"She's a griffin. And yes, they are everywhere," I lie, examining my surroundings to find an escape route.

"Why did you aim for the...King?" he asks, tightening his grip around me.

I could tell so many lies and continue the cat-and-mouse game I started years ago.

But I'm tired of it.

If killing the biggest threat to the Queen doesn't show I tried to help her, I don't know what will.

"Because if she dies, so will I," I say, verbalizing for the first time what I've been breaking my head over since Monsteress got hit by the first shard.

There's no guarantee I'm right. Maybe I will be just fine if Monsteress passes away. But it's a theory I don't want to test.

The shards alone convinced me I had to keep her safe. I never want to feel that kind of pain again.

He digs his heels into the soil, and we halt. "What do you mean, you will die if she dies?" His stare is blistering as his eyes wander over my face. Even without saying her name, he knows whom I'm referring to.

Rashly, I whip the back of my hand over my nose and cheeks, and when I inspect it, my stomach flips. He must be seeing what my father taught me to hide from a young age. The silver freckles that mark my face are out in the open for everyone to see. That alone should be enough for him to make the connection between Monsteress and me.

"I'm unsure how and why, but when she got hit by the shards, I could feel it. It's like her pain was mine."

Saying it out loud to someone feels so freeing. I could have gone with more lies, and maybe he would have believed me. But I need him to know that he might hurt his Queen if he hurts me. It also helps me lead him astray from more questions about Erinna.

He can't find out it was me.

"Did you tell anyone about this?" he asks, wrapping his arm around my shoulder to pull me against his chest to cover as much of my body as possible.

That's a reaction I didn't see coming, but of course, he's trying to shield me from harm. His response also shows me he believes me without a doubt.

"My father," I answer.

"Where is he?"

"I believe he's somewhere inside the Crymzon Palace. When the Crymzon Army raided our village, he was taken."

It's best to leave the part out that I was a prisoner, too. I don't know how to explain to him I managed to free myself.

"We need to get you to a healer and then find him," he says urgently.

My heart jumps into my throat.

Did I hear him correctly?

Is he really going to help me find my father?

Trying not to mess everything up, I shut my mouth and let him lead me through the empty streets and the courtyard into the palace.

I'm one step closer to finding my father and maybe even Aemilius. My stomach turns thinking about him carrying Monsteress. I've seen what Crymzon Magic can do. Therefore, I hold on to the belief that she forced him to switch sides because deep down, I don't know how I will react if I find out that he has been doing it with free will.

THIRTY-NINE

Cyrus

What am I supposed to do now?

I clearly can't go back after what I've done. Not only did I shoot my father, but I also watched as the souls I trapped in the Soulkeeper carried away my brother.

There was a chance I could command them to leave him alone. After all, I forced them into the Soulkeeper and established a *relationship* with them. It wasn't a healthy one, but better than being alone.

It was the right thing to try to save him. He's my brother, for Odione's sake! So why didn't I?

I need to go to Eternitie and tell my sister what happened. She will understand. She must.

There's no better Queen than Catalina after all the destruction our father and brother have brought to Escela.

As I stand in the middle of the chaos of the battlefield, my heart is heavy with conflicting emotions. The scent of death hangs heavily in the air as I survey the aftermath of the clash. The sun is still high in the sky, casting harsh shadows under the lifeless bodies scattered around me, a haunting testament to the violence that unfolded.

All of this could have been prevented. If my father had made better choices, he would still be here—and so would my brother.

They were the source of the torment and oppression of so many people, now lying motionless on the blood-stained ground. A mix of relief and sorrow washes over me. Relief because their demise means an end to their reign of terror. And sorrow because no matter how far we drifted apart, they were my family. No matter how painful, the bond of blood isn't easily severed. With their death, the throne passed to my sister, someone I love dearly. Yet, she might have been groomed to rule by our father's ruthless ways.

What if she has changed since I fled Eternitie? What if our father or brother, or maybe even both, got into her head?

No. I must believe she's still the same warm-hearted person I grew up with.

My inner turmoil deepens when I realize that in aiding Monsteress to victory, I played a role in toppling the oppressive regime of my bloodline.

Monsteress, whom I've come to tolerate, now holds the fate of my kingdom in her hands. My involuntary—and now voluntarily—allegiance to her is a testament to the complex moral choices I made before and during the battle, choices that will haunt me for the rest of my life.

As the soldiers tend to the bodies of the fallen, chopping their heads off and piling them up, I grapple with the uncertainty of my future. Should I return to my homeland despite the danger my sister might pose? Or should I seek refuge in Starstrand, where Liza is waiting for me?

It would offer me protection and a fresh start. But first, I need to face Monsteress again and beg her to release the Lady of Fate and Devana's father.

Devana.

How have I not thought of her before now?

Frantically, I scan the human piles for her. Devana doesn't shy away from a fight. If she marched with the Brass Army into the battle, she'd either be on the run right now after the war was lost or somewhere here.

Lost in thought after I can't find any trace of her, I approach a solitary dead tree on the outskirts of the battlefield. It stands tall and unwavering, its branches reaching out as if offering guidance. As I lean against its trunk, I close my eyes and let the winds of fate blow over me.

My heart sways between the love for my sister and the desire for a better future in a new kingdom, far away from all the bloodshed and violence.

Images of my childhood flash before me, memories of laughter and hugs mixed with images of cruelty and loneliness. I know I can never be free if I return to Eternitie, but leaving means escaping my past and embracing a new, uncertain future.

As the sun descends, its warm light illuminating the battlefield, a decision takes shape in my mind.

I know what I have to do.

To honor my sister's image and ensure a brighter future for my people, I have to follow my conscience and remain dead to Eternitie.

With a bit of luck, maybe none of the returning Eternians have seen me. And even if they did, who would believe them that the deceased Prince of Eternitie, who had the most prominent funeral to date because my father needed to make a statement, is still alive?

I know I wouldn't.

The smell of burned flesh and hair stings my nostrils as I wander to the Crymzon Gate.

How many times do I have to return to this godforsaken place to be finally rid of it? At this point, Monsteress should hand me a Crymzon armor to blend in, and allow me to come and go as I please.

No. This will be my last venture to Crymzon. Monsteress agreed to let the Lady of Fate and Wayne go. Once I have them, there's no reason for me to come close to this overheated kingdom ever again.

FORTY

Khaos

If Soulin finds out I'm using a healer to treat a stranger, she will probably lose her mind. But there's also the possibility that she's already aware of who this woman is and what she means to her. It wouldn't be the first secret she's kept from me.

I could have healed her, but those damn shards still prevent me from ciphering my magic. And to make matters worse, the chest wound I earned on the battlefield in Terminus is burning hot to the touch and bothering me.

Healers rush to our aid, tending to our wounds. My gaze never leaves the woman, her beauty striking me, even in her sorry state.

Who is she, and why did she risk her life to help Soulin?

I guess the answer is clear: she doesn't want to die. Fighting in a battle is one thing, surviving a totally different one. There are not a lot of female soldiers without magic. At least, that's what I noticed marching through the Brass Army.

As we rest in my chamber, I find myself intrigued and perplexed by the woman's connection to Soulin.

How is it possible that they share a Connection? From the sounds of it, it runs even deeper than our Soulmate Connection. If one of us dies, the other can still reach an old age. The wound of the loss might never fade, but it's not a death sentence.

So how is it possible that a stranger I've never seen before is connected to her?

Whispers of a Connection between three people have circulated among the soldiers, but the truth has remained elusive until now.

But there's also a chance that she's lying. What if I brought a threat into the palace?

Summoning my strength after the healer removes the last shard, I approach her as the other healer still tends to her wounds on my bed.

However, I can't reach her because the griffin, loyal and fiercely protective, barres my path with an intimidating glare, its large wings flaring as it pants. I can sense the griffin's intent clearly without being an animal whisperer: either leave her alone or face my wrath.

I need her to talk.

Undeterred, I speak softly, "I mean no harm to her. I only seek answers."

The griffin regards me warily but seems to acknowledge my sincerity. It steps back slightly, allowing me to enter the small space between it and the bed. The woman watches the healer as he uses his magic to restore her.

How is she so fucking calm?

If I were connected to the most hated person in the land as a person without magic, I would shit my pants.

Well, maybe not literally, but I wouldn't just lay there and stare at a healer.

As he turns his back to me to leave the room, I whisper my questions to the woman, ensuring no one else can hear me. "Who are you? Why did you stay away for so long? And what ties you to my Queen?"

Moments pass, and the woman stirs. Her eyes flutter shut and open, revealing a vibrant shade of amber that seems to suck me in.

"I'm Devana," she whispers, her voice melodic as she matches my tone. "I came here to search for my father. That's when I noticed I could feel the Queen's pain. I saw her getting hit by the shards, and it felt like they're wounding me too."

Slowly, I nod my head.

There are no similarities between Soulin and Devana, save the silver freckles covering their faces.

I'm readying myself to ask my next question when she speaks up first. "You're nothing like I imagined a Crymzon Soldier to be."

I raise my eyebrows. "Because we're known for our brutality?"

"Because no one with a soft heart like yours should stand beside a monster."

My gut wrenches at her insult. First, she called Soulin a monster, and second, she thinks I'm a fool.

"There's so much more to her than the name she was given."

I should have kept my mouth shut, but the calm way she gave me that statement rubbed me wrong.

"Don't defend her," she says, stretching out her legs before throwing them over the edge of the bed.

"I'm able to defend her because I'm the only one who truly knows her," I growl back at her.

The creature behind me makes a scratching noise, reminding me we're not alone.

"I'm also connected to her," I say, trying to ease the tension before her beast jumps me. "It's different from yours, but I can feel her pain. But I still can't quite understand what binds you two together. My connection to her is simple. But yours? I don't know what to make of it."

"Do you think I chose this? Do you really think I want to be connected to *her*?" Devana asks, furious. "All I want is to have my father back and leave this kingdom."

"I agreed to find your father, but I can't let you go until I can back up your story."

Her face drops. "But I can't stay here."

"You don't have another choice. Until I'm certain my Queen isn't in danger, you will remain here. I promise I will keep you safe."

She throws her hands in the air. "No one is safe in Crymzon. Your Queen has showed repeatedly that her subjects mean nothing to her. I mean, the palace doesn't even have any guards patrolling the corridors. I haven't seen a single soul since we got into the kingdom. Where is everyone?"

"That's none of your concern," I answer, letting her test her feet. She walks to the window, first shaky, then gaining steadiness with each step. "Please remember how you ended up connecting to Queen Soulin."

"It's a long story," she says, looking out the window.

"You're in luck. I have all the time in the world."

Devana sights and tells her story, starting when she was a newborn. I listen intently, absorbing her words like a thirsty man in the desert, finding an oasis. Her story unfolds, revealing that her mother abandoned her, and her father took her away from their kingdom to protect her. She details how he trained her in the Confines to defend herself and taught her how to live her life with the constant pain she experiences. She doesn't shy away from telling me that her Connection to Soulin might be why she has experienced muscle soreness and weakness, but she's unsure.

A tear rolls down her cheek when she tells me about her Glimmarum—the griffin currently breathing down my neck.

As the conversation deepens, I feel profound trust and admiration for Devana. Her sacrifice and dedication to her father resonates deeply with me, and so does her hard work to strengthen her body and mind.

"I've told no one my story," she says, coming to an end.

"So why tell me?"

"Because if I ever want to see my father again, I must trust you. You're not like the Crymzon Queen. I still don't know why you stayed here, knowing what she's done and still doing."

The naïve trust she puts in me breaks my heart. If she had trusted any other Crymzonian with her background, I don't know if she would be safe now. It also shows me she's easy to persuade, making it more complex.

"No one else can know about this. You hear me? Promise me to keep it to yourself until I figure out what to do with you."

She turns to face me. "I've fought my entire life. Against the pain, the rejection, and fate working against me. I'm exhausted."

So am I, but I don't voice it.

"Just stay here. Do *not* leave the room!"

"Where are you going?"

I walk to the door and grab the handle. "I will find your father. In the meantime, I need you to stay put. If anyone finds out I brought an Ordinary into the palace, we're both in deep shit."

"His name is Wayne," she says quickly just before I leave the room and close it carefully behind me.

My magic still hasn't returned; otherwise, I would seal the door behind me to assure her safety—and mine.

Trusting her to stick to her word is unwise, but I have no choice.

FORTY-ONE

Queen Soulin

As I stand before the ancient stone door in the palace's heart, I feel a strange and powerful energy emanating from within. For the last hours, my magic has been gone because of the shards, leaving me feeling disconnected from the essence of my being.

After having more magic than any other living being, and being stripped of it again, is cruel. But now, something is changing. The spark of magic within me begins to flicker and glow, slowly rekindling like a dormant flame awakening from a long slumber.

Thank Lunra for extracting the shards worked. I was getting worried that I would never feel this buzzing sensation in my veins again.

With a deep breath, I focus my thoughts, trying to remember anything that can help me open this door. As I reach out my hand towards the stone slab, a glimmering aura envelops my fingers, tracing complex patterns in the air. The door trembles under the touch of my magic. Ancient runes carved upon its surface sparkle to life.

With a whisper, I call upon the memories of my ancestors—avoiding my father's reflections at all costs—and draw upon the knowledge passed down through generations. The door responds to my call, gradually creaking open as if welcoming my presence. Beyond it lies Librascendia, the forbidden library my father sealed off, hidden from the world for decades.

When I step inside, a wave of ancient wisdom washes over me. The room is vast, shelves upon shelves stretching far into the distance, filled with books and artifacts of long-forgotten lore. The air is thick with the scent of dust and magic, and I know I'm about to enter a room few have ever witnessed.

Moving deeper into the library, my magical senses heighten, and I feel the enchantments' pulse within the room. Some books glow with gentle luminescence, whispering secrets of forgotten spells, while others hum with a power waiting to be harnessed.

My fingers trail the dusty spines, drawn to a particularly ancient tome with red letters. As I continue my exploration, I encounter magical artifacts I've only heard of in legends—enchanted amulets, crystal orbs, and potions of different hues.

Suddenly, a peculiar movement catches my eye. A sinuous black liquid snakes toward me, seemingly drawn to my magic. Before my eyes, the mysterious liquid transforms into a solid form, merging into the shape of a book.

Transfixed, I reach out to grasp the book, and as my fingers touch the cool surface, a surge of emotions washes over me. It floats towards me. The pages flip on their own, revealing obsolete texts and arcane symbols that dance in the air.

I know I should be more careful. I've heard the rumors that knowledge comes with a price in this enchanted library. Those who dare to seek its wisdom must navigate through mazes of enchantments, wards, and riddles. Its alluring and perilous secrets beckon to those who crave forbidden knowledge and are willing to face the consequences of their curiosity.

Am I really ready for this?

Thinking of my mother, her fingertip so close to mine, and the smile my father wore when he took her from me again brings the rage simmering in me to glow again. Otyx took it too far. He's used my entire family against me, from my brother to my father and mother.

Plus, I'm not just doing this for my family. I'm doing this to keep my kingdom safe.

Carefully, I flip the book's pages. It contains forgotten histories of the Gods and Crymzon, secrets long guarded by my ancestors, and untold tales of magic lost to time.

The information of centuries zooming through my brain is too much to bear. But when I try to lift my fingers off the cover, black liquid seeps out of its pores, enclosing my hand.

Fear grips me as my palm fuses with the book, and before I can let out a scream, my surroundings blur and vanish.

No. No. No!

In my panicked state, magic pulsates out of me, but even that isn't enough to stop what is happening.

I should have stayed out of Librascendia. I knew the risks and chose to ignore them. Look where it led me.

I'm back on the battlefield, facing the once formidable circular stonewall around Crymzon that has long protected my land. It crumbles under the relentless assault of an unfamiliar enemy. Red armored soldiers surged forward, their sinister presence casting a foreboding shadow over the once vibrant crimson desert.

Confused and disoriented, I stand in the turmoil's heart, the ground trembling beneath my feet with each impact of battering rams against the ancient wall. The thunderous clash of swords and the anguished cries of fallen soldiers echo through the air, leaving my senses overwhelmed. It all feels unnervingly real.

But how can that be?

Eternitie didn't attack the Crymzon Wall. King Citeus made it nowhere near it.

As I scan the faces of the surrounding warriors, a sense of recognition washes over me. Their armor, decorated with symbols of a long-forgotten lineage, bears striking similarities to my ancestors' portraits that adorn the Crymzon Palace's walls. A chilling realization dawns upon me; I'm witnessing the war of my bloodline long before I was born.

My mind swirls with questions, yet there's no time for answers as I find myself amid a desperate defense against the encroaching darkness. The Crymzonians surrounding me seem ethereal, their eyes glowing with an otherworldly malevolence as they fight back dark-armored soldiers. The attackers fight with uncanny precision, as if guided by an unseen force that seeks to extinguish the light of my kingdom.

Amid the clashing of weapons and sizzling magical attacks, my eyes meet with those of a dark warrior, his gaze hauntingly familiar. Their black eyes and pale skin catapult me back to the battle in Terminus.

Those aren't any soldiers attacking Crymzon. They're Otyx's resurrected creations.

A man steps before me, facing a hoard of incoming Undead. He resembles my father, his red curly hair matted with sweat and blood.

King Quentin.

I only know him through paintings and stories passed down from generations, but his likeness to the carving in the palace is uncanny.

Despite the intensity of the battle, the connection between us transcends time. I can feel his strength and hear his worry about keeping his people safe.

As the battle rages on, the swirling darkness enclosing Crymzon seems to thicken, attempting to swallow everything in its path.

My heart races, not knowing the outcome. How have I never heard of Crymzon being attacked? The peace treaty between the kingdoms was signed a millennium ago, so why is my great-great-great-grandfather fighting?

Suddenly, the chaotic scene stills, and all eyes turn to a figure emerging from the depths of the darkness.

It's a man.

He stands tall and imposing, an enigmatic figure wrapped in an aura of darkness. He wears nothing but a skirt made of smoke that clings to his muscular frame, barely concealing his raw power. His chest and arms are etched with sinewy muscles, and each ripple veiled in a thin shroud of darkness that seems to writhe and pulse with inner energy.

His face, a haunting visage, resembles more a skull than that of a living being. Deep-set eye sockets hold orbs of smoldering crimson, burning with an intensity that pierces through the very souls of those who dare to meet his gaze. Jagged lines are etched across his cheeks, resembling ancient runes of a forgotten language.

A cloak of swirling darkness billows behind him. The inky tendrils of the cloak reach out like shadowy fingers, dancing and twisting in a mesmerizing display of power. It whispers secrets of a forgotten realm and wields the enigmatic energy of the abyss.

In a breathtaking display, wings made of smoke stretch from his back, reminiscent of a mythical creature born of darkness and chaos. His wings are majestic, appearing as though they could carry him effortlessly through the boundless expanse of the night sky. Their edges blur and flow like liquid smoke, making them seem delicate and tangible.

Though his appearance is daunting, there's an undeniable magnetism to him. He emanates an aura of strength and an indomitable will that draws me closer despite the unsettling nature of his presence.

As he moves, the ground beneath my feet trembles.

In his eyes burns agony, yet a glimmer of mortality remains, hinting at the complex soul hidden behind the cryptic façade. He's a living embodiment of darkness and strength, a being so dark that even my heart skips a beat.

Undoubtedly, I'm looking at Otyx—the God of the Underworld.

He stands before me, his presence commanding fear. In his eyes, I see the embodiment of the forces of darkness that plague my reign.

Time slows as Otyx raises his hand, an ominous force gathering around him. In that moment, I feel the weight of generations past and the hope of generations to come rest upon my shoulders.

Summoning all my courage, I lift a sword off the ground and high into the air, reflecting the flickering light of the crumbling wall. With a cry, I charge toward the God of the Underworld, defying the darkness that seeks to consume Crymzon.

The clash of our opposing forces shakes the foundation of the battlefield, and for a brief moment, I can't breathe.

As my blade collides with the God's dark energy, a blinding flash of light engulfs us. And in that blinding moment, I feel the weight of history and destiny merge into one. The darkness recedes, and the swirling vortex dissipates, leaving the desert eerily quiet.

And then, just as suddenly as I was transported back in time, I find myself in the present again.

The liquid lets go of my hand.

That's when I realize that the return of Otyx isn't a mere coincidence, but a destiny that has been waiting for me.

He has done this before.

My father's decision to seal off Librascendia was out of fear. He knew Crymzon had fallen under Otyx before, and instead of protecting his kingdom by letting me in on our history, he hid it from me.

"How can I stop him?" I ask the book, immediately feeling foolish for talking to an object.

The book shakes, threatening to fall out of my hands. Carefully, I lift the cover and almost drop it when it flaps through its pages until it stops at the last chapter—the words on its page leap to life, swirling with a brilliance that nearly blinds me. The language is unfamiliar, yet I can understand every word as if the knowledge is etched into my soul.

My eyes skip over the words until I get to a part that catches my attention.

There was an age when magic was rampant and unbridled. Ancient sorcerers created unique stones to keep such potent forces in check. But over time, the knowledge of their existence faded into obscurity until—someday—they will resurface, threatening the kingdoms' very foundations.

The Lady of Fate spoke of unique stones, and just a few hours ago, my magic was depleted by a bunch of shards.

This can't be a coincidence.

Minutes turn into hours as I immerse myself in the forbidden book. With each passing moment, the connection to the ancient wisdom solidifies. I experiment with spells that have been dormant for centuries, breathing new life into forgotten incantations and weaving them into my magic.

By the time I put the book down, I still don't have an answer to how to stop Otyx, but I have a plan.

FORTY-TWO

Cyrus

How often can I return to Crymzon and walk out of it with my head still attached to my shoulders? It seems like that's the game I'm playing.

I climb the steps to the palace entrance hall. At this point, I don't expect guards to linger around every corner. Since I was first captured, this kingdom has turned from a bustling place into a ghostly one.

"If that isn't the dead prince," a voice says from the shadows of the staircase, forcing the hair on my neck to stand.

I stop in my tracks as the soldier with the scar on his face steps into the light, a smile forming on his lips.

"You know, I wouldn't have figured it out if it wasn't for your brother. The resemblance between you two is just...haunting."

"A 'thank you for saving my Queen's life *again'* would have done the job," I answer, trying to step past him, but he blocks my way.

"Where do you think you're going?"

"I need to speak to the Queen."

"Just because you *think* you saved her doesn't give you any right to march in here, demanding an audience with her. After all, you didn't bring her to safety."

I fucking know that. I would have carried her to the palace if my brother hadn't tackled me.

"I killed my father for her," I growl as bile rises in my throat again, thinking of the hole in his head.

The soldier looks at me, his face unreadable. For a moment, we stand there until he breaks the silence. "What do you want?"

"I've come here to ask the Queen to hold up the end of her bargain. She promised me to free two of her prisoners in return for information."

"What kind of information?"

Ugh. I could mess with him. It would be too easy to make him lose his temper, but I think better of it.

"I informed her of my father's plan to attack Crymzon."

The soldier stares at me. "You almost had me," he says, a wicked grin forming on his lips. "You know what gave you away?" He pauses for a dramatic moment. "Queen Soulin doesn't make promises."

My stomach drops.

This can't be true. She agreed to let them go if I was correct.

"My apologies. I worded it wrong. She agreed to let them go, and I'm here to collect them."

"Let's say I believe you. Who is important enough for you to kill your family members? Please don't tell me you're doing this for a woman."

This round goes to him. The wound of my father's passing and my brother's disappearance is still too fresh to discuss. I'm unsure if I'll ever get over what I've done.

I also don't know how much he knows. Does he know the Queen keeps the Lady of Fate here? Is that common knowledge?

"It's a blacksmith and an old woman," I answer generically.

"Let me guess. His name is Wayne," he says, and the blood in my veins freezes. "So you're doing it for a woman, after all. I can't hand him over."

I take a step towards him. "Why?"

"I don't owe you an explanation. I will give you the old woman and never want to see your face again."

My heart flutters. "She is here for him, isn't she? Devana."

"Guards," he yells, ignoring my question, and within seconds, I hear the clicking noises of metal boots on the hard floor. "Take this man to the prison to retrieve an old woman and get him out of here before I change my mind."

"She's not there," I say, standing my ground. "I already looked."

His grin widens. "Then you're out of luck. Now go."

"I can't," I say, shifting my weight to sit on the stone floor.

"Are you fucking kidding me? You think sitting down will stop me from throwing you out of here? Have you forgotten that we have magic?"

Another point for him.

Yes, for a split second, I forgot about it. He can probably lift me into the air with a simple move of his finger and not even break out in a sweat.

"Please let me talk to the Queen," I beg, looking up at him.

"Every other Eternian out there today had more guts than you," he says, continuing his insults. "You're lucky that Queen Soulin is so generous."

I snort and almost choke on my laugh. "Oh, you're serious?" I ask when his face doesn't move. The Queen is everything but generous, but he should know that firsthand.

"What do you want us to do with him?" a soldier beside him asks, pointing at me.

"Clean him up before bringing him to the Queen. I can't have him step before her looking like this," he says, stepping away. "And yes, she's here. I can either bring you to her, or you can wait for an audience with Queen Soulin."

My heart jumps into my throat. What a cruel thing to do. I know he wants to be the one saving the Queen over and over again to demonstrate his worth. I didn't save her because I wanted to, but because I *had* to.

He knows by forcing me to choose, I will give him the answer to what I want most. I can't risk it. He will use it against me.

But I want both. I want to be reunited with Devana again. I haven't seen her since this guy raided our village and took us prisoners. My entire being longs to check on her and see if she's alright.

But I also promised to return the Lady of Fate to Liza. Her life depends on it, and so does mine if I want to start my new life in Starstrand. She has been through so much, and only her grandma can give Liza her old life back and her wings.

"Tell your Queen I'm here," I say, holding his stony gaze.

It's the right thing to do. If Devana is here to get her father back, she will be safe once he's returned to her. She doesn't need my help.

Liza does. For everything she has done for me—giving me a home, sharing her food with me, and always being there for me, no questions asked—it's my turn to repay her.

The man turns to the soldier. "Clean him up and bring him to my chamber. I will get him once it's time," he says, smiling, and every fiber in my body tells me he's enjoying this way too much.

I don't trust him as much as I can throw him, and the turned-up corners of his mouth should alarm me more than what I'm currently feeling. But I'm tired.

This is going to be my last task to start my new life. And maybe—no, I'm certain—I will find the strength to search for Devana once I have my life back in order.

FORTY-THREE

Khaos

I'm not a fucking babysitter.

Even a blind person can see what he wants. I practically felt his emotions running through his body when he asked me if Devana was close.

I wish I could say why I'm entertaining his longing, maybe because he reminded me of myself. The way I used to feel—and still feel—every time Soulin is around. The pure desire to be close to her and spend every moment of my life with her.

Or because even though I dislike him, he saved Soulin more times than I can count. Because of him, she's still here.

Thinking about their reunion, my face crunches with disgust. Lunra, have mercy. I didn't think this through. Either way, he will get his heart broken if Devana doesn't feel the same, or I will have their juices all over my chamber.

Fucking great.

But I can't change my mind now. I need to find Soulin.

It should have been the first thing once the battle was over. I should have gone with her, but I needed to learn more about that arrow.

Was it worth it to stay behind? Totally.

Not only did I find out that the coronation attacker is from Tenacoro, but I also found the only weakness Soulin has besides those shards—Devana.

Though I can feel Soulin through our Connection, I haven't reached out since I let go of her hand.

That bastard better get laid because he's probably the only one having fun any time soon. Soulin was already in a very unfamiliar state when I rejected her offer to take me to the palace. Who knows how badly she will chew my ass up when I stand before her again?

Why can't our Connection be easier?

My parents never said sharing your life with another person would be hard. They made it look like a piece of cake.

Starting in the throne room, I check every corridor and chamber for Soulin. With each door I close behind me, I'm getting more worried.

The flickering torches cast shadows on the stone walls, creating an atmosphere of uncertainty that mirrors my anxious heart. Every turn I take leads to empty chambers, each devoid of any sign of life. I call out her name, but there's no response, only the haunting silence that envelops the palace.

I shouldn't have let go of her.

As I continue, my walk turning into a jog, my mind replays scenes from the attack. The clash of swords, the thunderous sound of hooves and flying shards, and the screams of warriors fill my thoughts.

What if she never made it back? What if her wounds were deeper than I thought, and she collapsed on the way to the next healer?

The fear gnaws at me with every passing moment.

Soulin.

Soulin?

I wait for an answer through our Connection, but it's silent.

A sense of isolation overwhelms me as I realize no guards or servants are in sight. The palace feels lonely and abandoned.

Where did everyone go? Is there some dreadful event I'm unaware of?

I've noticed that fewer Crymzonians roam the palace' corridors since I left for Terminus, but this emptiness is new.

Suddenly, the distant sound of approaching footsteps reverberates through the walls. I strain to listen, hoping it might be Soulin, but the steps are heavy and uneven, accompanied by painful groans.

It has to be the wounded soldiers returning from the battlefield, bearing the burden of war's toll.

Could Soulin be with them? Could she have stayed behind to help them?

I quicken my pace, following the trail of wounded soldiers' screams until I reach the nearest window, looking over Crymzon's streets.

There, I see the agony etched on their faces, each carrying scars of bravery and sacrifice.

Yet, among the injured, there's no sign of her signature red dress.

My worry intensifies, and I feel a heavy weight in my chest as I retreat into the corridor, desperate to find her.

There's only one area I haven't checked - the stone door that has permanently been closed, mysterious, and hidden from sight.

There's no way Soulin is in there. This door hasn't opened since King Obsidian died.

But it's the last place I must check before rounding up the soldiers again to search for her.

Curiously, I approach the massive stone door, running my fingers over the rough surface.

Even if she's in there—unlikely but not impossible—how am I supposed to get it open to check? It's enchanted, a secret passage unknown to anyone but the ruler of the Crymzon Throne.

Summoning my strength because my magic still hasn't returned, I push the heavy door with all my might, and it creaks open, revealing a breathtaking sight. A vast library unfolds before me, bathed in the soft glow of sunlight.

And there, standing right before me, is Soulin, looking refreshed and serene. Her regal attire has been replaced with a simple red gown.

She turns to me, her eyes bright. I haven't seen that sparkle in years.

"I know what to do," she whispers, tears glistening in her eyes.

I rush to her side, wrapping her in a tight embrace. "I was so worried. I couldn't find you anywhere."

She caresses my cheek, offering a reassuring smile. "I needed time alone, away from the chaos of the palace and the battlefield."

"Don't do that again," I say, cupping her face to look into her glowing emerald eyes.

I was so frightened I had lost the last piece of the Soulin I grew up with when I looked into those same eyes after the battle. Honestly, I was scared to find her and confirm the suspicion I already had—she finally snapped.

"It happened before," Soulin says, her face lit up like the night sky during a meteor shower.

I shake my head. "What do you mean?"

"Otyx. I thought he was doing this all because of me. But it's not the first time he attacked Crymzon."

"How do you know that?"

"Because I've seen it."

I grab her hands and pull her closer. "Nothing you say makes sense. Has a healer checked on you?"

She pushes herself out of my embrace and stares at me. "Khaos Zedohr. How long have you known me?"

"I don't know how this has anything to do with this."

"From all the people in Crymzon, I expect you to believe me. Why would I make this up?"

"The same reason you lied to me about the prison," I say and immediately regret my words.

Shit. That's not how I wanted her to discover that I know about the tunnels.

She grabs me by the collar and pulls me inside the library before she uses her magic to slam the door behind us shut. "How did you find out?"

"That you're holding all Crymzonians underground? I went to check on the prisoners after I received a lead from an old man."

Soulin turns around and rubs her chin. "I knew it. Conrad notices more than he wants me to believe. I need to talk to him."

"Who is Conrad?"

"He used to be one of my father's trustees."

"I thought you...I mean...didn't they all—"

"Die in the throne room? That's what I thought. But somehow, he slipped through the cracks. He turned out useful. He returned from Terminus with the Painite."

"I thought you—"

She interrupts me. "It would have been me if I hadn't left him behind to search for you instead."

My mouth goes dry. I wondered how she made it to my side during the battle in Terminus. When I searched for her, she was nowhere near. Then, after I was stabbed, I could hear her voice. Far away, but she was there.

Now that I know it wasn't a coincidence that she found me, I don't have the guts to let her go into detail. Instead, my mind goes back to Devana.

"There's something we need to discuss," I say, ignoring everything she has said since I found her. "What do you know about other Connections that differ from a Soulmate Connection?"

She cocks her head. "I've never heard of any other ones besides the Soulmate Connection. Why?"

"What would you say if I told you I met a woman who claims to be connected to you?"

Her face drops as she takes a moment to respond. "The woman on the battlefield with the silver freckles," she says, deep in thought.

"You know her?"

She shakes her head. "Of course not. But I saw her when the Nullstone hit me. She acted like it was affecting her too, but I didn't see any wounds on her. And to make matters worse, those shards King Citeus used to disable our magic, apparently more stones are out there with similar wicked side effects."

"I better not ask how you know that," I say, looking past her at the books crammed into every shelf and corner. "Anyway, she's in my chamber."

Soulin's pleasant facial expression turns dark in an instant. "Your chamber?"

Gods be damned.

"It's not what it sounds like. I brought her to my chamber because I didn't know where else to hide her. And she's not alone," I add, trying to ease her mind.

"Let me guess? You paired the Tenacorian with a nice Starstrandian to have a variety to return to when I'm not around."

My face heats. "Stop it, Soulin. If you haven't figured out that you're the *only* one I want, I can't help you," I say, anger boiling inside me.

How can she be so jealous?

Jealous.

Wait a minute. Jealousy would mean that she's possessive of me.

"Then who's with her?"

"The Prince of Eternitie," I say, watching her face for any cues.

As expected, Soulin doesn't seem confused. She knew all along who he was and didn't tell me.

"Did you drag him back to my palace, too?" she asks, her lips pressed into a fine line.

"He actually came here freely. He says you agreed to hand over two prisoners."

Talking to herself, Soulin walks back and forth between the shelves before she comes to a halt.

"Tell him he can have them," she says sternly, lifting one finger. "Under one condition. He can never show his face here again. I don't want to be involved in any of the politics once it comes out that he killed his father. Rumors will be enough to make it sound like I forced his hand to save my life."

Her reasoning makes sense. "Can I ask who the old lady is?"

Soulin laughs. "I see he didn't trust you with that information. He's trying to return the Lady of Fate to Starstrand. I guess he's trying to impress his girl with this heroic gesture."

My mind spins. I didn't even know she was missing. Queen Caecilia never made it known that she was not in Starstrand. I don't have enough energy left to be surprised that Soulin somehow got her hands on her.

But why would Devana be interested in retrieving the Lady of Fate?

"You disagree. Why's that?" she asks, her eyes scanning my face.

"I got the impression that he's interested in Devana."

Disgust washes over her face. "And you think giving them your chamber to themselves is a good idea?" A laugh rumbles through her. "No. The woman you retrieved from his hut is his lover."

I bite my lip to swallow my following words.

"Say it," she says, stepping closer and running her fingers over my chest.

"I think you're wrong." My heart stops as I say the last part. Few people have disagreed with Soulin and still have their heads attached to tell the tale. But I shouldn't be so afraid to voice my opinion. Before our Soulmate Connection snapped into place, I never had a problem proving my point to her.

So, what has changed?

"Bring them to the throne room," Soulin says, a smile forming on her lips. "And if I'm right about the woman he chases, you owe me a favor."

"And if I am?"

"I'll let you live," she answers, her grin widening.

If I win—and I certainly will—I will collect the favor she knows she owes me.

"Fine," I say, returning the smile.

FORTY-FOUR

Devana

As the sun dips below the horizon, I sit nervously on the bed, my heart pounding like the beat of distant thunder. The anticipation of my father's return has kept me restless as I pace anxiously between bed and window. The walls seem to close around me, suffocating me the longer I wait, and my anxiety grows with each passing moment.

There's nothing to do in his room.

No books. No gimmicks. Nothing in this room screams that someone lives here.

Erinna follows me nervously as I stand up from the bed again to check the window for signs of life.

When I sit down after a while, something hard bangs against my leg.

I push my hand into my pocket, and my muscles stiffen when I feel the gaping hole.

The Chrono-Locator.

I completely forgot about it.

Taking off the coat I was handed before leaving Eternitie, I rip the bottom seam open, and the device bounces onto the bed.

The Chrono-Locator is as small as a pocket watch, yet it means so much to me. Pressing it against my chest, I think about the man gifting it to me. If I ever see him again, I must thank him for giving me a small piece of hope when everything seemed hopeless.

Time crawls as I fidget with the device. Over and over again, I clutch it tightly in my hand, wishing it would show more than just Eternitie.

Suddenly, a creaking sound echoes through the chamber, and the heavy door opens. My heart leaps, and a mixture of relief and anticipation fills me.

But as the door swings fully ajar, my eyes meet not the familiar face of my father but the intense gaze of the man I thought I would never see again up close–Aemilius.

Time seems to freeze as we stand there, both surprised to encounter each other in such a peculiar circumstance. A whirlwind of emotions threatens to consume me as I struggle to make sense of the situation. My mind wants to scold him for showing up at this very moment after I've seen him carrying Monsteress, but my heart rejoices at the sight of him.

When I search the room for Erinna, I catch a glimpse of her feathers outside the window before the wind carries her away.

Fucking coward.

She's supposed to be by my side at all times. Why did she leave?

"Aemilius," I stammer, my voice betraying my inner turmoil as I turn back to him.

He cringes at his name but steps into the room, closing the door behind him. "I didn't expect to find you here," he admits, his voice tinged with confusion.

"I could say the same," I reply, regaining my composure. "I'm here because...my father, he's missing."

A flicker of guilt crosses his face, and I wonder if he knows more than he lets on.

We have grown close in secret, knowing that everything we say living in the Confines could be used against us at some point.

How many times did I want to tell him how I ended up living as an Ordinary, and I couldn't because my father's safety was more important than any feelings for a man?

Now, during my desperate search for my father, I can't ignore my tumultuous feelings for him.

He's here.

He's real.

He's a piece of home I've been missing since we got dragged to Crymzon.

"I know," Aemilius says softly, stepping closer to me, his eyes skipping over the freckles I've been concealing from him. "Queen Caecilia told me about your venture to Eternitie."

How is that possible? Monsteress wouldn't have let him go freely. So how come he met the Queen of Starstrand and still fought alongside Crymzon? Something doesn't add up.

I hesitate, torn between confiding in him and keeping my emotions in check. "I saw you out there. You were helping *her*." The bite in my tone is enough to make him cringe.

"I don't know how to explain everything to you," he says, his eyes filled with sadness.

"Don't. Just don't. I'm here for my father," I answer, walking back to the bed because I might lose myself if I look at him any longer.

"I owe you the truth," he begins, following me to the bed.

"Please don't," I beg, looking into his brown eyes.

For a moment, I want to forget about my quest, about my missing father, as the warmth of his smile envelops me. Our past encounters have been fleeting, stolen moments while training or brief glances across the crowded village square. Now, fate has brought us together at the most inconvenient of times.

As he reaches out, our hands brush slightly, setting my heart into an erratic dance. The urgency of finding my father slowly intertwines with the thrill of being close to him.

"Why are you doing this to me?" I ask when my hope to ignore him fades like the dying embers of a fire.

"I don't know what you're referring to."

"Why do you show up now? Where were you when I needed you?" I ask, out of breath.

"I don't know where to start," he says, lowering his eyes. "But if I don't do this now, I will never find the courage again," he says, meeting my gaze.

He steps forward and pushes a strand of my curls behind my ear before he leans forward to press his lips gently on mine. I close my eyes as heat licks through me.

I wanted this for such a long time. So long, I can't even remember when it started.

Couldn't he have done this when our world was still perfect living in the Confines?

"I needed to do this before the illusion of Devana and Aemilius breaks," he says, taking a step back again. "Before you realize who I really am."

The warmth building in my body turns to ice. "You're scaring me. What's going on?"

"My name isn't Aemilius Vosdon," he says, studying me. "I made that name up."

"It's just a name. Who cares what name you chose?"

He swallows hard. "Because my real name is Cyrus Matrus."

The world around me crumbles.

"No," I whisper, holding on to the name he introduced himself to me.

The longer I stare at him in silence, the more I see the resemblance between him and his father.

"Please tell me that's not true," I say, tears welling in my eyes.

He lowers his head and takes another step away from me. "I'm sorry. I should have told you, but I was scared. When I arrived in the village, I didn't know whom I could trust."

"You're a Prince? *The* Prince of Eternitie?"

"The *deceased* Prince of Eternitie," he says, forcing a smile on his lips to lighten up my mood.

"How can you think this is remotely funny?" I say, bolting forward to slam my fist into his chest.

He gasps, and when I lift my hand again, he grabs it mid-air. "I hate it as much as you do."

"That's the problem. I don't hate it. I can't believe you didn't trust me enough to include me in your secret," I say, looking down. "But it makes my confession so much easier."

His eyebrows shoot up, and I blur the words out before I can change my mind. "My father trained me to assassinate Monsteress. When I was a teenager, I took a shot at her, but the man who brought me here today shielded her at the last moment." I take a deep breath. "And I'm glad he did because I just found out I'm somehow connected to her."

His eyes widen. "You're...connected to...Monsteress?"

"I know it sounds baffling, but every time she got hurt, I could feel the pain inflicted on her. It felt like her pain was mine."

He blinks a few times, his eyes darting through the room like he's trying to connect invisible dots.

"Your freckles," he says calmly, finally looking at me again.

"We were born under the same star constellation, taking our first breaths at the same time," I answer, lifting my hand to cover them.

"Don't," he says, reaching for my hand, and electricity sparks through me when our skin connects.

He pulls me into his arms and presses his body against me, tender enough for me to shift out of it if I wanted to.

But I don't back away from him. Instead, I wrap my arms around him and lean my head against his chest.

"I guess we're both not perfect," he says, his chest vibrating under his laugh.

"You...you're not repelled by it?"

"I don't think there's anything you can do to change my mind about you," he chuckles.

I lift my head to look into his eyes. On my way, my gaze stops on his lips. I've dreamed of kissing them countless nights laying in my tiny hut on the other side of the village. And now that the moment is finally here, anxiety gets the better of me.

We already kissed. So why is it so hard to do it again?

In the back of my mind, guilt nags at me. How can I think of kissing a man when my father is still missing?

Yet, with each inhale and exhale, I find myself drawn to Cyrus, unable to resist the magnetic pull that fate has thrust upon us.

"You will get him back," he says as if he can read my mind.

"How do you know?"

"Because the Queen isn't as heartless as people make her out to be. She's done cruel things, don't get me wrong, and I've seen what she's capable of when rage consumes her. But I truly believe there's more to her than we can see."

I've heard similar words before. Then, I didn't want to believe them because I didn't trust the man who spoke them.

But Cyrus?

Yes, he lied about his name. But everything else about him is pure. Having an eye for detail, his building skills, the clumsy way he holds a sword, and the depth he cares for everyone around him are just a few things I fell in love with.

If I can't trust Cyrus, no one else deserves it.

Knowing that I'm bonded to someone who isn't as ruthless as I thought she was and receiving the reassurance that I will see my father again lifts a massive weight off my shoulders.

And in that freeing moment, I step on my tippy toes and kiss him.

When our lips connect again, my core sets on fire. As he brushes his lips against mine, I can feel his eagerness with each heartbeat. He sucks my lip into his mouth, forcing me to move restlessly against him.

Out of breath, I pull away and get lost in his darkened eyes. "I've never done this before," I whisper, giving him a way out.

A chuckle reverberates through him, making me cringe. "Neither have I," he says, pushing another strand of my hair out of the way.

FORTY-FIVE

CYRUS

Please tell me I didn't just spill that I'm still a virgin.

My cheeks glow, and I laugh harder to cover up my mistake.

It's true. All of it.

I never had a romantic relationship with anyone. How could I when my brother brushed over almost every female allowed into the Brass Palace? I didn't want to double-dip what he already had.

Just thinking about it makes me recoil, and Devana is alert enough to notice it.

"Stop the bullshit. You lived with Liza in a hut, and before that, you had an entire kingdom to your feet. You want me to believe that nothing happened before we met?"

"I wish it wasn't true," I say, my body glowing at this point. "Being the Prince of Eternitie wasn't as great as you make it out to be. It's lonely. As my father's least favorite son, I didn't have the same freedom Cyprian had."

The image of him being dragged away by the souls I called my 'friends' comes back to me. They know how much I struggled to be secluded.

Why else would I build a device to force creatures to communicate with me?

Devana cocks her head, a smile tugging at the corners of her mouth. "I was just messing with you. I think it's adorable you waited for the right person."

That also doesn't seem right. I wouldn't say I waited. I was forced to wait. Did I have the urge to get the feeling of something other than my hand around my cock? For sure. But the chance never presented itself to hit that offer up.

"Relax," Devana says, trailing her finger under my chin to bring me back to her. "This is going to make this so much more special."

When I realize what she's saying, my hands and knees shake.

I want this. I want her.

But what if I'm bad at it? What if she regrets her first time because I can't get a hang of it?

She steps back, and I notice she's wearing the same uniform as my brother. I watch her unbutton her white blouse—one button at a time.

Where's that damn coat every other Eternian was wearing? Where is it? This is going too fast!

I'm about to tell her I'm not ready to take things further when she slowly opens the thin fabric, revealing her breasts.

I almost choke on how beautiful they are. So far, I've only seen pictures in drawings my brother kept in his room for unknown reasons. Even Liza made sure to cover them at all times when I tended the wounds on her back.

"Are you okay?" she asks, worry flashing over her face. "Am I doing this wrong?"

"There's nothing wrong with you," I say, filling the space between us. "Are you certain you want to do this?" I ask, my finger only inches from her sensitive, exposed skin.

"I've dreamt of this moment so many times," she says, her boldness igniting the fire inside me.

I can feel my cock pressing against the clothes the guard handed me after the shower. Devana also seems to notice when she presses her hips against me. As she grinds against me, dropping her shirt to the ground, I cup her breast with my hand. Not only is her skin soft and beautiful, but her nipple is hard, and every time I touch it, she lets out a quiet groan.

Her noises are delicious and force me to raise my other hand to do the same with her nipple. More heat rushes into my cock, driving me to twitch against her. Without warning, she lifts her hands to pull my loose shirt up my stomach and over my shoulders and head, breaking the hold I have on her.

"Another thing I imagined doing countless times," she says, pulling me closer to press her bare chest against mine. My skin is on fire when we touch. Leaning down, I press a kiss to her head, savoring every moment of our exposed position.

She looks up at me, her amber eyes drowning out every insecurity I still have.

She wants me as much as I want her.

I wrap my hands around her and hoist her up. Gently, she wraps her legs around my hips, anchoring herself to me before I carry her to the bed behind her. Carefully, I let her down, and a chuckle escapes my throat when I see the coat sprawled out on it.

There's that damn coat I wished for just moments ago to slow everything down.

Hastily, she grabs it to push it to the side before she reaches out to my waistband, undoing the loose knot I made to keep it in place. Her fingers tremble slightly as she undoes it. Is she cold or just as nervous as I am?

Without warning, my pants glide to the ground, and her eyes are on the same level as my cock.

Another wave of heat rushes through me and into my face.

"Wow," she says, hesitantly staring at me.

This has been my worry since I heard my brother talk about sizes when I became a young man. Is he too small?

Devana takes one more look at my cock before curling her hand around my shaft.

Every nerve ending in my body screams for more when she gently glides her palm over me. A groan escapes my throat, and I need to throw my head back to concentrate on not coming right away.

Her hand feels so much nicer around my cock than any hand job I've ever done to myself.

"Don't stop," I say when her grip tightens.

This is the most selfish thing I've done to date. I should attend to her needs and get her undressed to taste her, but my toes curl so much that I can't think of anything else but her hand around me.

"Come here," she says, letting go of me to tap the spot beside her.

This brings me back from the trance I was in. I want to beg her to continue, but if she does, this is over before it even starts.

Eyeing me, she opens the buckle, holding her pants in place, and my gaze is on her as she shimmies out of them, panties included. My fingers tremble when I see her naked before me.

"You're divine," I say, my eyes trailing over her sharp collarbones, over her breast, down her stomach to her core.

"You can touch me," she says, giggling.

Suppressing the urge to crawl on top of her and pressing my dick right into her like my instincts demand, I lay her down on the bed and find a comfortable spot beside her. Trailing a finger over her nipple, down and down to her most sensitive spot, I inhale sharply before my fingers venture to a place they have never been.

Her lips are sleek as I explore her sex.

Does that mean she likes it? Is it like the pre-cum glistening on my tip as I spread her lips to feel my way to the center of her core?

Devana moans into my ear as I find her entrance and carefully stick a finger inside her. It's wet and tight. She grabs my hand to move it in and out of her, showing me the pace she likes the most. Her other hand curls around my dick, and when she strokes me, my mind goes straight to her vagina.

To be inside her right now.

Closing my eyes, I hear her heavy breathing and the image lying on top of her. Moving my hand at her desired speed, I open my eyes to see her using her other hand to rub a spot I haven't noticed before.

It's so fucking sexy that I bite my lip not to react.

Her grasp around my length tightens, and she picks up speed. Closing my eyes again, I take her strokes in.

And then...panic sets in.

I'm not fast enough to turn away from her as my cum releases. As the heat and moans consume me, I try to open my eyes to see her reaction.

When I'm done, it's all over her.

Her belly. Her hip. Even her breasts.

"Gods be damned," I breathe, hastily grabbing the next thing close to me to clean her up.

Her face is blank until a laugh erupts out of her, forcing my cum to slide over her skin.

"I think we did it wrong," she says, laughing as she releases my pulsating dick.

"I'm so sorry," I whisper, wiping her clean with the corner of a thin blanket. "This is so embarrassing. You were so wet. I...just—"

"It's fine," she says, grabbing the fabric from me to clean off the rest of my embarrassment. "My lips are sealed." She taps her lips with her finger, and my eyes follow.

"Let me test it," I say, working through my shame.

"Cyrus," she whispers as I lean in to kiss her.

My name.

She used my real name.

"It sounds like a prayer on your lips," I say before kissing her.

Her lips are so soft and full, and when she parts them for me to let me taste her, my desire to bury myself inside of her catches fire again.

"What the fuck?" a male voice asks behind me.

I turn around, and when my eyes meet with the soldier's, embarrassment washes over me again.

Shit!

FORTY-SIX

DEVANA

Scrambling for the cum coated blanket, I cover as much of my body as possible.

"Get dressed," Khaos barks, leaving the room and slamming the door behind him shut.

I swear I saw a light smile in the corners of his mouth, but I can't be sure because who would laugh at finding his bed covered in other people's fluids?

Jumping for my clothes, I dress myself at record speed, and when I turn to Cyrus, I see him waiting for me.

"How long was he standing there?" he asks, his face pale as snow.

"I don't know," I answer, putting on my second boot. "Let's hope he just got here."

How can such a massive man be so quiet?

But I'm not worried about him seeing me naked. I'm nervous about how Cyrus feels after he ejaculated all over me and, to make matters worse, might have been caught by another man doing so.

I don't mind it. It wasn't how I imagined our first intimate encounter, but his early release made me even hornier.

He liked what he saw.

He liked it so much that he couldn't contain himself.

"If he saw—"

I cut him off. "He didn't," I lie, grabbing his hand to squeeze it. "Look at me, Cyrus. And even if he did, it doesn't matter. We're about to leave this place and never look back."

I'm unsure how many lies I can tell without him catching me.

In the time I waited for Khaos' return, I thought of all the probable outcomes if I ran into Monsteress. She will unlikely let me go, knowing that I could be her ruin. I would be surprised if she did.

But if she forces me to stay close to her, the least I can do is free my father. He has given so much. Too much.

I want to see him happy after everything he's been through and done for me. I want him to open up a new forge and find a woman who fulfills all his wishes.

"We shouldn't let him wait," I say, pulling Cyrus behind me to the door.

On the other side, Khaos greets us with a smirk. "Did you at least both finish?" he asks, and I feel Cyrus's fingers cutting into my skin.

"Multiple times," I answer, smiling back at him. "How about you?"

Khaos bites his lip, his smirk vanishing. "The Queen requests your presence in the throne room," he says coldly, leading the way.

"You said you would bring my father to me," I say, looking over his shoulder.

"And let him walk in on his naked daughter?"

My cheeks heat, but I hold my head high as I push that thought away.

The entire way to the throne room, no one says another word. I want to break the silence and lighten the mood, but there's nothing to say.

The double door opens before us, and when I see my father at the feet of Monsteress, my heart lights up and breaks simultaneously.

I cling to Cyrus' arm, seeking solace in his presence as we await the release of my father and the old woman beside him, who are huddled together.

As Khaos approaches the dais with a stoic expression, he bows respectfully before his Queen, keeping us within his line of sight.

Monsteress' eyes, sharp as daggers, narrow on us before she settles on me. "Why do you believe you're connected to me, girl?"

He told her. I knew it.

Tears well up in my eyes, but I hold my chin high, refusing to falter before the heartless monarch. "Your Majesty, I may not know you, but fate has brought us together. I feel a bond, an unspoken connection to your pain and suffering."

A sinister grin curls upon her lips. "Prove it then," she commands, her voice dripping with malice.

With a swift, calculated movement, she draws a dagger from beneath her dress and plunges it into her hand behind her back, hidden from my view. Blood drips onto the warm sandstone as she pulls the dagger out to show me she's not playing.

A scream escapes my lips, a chilling symphony of pain and defiance, as I feel something being rammed into my finger.

My eyes widen in horror as the pain slams into me.

I can't feel my finger.

It's gone.

Looking at my hand, I can still see my little finger attached to it, but my body tells me otherwise.

"Fix it," I beg, grabbing my little finger to press it as hard as possible to ease the pain. If I put enough pressure on it, I may feel it again.

The room falls into a stunned silence, broken only by my cries.

Monsteress' face betrays a mix of astonishment and curiosity. "You're either an outstanding performer, or truly connected to me by some strange twist of fate," she remarks coldly.

My breaths come in ragged gasps, but my eyes remain locked with the Queen's, unyielding. "I do *not* seek to understand the whims of destiny, Your Majesty. I only know that compassion and empathy bind us, even across the chasm of rank and circumstance."

"Enough of this sentimental bullshit," she snaps, motioning for Khaos to release the prisoners. "Take them away and be done with it. And you," she points at me with her injured hand, revealing her missing finger, blood dripping from the wound. "Come here."

Clenching my teeth, I go to the dais, catching a good look at my father and the old woman, her eyes milky and blind.

This is it.

This is the moment she tells me I can't leave.

"Hurry," she says, tapping her fingers against the throne.

I don't understand. She should show signs of pain like I do. Instead, her wicked smile widens when I reach her.

With an inhuman speed, she grabs me by my shoulder and pulls me in.

"Let her go!" Cyrus yells from afar as my ears ring.

"You shut up. You should know that I don't listen to anyone," she barks over my shoulder, her gaze returning to me.

I hear him struggle behind me, but I know he's no match for Khaos.

"You weren't lying after all," she says, her eyes running over my freckles. "I hate to do this, but I have bigger fish to fry."

Her other hand shoots to my throat, and her grip tightens. When my vision blurs, she suddenly releases me. Falling to my knees, I scratch my throat, inhaling as much air as possible.

What did she do to me?

"I need you to go somewhere where no one can find you. If you run into trouble, think of me, and I will hunt you down."

Her words linger in the air like poisonous smoke.

I have little time to think about her words because she might change her mind if I wait too long.

Crawling, I turn away from her, and when my pulse finally goes down, and my legs listen to my commands again, I stand up and run. Adrenaline rushes through me, making me forget the pain in my shoulder and finger.

"Let's go," I say, digging my heels into the ground to stop before my father.

"Devana," he whispers, reaching for my face.

"Not now. We must go."

I push my shoulder under his arm to support him, and together, we stumble out of the throne room, trailing Cyrus, who's helping the woman.

I'm not sure who she is and why Cyrus needs her, but that is also a conversation for another day. Right now, we must bring as many miles between Crymzon and us as we can.

"She marked you," Cyrus says, slowing his step as we reach the gate.

"What?"

"Her hand. It's visible on your throat."

Marked me? For what?

"Don't worry. I will make you the most beautiful necklace to cover it up," my father says, his words slurred.

He's not doing well. I need to get him to a healer somehow.

Pushing that thought of my throat aside, I stare into the dark landscape surrounding us as the gate closes behind us. "Where to?"

"Starstrand," Cyrus says with a firm tone.

I shake my head, my legs trembling under my father's weight. "I can't go there. She said I need to find a place where no one can find me."

"Come with me," Cyrus pleads. "I need to return her to Starstrand for Liza. After that, I will go wherever you want me to."

What if Monsteress finds out? Is the mark also a tracker?

"Please," he says, his voice thick. "I will take care of you two."

"We'll never make it. My father is too weak," I say, shifting his weight to ease the pressure on my shoulder.

"There is a way," Cyrus says, stepping back.

I almost recoil when two massive wings appear behind him.

"Are those...clouds?" I ask, studying his featherless, fluffy wings protruding from his shoulder blades. "That's not possible."

"We'll have enough time to catch up once we're safe," he says, turning to the old woman. "May I?" he asks, holding his arms out to pick her up.

When she looks at him, moonlight dancing in her silver irises, I choke on my spit.

She was blind. I saw her milky eyes in the throne room. I would bet my life on it.

"I might be old, but not useless," she says, unleashing another set of feathered wings behind her.

What in Emara's name is going on? Are my father and I the only ones without wings?

That's when it hits me.

I have wings. They might not be attached to me, but my wings are strong enough to carry my father and me.

Shifting my weight again to free a hand, I lift my necklace and blow into the feather.

The moon darkens above us, and I don't have to look up to know Erinna is always close.

FORTY-SEVEN

Queen Soulin

It was easy to find the man Cyrus was looking for. Using my magic, I send waves through the palace, detecting him stuck under the staircase of the East Tower. How he got there without using magic or hammering a hole into a wall is even a mystery to me.

He looked more dead than alive when I found him, and under no circumstances could I return him like that to Cyrus. My first thought was to call a healer, but since my magic is back to its full potential, it only takes a little spark to pull him back from death's edge and rehydrate him.

As for the Lady of Fate, I hope she perks back up once starlight shines upon her again. No magic in this world is strong enough to return her shriveling body to the beautiful woman she once was.

After handing over the Lady of Fate and Devana's father and giving Devana a warning, Khaos stands before me, his eyebrows knitted together.

"Was that really necessary?" he asks, rubbing his forehead.

"You would rather see her locked away?"

"That's not what I mean."

"Then, yes. My magic prevents me from feeling her pain. Tell me, how else am I supposed to know if she needs help? I don't know what will happen to me if she dies."

"So why let her go?"

Khaos knows it all. Every single *bad-good* thing I've done. From making it appear that I punish my people to the outside world, but actually, they're safe and sound below the prison, to trying to look like the worst bitch this planet has seen just to repel other people to walk all over me.

He knows my weaknesses and my values.

"Because she has so much more to live for. She's still so young. And now she's free to experience a life I can never fathom to have. Maybe happiness is not in my cards, but that doesn't mean I must ruin it for everyone else."

Khaos' face softens as he takes me in—the raw, maskless me.

"There's something you need to see," he says, climbing the last steps of the dais to hold his hand in my direction.

"You know I don't have—"

"Time for it? Then make some."

His powerful hand is still outstretched to help me off the throne. I accept his offer and grab it. "What are you planning?"

"Oh, you'll like it," he says, intertwining his fingers with mine.

The warmth of his hand and the gentleness he pulls me into his arms show me I made the right choice.

There's no pretending anymore.

Even when he thought I was a monster, he stayed. Every time I gave him a reason to leave—even when I forced him out of Crymzon—he came back.

And I'm glad.

If there was ever a person made for me, it's Khaos.

Now I have to become that person he sees in me—starting behind closed doors because Otyx is still out there, and I can't risk delivering Khaos on a silver plate.

"I need to cover your eyes for this one," he says, moving my back against his chest.

The heat spreading through my body when my shoulders meet his muscular chest almost sets me on fire.

"Do you trust me?"

He hasn't given me any reason not to.

Instead of answering, I press my ass against his cock, forcing a light moan out of him.

Reaching over my shoulders, he presses his hands against my eyes, and I close them, giving him complete control over my body.

"Don't let me regret it," I whisper, feeling his excitement through our connection.

He's up to something.

Knowing the palace like the back of my hand, I realize where he's taking me.

"Keep your eyes closed," he says, removing one hand to open the door before pressing his chest against me again to push me into the room.

"What do you smell?" he asks, a chuckle reverberating through him.

I take a deep sniff, and when my nostrils fill with the musky smell of sweat and cum, I almost gag.

"Are you fucking serious?" I yell, swatting his hand away to break out of his grasp.

"Well, it smells nasty, but victory smells different to every person," he says.

A tear rolls down his face because he's laughing too hard. "You owe me a favor."

"You dragged me here to prove your point?"

"I learned from the best," he winks at me, and another tear escapes his pinched eye.

My body shakes with disgust. "That's so gross. I can't believe you did this to me."

"How else are you going to believe me that I won?"

"Let's say I agree with your victory. What favor do you want?"

He closes the distance between us and presses his chest against mine. "One night with you. *Alone.*"

My heart stops for a beat.

He could have asked for anything. A throne. His title back. Freedom.

Instead, he chose me.

Leaning down, he lifts my chin and presses a passionate kiss on my lips.

He wants me *now. Here.*

"That's not going to happen," I say, pushing him off me.

The light in his eyes dies, and so does his smile.

Gently, I take his hand in mine. "You can never return to this room again," I say with a smile. "It's time you move your belongings to *our* chambers."

The chambers were designed just for me and my future Soulmate when I was born. It's not in the West Wing where every other monarch lived before me because those chambers were reserved for my brother, the Crown Prince.

I still can't bring upon myself to venture to that part of the palace, but I also never meant to move there.

"That's not funny. Don't play with me," Khaos says, shaking his head slightly.

"You're more than welcome to roll around in someone else's cum, if that's what you're into," I answer, pressing my lips together to prevent myself from laughing.

Khaos is so fast at grabbing me by my hips and throwing me over his shoulder that I only manage to let out an embarrassing squeaking noise.

"I'm going to do it the right way. My cum will drip from your pretty little pussy onto your bed while you beg me for more."

His words send shivers down my spine.

He's everything I want—and more.

I don't have to tell him where our new chambers are. When I was little, I always pointed them out as I passed them, sometimes even sneaking inside with Khaos in my arms to show him what my future would look like.

Since my coronation, I haven't set foot into them again.

How could I?

I promised myself that I would never yield to a Connection with another being.

For what purpose? To be vulnerable?

Entering the chambers with Khaos again wipes away all the negative thoughts I connected with this place.

We're here again. Together.

But there's no sneaking or hushed voices to keep us from getting caught.

He closes the door behind us, walks to the oversized bed in the far corner of the room, and lets me down gently.

"Since the first time we set foot in here, I always dreamt of you choosing me," he says, looking around the vast room. "I always imagined how I would decorate it with you. Beautiful colors covering the walls. A bed right below the window so we can gaze at the moon. A mirror big enough to cover an entire wall so I can always see you."

Oh, I dreamt of it, too. But a child made those dreams.

"Stop talking," I say, extending my legs to tap them around him.

He stumbles forward and comes to a halt at the edge of the bed.

"Your time just started," I purr, my eyes resting on his hard cock straining against his pants.

I don't have to tell him twice. Swiftly, he pulls off his shirt and releases the cord, holding his pants in place.

I watch as he steps out of them. My mouth waters, and my core clenches when I see his excitement glistening on his tip.

He lowers himself to my level, and his dark irises search mine. "I want to wake up beside you," he says, his eyes pleading for an answer.

He already voiced his favor. But how can I say *no?* "I promise," I whisper back, and he inhales sharply.

I never make promises. First, because most of them I can't keep. And second, because I hate keeping them.

He knows that.

So when I say that I will be next to him when he opens his eyes, I mean it.

No matter what happens, I can't fuck this up.

His smile is bright enough to lighten up the entire room, but his eyes turn dark fast when I wrap my legs around him again, pulling him closer. He's still standing before the bed, his cock at my entrance when I anker him in place.

"You will be the death of me, Soulin," he growls, towering over me to kiss his way up and down my neck.

I lose myself in his touch as he slides my dress over my ass to my shoulders.

"You're not wearing anything beneath," he says, out of breath, cupping my breasts the second they jump free.

"Maybe I wanted you to win," I laugh, sliding my hip to the side to give him entrance.

He slides inside me with a big thrust, his body shaking as he rolls his hip to savor the feeling.

"You're so fucking tight," he growls, thrusting into me again to stretch me.

I claw my nails into the sheets.

It feels so good. So good that when he finds a rhythm in his movement, I can't stop moaning.

He grabs my ass, and I relax my thighs around him to give him more room.

Pressure builds up inside of me.

"Harder," I moan, arching my back until I can feel him hitting the spot inside me I didn't know existed.

Picking up speed, his thighs clap against my ass, and his groans deepen.

He's as close as I am. Maybe even closer.

I wince as he takes one of his hands away from my backside to trail it down my stomach until his thumb presses on my clit.

"You like that?" he asks, rubbing it in a circular motion as he pounds into me.

My moans are enough as an answer when I fall over the edge.

He makes me ride my release, my vagina and stomach contracting as pleasure washes over me again and again. And just when I think I have experienced all of it, he groans as his warm cum fills me.

"Oh, fuck," he says, his breath hot on my face when he leans down to kiss me. "Let's bathe and do it again."

He's still inside me, so how can he already demand more?

But I want more, too. I want his fingers to touch every part of my body. I want him to worship me and thrust into me until we both can't take it anymore.

I also want to repay him for tongue fucking me in the Throne Room right after he returned from Tenacoro. I know I made up for it by sucking him off. Despite that, I want more of him.

There are so many things I want to do to him. Experience with him. This night won't be enough to cover half of it.

"After you," he says, pulling out of me and reaching for my hands to help me off the bed.

As he walks behind me, I can feel his gaze devouring me. "I will never get enough of this view," he says, grabbing my ass.

FORTY-EIGHT

Queen Soulin

When I awake, Khaos lies beside me, a smile curving his lips.

"What are you staring at?" I mumble, turning away from him to rub my eyes.

Somehow, I slept through the entire day. I don't know the last time I woke up refreshed. Sore but refreshed.

"How are you feeling?" he asks, scooting closer to press his erection against my ass while trailing my bare arm with his fingers.

"Like I need to use half of my power to restore my pussy," I chuckle, leaning into him.

"So you're saying there's time for more?" he teases, wrapping his arms around me.

"You're insufferable," I laugh, grabbing his hand to bite into his finger.

"Ouch," he says, pulling it away. "What was that for?"

"A little pain to bring you back to reality," I say, shifting my weight to face him.

He's handsome. Despite the scar covering the left side of his face and the charcoal one on his chest, he's perfect.

No, I take that back. His scars make him perfect. They are a sign of his loyalty to the people he cares for. A sign that he risked his life to support me.

"I need you to check on the prisoners," I say, tracing the soft scar tissue. "I also need you to write a letter to Queen Catalina Matrus with our deepest apologies for her recent losses. Sign it with King Khaos SinClaret."

"But—"

"Don't worry. We will complete our Connection Ceremony under Lunra's supervision before the letter can reach Eternitie."

"But—"

"We also need to call in a Council meeting. If—"

"It's the day you were born," he cuts in, pressing his finger against my lips to stop me from talking.

Indeed, it is.

The day my mother spent hours pushing to bring me into this world. The day my father named me Soulin, seeing my red hair for the first time. The day my fate was decided, making me the executioner of my family.

"And we treat it like any other day," I say, almost biting his finger again.

Khaos notices the defiance in my words and backs off.

"That's a lot for a first day," he says, rubbing his chin. "But can we talk about our Connection Ceremony first? Is that really what you want?"

There are things we don't talk about. Like how I lost my virginity. Or how many females he's been with since I became Queen. I'm also bad at voicing my feelings.

I know Khaos would never dismiss me, but the fear lingers inside me.

"This was my way of asking you if you would like to complete our Connection," I say, the choice of my words making me cringe.

For Lunra's sake. We fucked all night. Again and again, until we couldn't move anymore.

How can I still be so stuck up after he made me experience one orgasm after another?

And it's Khaos I'm talking to—the only person on this planet who never stopped believing in me.

"Let's try this again," I say, shaking my head. "I want you. I want you by my side for the rest of my nights. I want to wake up beside you, knowing you will never leave. And even though I can't promise to be the best Soulmate, I will try. I will try every day until death do us apart."

Saying the words out loud feels freeing.

His chin wobbles, and tears dwell in his eyes.

"Are you crying?" I snap, punching his chest. "No, I'm not doing that. Suck those tears up," I warn him.

Khaos laughs, burying his face in my chest. "I can't wait for the Ceremony," he says, kissing me. "And for every night after that."

There are still a few things I haven't been able to tell Khaos.

While he is busy working down the list of tasks I gave him, I go to Librascendia. If he knew my plan, he would never let me out of his sight.

Checking the little bag attached to my belt again, I wait for the black liquid to inch closer. It forms into a book, and I grab it to bring it to the table pressed against a high-ceiling window. Carefully, I open it and skim through it until I find the necessary information and place it on a plush velvet cushion.

I withdraw a delicate candle from within my bag's depths, placing it beside the book.

As the silver moon hangs low in the ink-black sky, my gown of blood red, embroidered with constellations, seems to come alive under the moon's gentle glow.

With a mere flick of my fingers, I ignite the candle with my magic.

Intricately etched symbols of the ancient language shimmer under the candle's glow, resonating with an unseen energy.

I must act with utmost care, for the ritual I'm about to perform requires precision and focus. I can't think about what will happen if I mess up.

From a crystal vial held within the folds of my cloak, I retrieve a ruby-red liquid, a rare and potent substance known only to the most skilled of enchanters. Its source is rumored to be tied to the depths of the Underworld itself. I drip the crimson liquid onto the flickering flame with steady hands and step back.

I'm not sure why my father had this liquid in his possession and even labeled it. Maybe it was handed down to him, and he didn't know. Or because he's used the same spell I'm about to do.

The book doesn't describe what reaction I should expect, but I step closer to inspect the candle when nothing happens.

Anger boils inside me when I realize it won't work.

Shit!

I expected it to fail, but I didn't think it would be the easiest part of the spell that gives me trouble.

There needs to be another way.

I already called Lunra. So did my parents, and their parents, and every generation before that.

My stomach turns when I think about the price—a soul.

There's no way I can bring a sacrifice into Librascendia.

Clenching my fists, I hammer them on the desk.

This was supposed to work!

Wait.

I called upon Lunra without a sacrifice. All I did was touch the Heiligbaum. Sure, there was more to it, pain and a nasty burn, but it worked.

The spell is in the book, and all I need is excruciating pain and burning skin—or something like that.

Looking at the candle, I lift my hand and place my palm over the flickering flame.

At first, I feel the warmth until it becomes a biting pain.

Red liquid. The spell demands red liquid.

With my other hand, I drive under my dress and press it against the whip curled around my thigh. Eventually, I find a spike sticking out and prick my finger.

Forcing my magic through my veins to stop the unbearable pain, I bring my bleeding finger over the flame and squeeze it with my thumb until a drop of my blood drops out.

As the liquid touches the candle's surface, a mesmerizing transformation unfolds before my eyes. The entire candle comes alive, the flames dancing with new intensity. The wax takes on a mysterious quality, becoming shadowy and see-through as if infused with the night's essence.

It's working.

It's working!

With unwavering focus, I flip to the next page, revealing the incantations one of my ancestors inscribed. Speaking the sacred words with a voice that resonates like a haunting melody, I begin to weave the magic that will call upon the God of the Underworld.

A palpable presence fills the air as I delve into the deepest and darkest part of Escela with my conscience.

The chant grows darker and more profound, mingling with my magic. Each verse strengthens the connection to the Underworld, and the barrier between our kingdoms thins.

The candle flickers and wanes, its light casting elongated shadows across the room.

My heart pounds with anticipation, knowing I'm about to encounter a being of unimaginable power—a God I've seen in a vision before.

As the last syllable of the incantation leaves my lips, a sudden hush falls upon the room. The candle, now burning low, trembles as if acknowledging the other being.

And then, in an instant, the flame extinguishes, plunging the chamber into darkness.

In the darkness, I sense him, a force that I know can only belong to the God I summoned. As my eyes adjust to the lack of light, I see a faint silhouette taking form before me.

It's him—Otyx, the God of the Underworld, with smoking wings and all.

His eyes glow like molten rubies, and a cloak of shadows envelops him, swirling like tendrils of smoke.

He regards me with curiosity and intrigue, as if he has been summoned from his realm but not wholly displeased by it.

Silence lingers in the room, broken only by the soft crackle of the extinguished candle.

We lock eyes, and my anger deepens when I see the smile on his face.

"This is your cue to address me, mortal," he says, his voice so deep but vibrant that it reverberates through me.

"What do you want, Otyx?" I ask, aware I'm skipping the protocol I've been taught.

He holds his extremely muscular stomach and laughs. "And therefore, I love playing with Crymzonians the most. Your hair really matches your personality."

With courage and determination in my heart, I take a step forward, prepared to try the unknown.

"This is my only warning. Leave us mortals alone," I say, my voice unwavering.

"Or you do what? Burn your hand again to get a look at me?"

Ignoring his insult, I take another step forward. "Do I have your word?"

"You're brave. I admire your attempt to save your people. But I have to decline. It's just too much fun. And now that you dipped your fingers into Blood Magic, I can't wait to see how this unfolds."

Blood Magic? What is he talking about?

I just used the spell from the book.

As I move even closer, the God of the Underworld inclines his head ever so slightly. "You don't know, do you? By using Blood Magic, you've opened up a portal to my kingdom," he laughs, pointing out the window. "There's a reason this kind of magic is forbidden. But thanks to you, I can unleash Hell on Escela."

As he throws his head back to let out an ear-shattering laugh, I grab into the bag tangling behind me and grab the biggest piece of Nullstone retrieved from my neck.

Launching forward, I slam the sharp end into his chest, and when he realizes my attack, I twist the shard and use the last of my remaining magic to splinter it into a million pieces.

The scream from Otyx's mouth almost splits my eardrums as I fall to the ground.

Another scream, more human and frail, sends shivers down my spine. When Otyx's body fades before my eyes, I see Khaos leaning against the open door, pressing his hands against his chest.

Black liquid stains his shirt. When he looks at me, his face contorted with pain and surprise, I'm not fast enough without my magic to reach him before he collapses and his pupils dilate.

What have I done?

ABOUT THE AUTHOR

C.K. Franziska is the author of the finished A *Speck of Darkness* series, and her second series, The Crymzon Chronicles. She is the wife of a traveler, as well as the mother of two mini versions of herself and way too many pets. In her spare time, she is also a photographer, traveler, full-time entertainer, and animal lover. She does her best writing at night, at the beach listening to the waves, or while camping. C.K. loves to play make-believe, transporting readers to a place where the heroes have to step out of the seemingly endless cycle of family curses, where the magic is as beautiful and untamable as we think, and where every person deserves to be celebrated.

Made in the USA
Columbia, SC
25 February 2024

6764f342-fa20-46f8-9f95-8e16f844753bR01